# The Truth About Jacob Marley

# THE TRUTH ABOUT JACOB MARLEY

A NOVEL BY

## GEORGE RAPIER

TWIN
OAKS
PRESS

ISBN-13: 978-1-937937-24-9

First Paperback Edition
November 2020

Printed in The United States of America

Twin Oaks Press
twinoakspress@gmail.com
www.twinoakspress.com

Design
Art Growden

*To Jessica*

# Chapter 1

## A Shifting of the Earth

Marley was alive, to begin with.

In spite of everything you may have heard or read, the man was actually *alive* on the night in question—by which I mean the Christmas Eve on which my uncle underwent a profound change in his philosophy of life. The world believes Marley died much earlier, exactly seven years prior to that fateful night. But I must refute that version of the story, no matter how many comparisons are made between Mr. Marley and a door-nail or a coffin-nail. Those are merely overstatements designed to prepare the reader to believe the unbelievable, or even the supernatural.

To reiterate, Jacob Marley was not dead on that occasion and therefore not a ghost.

My name is Frederick Truelock. I am composing this memoir to set straight the true events of Christmas, 1841. I am older now and retired from public life. Over the years, it has irritated me that no one heeded my challenge of the details found in the extravagant fantasy.

My exasperation may appear strange in view of the general

acclaim afforded that narrative. That was put forward as a piece of fiction, of course, and as such is highly esteemed far and wide. The reader of the present work may well ask why anyone should contest the accuracy of something fictional! But was it a mere fable? My purpose is not to disparage the previous narrative but rather to divulge the underpinnings on which that story was constructed—for such a basis absolutely exists.

Furthermore, it so happens I am the only person still living who can refute the notion that the real Jacob Marley was deceased on the night in question. Nor is that the only matter to be explained. There is much more. Now, with ample time at my disposal, I will set down my version of those events.

If you would like to know what really happened to Jacob Marley—and what extraordinary event transformed the character of my uncle, Ebenezer Scrooge—pray continue.

I begin my account many years before the night under discussion.

⋙⟡⋘

My family came to London from a provincial city in Lancashire. At the time, I was but three years old, an only child. When I grew a little older, my mother would often speak of her early days and told me many family stories, not all of them proper tales for children. Her father, my maternal grandfather, was a hard man, she asserted. Many of his actions were cruel and of a sort that I would rather forget. From the tales Mother told me, I gathered he was a domineering tyrant and habitual drunkard. In trying to defend him, she suggested that because he was widowed, their home lacked the usual mitigating influence of a woman. This explanation rang hollow to me, even though I was still a child.

Nevertheless, one of the happier stories involved her brother, Ebenezer, who attended a public school quite some distance away. This school was of the lowest rank in the kingdom. It produced no great scholars or statesmen but merely provided a place for a gentleman to banish an unwanted male offspring. Furthermore, Ebenezer was kept at school during most holidays, an arrangement specified by my grandfather, though there was no particular reason for it other than to save the gentleman travel expenses. As a result, my mother rarely saw her brother in her younger years.

Ebenezer even remained at school during the Christmas recess, a time when the other students departed for their homes, singing carols and full of merriment. It nettled the lad to remain in that drafty place for the entire holiday, in the full embrace of winter, alone. His only consolation was in reading books by the fire, mostly adventure stories popular with boys his age.

But one year at Christmas-time he was astonished to have a visitor come to see him. It was my mother, who had come to fetch him home! She joyously explained to her brother that their father's heart had softened. Moreover, he now considered the lad entirely grown up, a man, and thus he did not need to remain there. And so at last young Ebenezer was able to leave and never return to that broken-down institution.

"But why did Grandfather change his mind?" I asked my mother.

"I'm not sure, Freddy," she said. "I believe someone made him feel remorse about his treatment of his only son. And I have a notion who it was. At the time, Father was courting a lady who might have suggested such a thing; she is the likeliest person."

I should mention here that my mother had a personal motto of sorts: "Every seven years, behold a shifting of the earth!" As a small child I took this to be a quotation from Scripture, but later I discovered it was only a peculiar saying of hers. At any rate, that's how she regarded her father's unexpected change of heart: it amounted to nothing less than the earth moving.

"What happened after he returned home?" I asked. "Did he get on with his father?"

"Not really," she answered dully.

She told me that Ebenezer remained a moody boy and avoided everyone but herself. A few years later he apprenticed himself to a businessman who owned a warehouse in a nearby city and so moved there. He excelled in bookkeeping and succeeded splendidly in his new position.

"And, you may not believe it," she added with a twinkle in her eye, "but he behaved quite sociably in those days. He even courted a local girl for several years."

"Go on!" I cried. "Uncle Ebenezer? What happened? Did they marry?"

"I'm afraid not. The young lady broke off their engagement. Perhaps he dallied too long, afraid to take the final step. At any rate, your uncle was so downhearted about it that he decided to depart for London and seek his fortune in the capital."

That decision puzzled me, for at that early age I understood little of the interplay between young men and young women.

"As it happened, Freddy, he left seven years after he returned from the boarding school." I nodded, not understanding her point at the time. After he left, she heard little from her brother for a considerable period.

Then their father suddenly died. By then the man was nearly destitute, having squandered a considerable fortune. But Ebenezer did not return to Lancashire for the funeral, for he still nursed a childhood grudge. By then my mother had already married and begun to make a home for my father, the late John Truelock. On the occasion of her marriage, her brother sent a letter of congratulations and a gift.

He did so again when I was born.

I have few childhood memories of Lancashire. I was told that for a long time my father looked for an opportunity to better himself there but had no luck in doing so. After receiving an offer from a friend in the wine trade, he accepted, though the position was in London. Nevertheless we all removed to London. It was a bold gamble on his part. But there he prospered as a wholesale purveyor of wine, and there I grew to manhood.

By this time my Uncle Ebenezer was already immersed in the running of his business. Yet a genial relationship was rekindled between him and my mother. I think each was happy to have a relative living in town, if only to visit occasionally and discuss their salad days.

I had a similar sentiment, even at a young age. Here was someone, my Uncle Ebenezer, the only relative with whom I was acquainted outside the immediate family. He used to bring me sweets, and I always looked forward to seeing him, though conversation between us was slight.

And now we come to Mr. Marley.

Jacob Marley was of course my uncle's friend and business partner. In my early years I recall both men coming to our house on feast days, especially Christmas. My uncle would smile at me, but he never knew what exactly to say to a child. His partner, on the other hand, was garrulous to a fault and tried to befriend me through formulaic phrases meant to cajole a boy.

"Ahoy, Master Fred," he would sometimes begin, remembering I once vowed to become a sailor when I grew up. "Can you clamber up the mast to the crow's nest today? Eh? We need your eagle-eye to lead us to the punch bowl."

When I was small, I loved hearing this sort of banter and doted upon Mr. Marley.

But as I grew older, such talk embarrassed me. Still, he would try to amuse me in this fashion for a minute or two and I would laugh to be polite. Mr. Marley would soon leave off his nautical patter as the adults began to engage in conversation.

I sensed that neither visitor was overfond of children.

Physically, the two were completely different. My uncle was tall and gaunt and possessed a strong chin. Marley was shorter and rotund and wore a pigtail down to his shoulders, a fashion I never quite understood. Even though they came round several times a year, I observed that, after eating and communing a bit with my parents, both men grew eager to depart, supplying some feeble excuse as a reason.

After they left, Mother and Father would sometimes talk. One time their conversation went somewhat as follows.

"Mr. Marley seems to be losing a bit of his 'extra baggage,'" my father muttered as he tapped his pipe.

"Really? I hadn't noticed," replied Mother. "That would be difficult, considering how he devours my plum pudding."

Father chuckled and said nothing more about it. But I agreed with him. Children are often perceptive, and I'd seen Mr. Marley three times that year. On the most recent occasion I, too, noticed that his waistcoat seemed a bit looser around his middle, and, being a child, I concluded he neglected to have it pressed.

As I said, Marley usually came with Uncle at Christmas. But one year my uncle came alone. My family was perhaps too conventional for Marley, I think. Eventually he stopped coming round altogether.

Members of my father's firm would sometimes appear as well, invariably bearing wine, and this made for a more lively affair. At these times my uncle would typically sit alone in the corner or by the fire, where he would drink his punch and smoke his pipe. He rarely took part in their conversation. I felt sorry for him sitting there by himself. Often he would leave early and abruptly.

Sometimes, prior to the arrival of the other guests, Uncle would inquire of Mother if there were any news from their home town. She was an inveterate letter-writer and kept up with all her childhood friends. Therefore, she would politely enumerate the latest happenings for him. I watched him nod and cluck his tongue, but rarely did he show much interest in the general news. Only once did I see him react, when the news came that a certain Mr. Fezziwig had died and been laid to rest. The news visibly saddened him.

Mother once remarked to Father that her brother cared naught about these country goings-on, except for news concerning one person in particular—his former fiancée, a woman named Belle—and that she, my mother, was loath to inform him time after time that the lady's marriage continued to be a happy one. After Mother received word that a fourth child was born to this lady, Scrooge stopped inquiring about happenings in the country.

As I grew taller and stronger, my uncle grew thinner and more reclusive. I reasoned this must be because he lived alone; consequently I wondered why he had never married. To me he looked distinguished and as able as any other gentleman to get a wife.

When I was about the age of ten or so, I bluntly put the question to him.

He was a bit shaken by my impertinence but explained that he was exceedingly poor when he arrived in the city and he'd had neither the money nor inclination to court.

"Yes, Uncle," I said, "but now you're rich, are you not?"

"Not rich enough for that enterprise," he growled.

At this point my father wisely intervened by sending me to fetch his spectacles.

After Marley stopped visiting, my uncle gradually curtailed his attendance as well, perhaps because he was then so outnumbered by my father's associates. When he did come, he appeared distracted, sat by the fire, and was not disposed to linger. He always complained of having too much work to do, saying that their firm, Scrooge & Marley, was expanding and thriving, which meant his work continued to increase.

Several years passed. Then one day in early spring, my mother died suddenly of pneumonia at the age of thirty-nine. I was but twelve years of age. All of us were prostrate with grief. Even Uncle Ebenezer wept at her funeral, which shocked me, since I had never seen him show emotion before, save the one time when he heard about Mr. Fezziwig's passing. After the last clod of earth was thrown upon her coffin, Uncle Ebenezer went home and came to visit us no longer, though Father often invited him.

As cruel fate would have it, my father himself died seven years afterwards—of apoplexy, so the doctor said. This blow was also a mighty one to me but not as devastating as the previous calamity, partly because it did not take me completely by surprise. I had marked the decline in Father's health in the intervening years and for some time feared he would leave me. Furthermore, by the time of his death, I was reading law at a good firm and was engaged to be married. My dear fiancée Emily became a bulwark for me during that time of grief.

The next year we wed. My bride and I took up residence in a small upstairs flat. My whole life lay before me, and so, with my wife's moral support, I was better able to weather this second misfortune. Thus I was at the age of twenty an orphan.

To my great distress, my uncle did not attend either Father's funeral or my wedding. He sent not the briefest note of sympathy for the former nor congratulations for the latter. I was angry about this. *Let the old fool go to the devil!* I thought and thanked heaven that my exemplary parents, the two people who gave me life, were so unlike that boorish relative.

I vowed never to have a thing to do with him again.

My father had been an affable man who took life as he found it. He enjoyed traveling to the Continent at the behest of his firm and spoke good French. He always behaved in a friendly manner and treated colleagues with respect. But it was the role of a well-heeled gentleman and family man that he relished above all. I later learned from one of his associates—Mr. Evans, a man who treated me kindly after his death—that my father was averse to sharp practices and never could be relied on to drive much of a bargain.

As one may suppose from the above, my father was not particularly ambitious, perhaps because he was of humble origin. I, on the other hand, did not feel the same way. I had been raised in a greater degree of comfort and in turn wanted grander things. I threw myself into my work to such a degree that I fairly neglected my bride. She was eager to start a family, whereas I was adamant we put that off until I had reached a certain level of eminence and accumulated enough savings to ensure that our lives, and those of our future children, would not be compromised.

We quarreled over this for many a night. She wept over my stubbornness and continued to bring it up. Not wishing to contend with her further, I refused to speak any more about the matter. Instead I redoubled my efforts to succeed in the law, and during the next year we barely spoke to each other.

One sunny afternoon in late summer I was hurrying to a meeting with a new client, a gentleman for whom I had drawn up a contract for use in a partnership. The man was financing a mining venture in the western Canadian wilderness. His office sat in a district full of all sorts of firms—banks, emporia, investment houses, small shops. I was late for the meeting and hastened to make up the time, paying little attention to where my feet took me . . . until I rounded a corner and was startled to behold the warehouse of Scrooge & Marley across the street.

For a long moment I did not move, as if under a spell. I

recalled standing in that very spot when I was a small boy, when my mother would occasionally visit her brother at his place of business. Memories from childhood flooded my mind as I cast back to those happier days, the days when Mr. Scrooge and Mr. Marley would sometimes visit our home.

The firm occupied only a portion of a larger building. I knew not what sort of wares were kept in the back, for I was familiar only with the front rooms: the reception room and the offices behind it, where my uncle was probably sitting at that very moment. The place was much smaller than I remembered—only a few yards of its brick faced the street—and the sign over the door was beginning to fade. There was but one small, smeary window which was nearly opaque. On that bright day I could see nothing through it at all. No sign of cheer or cordiality was to be found in the frontage. Even a smelly tannery nearby looked more inviting.

Before I regained my composure, Jacob Marley himself threw open the door and burst into the street. I hailed him at once, but he did not hear me or chose not to respond. He appeared red-faced and upset. Then he turned and strode quickly away. The man looked quite a bit older now, his hair graying down the pigtail, which was shorter than I remembered. Nor was he at all rotund as my memory had it but was now fairly slim. But it was certainly the same man, though I reckoned I hadn't seen the fellow in fifteen years. I called out to him again, more forcefully this time, but he paid no heed and soon disappeared into a throng of well-dressed gentlemen striding in the opposite direction.

I did not know exactly why I'd hailed the man, except perhaps to learn of my uncle's condition—to wit, whether he was in good health, whether he ever married, and so forth, for I was overcome by the pull of nostalgia, recalling my mother's endearing voice and manners. It struck me that within the building directly before me there remained my last link to her . . . in the person of my Uncle Ebenezer.

A dirty-faced urchin jostled my arm, trying pick my pocket, I suspect, and the full weight of the present-day world crashed on me. I felt quite at sea until I regained my sense of purpose. Then I laughed and shook my head at my own foolishness. Here I was, late to a meeting with my client, yet standing stock-still in this busy street, mawkishly reminiscing of my childhood and longing for the olden days. I rushed away.

Despite my apprehensions, the meeting with the client went swimmingly. The gentleman, a great ruddy bear of man, was himself tardy for our tete-a-tete and praised my punctuality. He was generally pleased with the wording of the contract I proposed, specifying only one change to the document. After shaking hands with him, I took my leave.

I could have taken a shorter route to my home, for I had no other items of business to attend to that day, but I soon found myself drifting through the streets exactly contrariwise to the way I'd come. It was, I believe, the persistent memory of my mother that drew me in that direction and caused me to stop once more at the building with the faded sign.

I decided to go in.

Two clerks were in the small reception area. I recognized neither of them.

"May I be of service, sir?" said one of the clerks as he sprang from his writing desk. He was a very small man with a fat little face.

"Yes," I replied. "I wonder if I might have a word with Mr. Scrooge."

"I shall put the matter to him at once," said the clerk with good cheer. "Who may I say is calling?"

"Mr. Truelock."

A few moments later my uncle himself appeared in the doorway of his inner office, looking somewhat confused. He studied me with a look of concern. "Fred? Is it really you? Is something wrong?"

"No, Uncle, I was merely traversing this street and passed by your front door and thought I should pay you a call."

"Well, now," he said. "I am rather busy at the moment. Oh, but do come in, nephew. Come in!"

I followed him into his office, as did the clerk, who stood in the doorway awaiting further instructions.

"That will be all, Cratchit," Uncle said and reached under his austere desk, which was covered with six or seven ledger books. He withdrew a bottle of claret and two glasses. As he poured, I studied him, thinking that he looked about the same as the image that lingered in my mind, though he now had something of a stoop.

We drank to each other's health, and he remarked that I had grown to be a tall man and a good-looking one as well.

"Your health seems quite good, Uncle," I observed.

"It is," he replied.

"And how is Mr. Marley?"

He frowned. "Better you didn't ask after the man. At present he is preoccupied with personal troubles."

"Oh? I take it he's not here, then."

"He took his leave earlier today, as is his habit more and more."

"I know. I passed him on the street earlier this afternoon," I said. "And I must say, he did not look at all well. Has he been ill?"

A stern look clouded his face. "Why do you ask after him so, Fred? He's no relation of yours, and these days I wish he were no partner of mine. Ill? He is only ill because of dissipation and unhealthy habits." He downed the rest of his wine and began to fidget.

"I'm truly sorry to hear such news," I said. I thought it best not to inquire further of Mr. Marley, nor to remind him that at one time his partner was something of a family friend. I let my remaining claret sit in the glass, afraid that as soon as I finished it my uncle would dismiss me.

As I sat there, I found I no longer felt so angry with him, though I'd harbored bad feelings a long time. I did not forget he failed to come to my wedding; yet, oddly, I now thought it would be a good thing if he could meet my wife.

"I am glad you are so hale, sir," I said. "Why not come to dinner tomorrow evening? My wife would love to meet you."

"Oh, yes, you are married now," he said, giving me a strange look. No doubt he'd forgotten. After a moment's hesitation he asked, "Do you have children, Fred?"

"No, sir. I do not feel that step is prudent yet." I briefly expounded my view on the matter and also summarized for him my budding career in the law. He nodded, pleased to hear of my progress.

"And yet," he continued, "I'll wager your wife does not care to wait until you have made a name for yourself before having that first child."

"Astute of you, sir," I answered. "Women rarely appreciate the concerns we men have, do they?"

He turned his head to the clouded window, a far-off look in his eyes. "Sometimes women know better, especially when it comes to family matters."

My mouth nearly fell open, struck as I was by this unexpected sentiment.

He looked back to me. "No," he said brusquely, "I'd better not come to see you. It might bring you bad luck." Then he stood up, a sure signal I had stayed long enough.

I gulped down the rest of the wine.

As I passed through the outer room I casually turned to the clerk. "Pardon me—Mr Cratchit, is it?"

"Yes, sir. Bob Cratchit, at your service."

"Well, tell me, Bob: What *does* Mr. Scrooge store in the warehouse? No one has ever told me."

"Why, cloth, sir. The finest cotton from Lancashire."

## CHAPTER 2

## HARD TIMES

Though I pondered my uncle's remark about women a good deal in the following weeks, I did not really change my mind about having a child. His words, however, forced me to own that a wall of silence now stood between my wife and myself. This weighed on me, as it appeared that the carefree early years of our married life had already passed by.

I knew of no other course but to work even more diligently in my position until I could afford the responsibility of a child. Thus I threw myself into the task.

My hard work did not go unnoticed. My superiors at the firm often praised my efforts, calling me "a young man with a future." These words were reassuring, but they were not accompanied by a rise in salary. It appeared I was mired in a slough and unable to progress as I ought. I was miserable.

The cold chill of autumn brought with it hard times. Prices of basic goods rose. Idling men who were out of work thronged the streets and made mischief. Many of them blamed their situation on the new steam-powered machinery and the factories that ran on them. Some even began a clandestine movement to destroy these engines of progress, as if destroying the machines could destroy the idea.

As for my household, I dismissed the one servant we employed, a woman who helped my wife clean our rooms twice a week. I knew we had to live as simply as we could. Emily, I'm happy to say, bore down and kept a tight rein on the household finances. Each of us pledged to the other that we would somehow weather these uncertain times.

Then, around the middle of December, fortune smiled on me. The firm had managed to prosper that year, and it was announced that the staff was to receive a Christmas bonus— not an extravagant amount, but large enough so that we might enjoy a festive holiday. This was enough to raise my spirits. But there was more good news. Before I left on the day of this announcement, my direct superior, Mr. Chauncey, called me aside to tell me the partners decided I deserved an increase in salary beginning in January. This, he said, was in recognition of my outstanding efforts on behalf of the firm.

Darkness had fallen when I arrived home that day. I do not remember if the air was cold or warm or whether the wind blew soft or hard. For I was under the spell of our good fortune.

My wife, Emily, however, scolded me for not tying my woolen scarf more tightly.

"Darling," I said, barely able to contain myself, "I have wonderful news."

"Yes, Frederick?" she said dully. She did not look at me, but picked up her knitting, unimpressed. She was long accustomed to encouraging words that meant nothing.

"Our fortunes have truly changed this time." Then I embraced her and told her what had happened. I could feel her relax as she shuddered in my arms and cried. But like prisoners released from the deepest dungeon, we hesitated to embrace the light, but kept to the shade awhile. We timidly conspired to make plans— sensible and moderate plans—as to how we should proceed.

"As for the bonus money," Emily said drying her tears, "I

believe we should employ it in the spirit it was given."

"And how would that be?" I asked.

"We should host a dinner on Christmas Day, a proper one, and invite our close friends to come. We shall cook a goose and have rum punch and trifle and play lots of silly games."

"But won't our guests feel as though . . ."

"As though we vaunt our good fortune?" she asked, divining my thought.

"Precisely, dear. Especially in these awful times."

She took my hand in hers. "Do not think of it that way, Fred. We are *sharing* our good fortune with dear friends, not vaunting it. It is Christmas, after all. There is no reason to hoard the money for some future need that may never arise. Think of the joy and encouragement it will bring, especially for those who struggle in these difficult days."

I stared at her in wonder. When I thus regarded her it was usually because of her beauty and the slight, delicate way she had of tilting her head and letting her long hair cascade down her neck. Now I was struck by her wisdom, the keen insight so well hidden within the trappings of her charms.

Uncle Ebenezer's words came back from memory then: *Sometimes women know best.* I realized he was not without his own wisdom, his born perhaps of bitter regret.

"I should like to invite my uncle," I blurted out.

She clapped her hands. "Capital! Do you think he will come?"

"I hope he will," I said. "I will beg him if I must!" Then we ate the cold chicken soup which was our supper. But we continued to talk and talk, excited and happy again. The wall of silence had toppled.

We took delight in making arrangements for the dinner. I have seldom been as happy as I was in the days leading up to that Christmas. A few friends, as well as Emily's mother and sisters, were delighted to attend. Our flat was not large, but we thought we could manage quite nicely. I wrote to invite Uncle Ebenezer, but he did not reply. Rather than write again, I resolved to go and ask him in person.

It was but two days before Christmas when I ventured again into the bustling district that was home to his business. I reached the final street near sunset. By this time a thick fog was stealing into the cracks and crevices of the old buildings and descending into the very cobblestones that lined the thoroughfare. Candles or oil lamps burned in nearly every window. Not many pedestrians strode past me as on that bright day in summer. Many of the walkers merely shuffled by at a laggardly pace, as if the destinations to which they trudged held nothing better to offer than the fog now enfolding them. It was altogether a dreary scene.

Still, I kept up my good cheer as I walked, imagining the joy I would have in making my friends' Christmas a happy one and my uncle's as well, I hoped.

When I arrived at my destination, however, I nearly lost my nerve. Perhaps I was on a fool's errand, I thought. The darkening day made the Scrooge & Marley sign hard to read. In the nearly opaque window I detected the eerie and distorted glow of a faint light as it struggled to pierce the grease and dirt.

Nevertheless, I went in.

Only the smaller clerk, Cratchit, was to be found at his post. He wore a long, shabby white comforter wound tightly about his neck in an effort to keep warm. On the street I had been unaware of any great lessening of the temperature; yet once inside the building, I noticed a pronounced chill.

The man made a little bow, but showed little life. He looked bone-weary.

"Don't you remember me, Mr. Cratchit?" I asked, smiling,

hoping to enliven him a bit.

"Why, no, sir," he said, looking at me carefully. Then: "Hold on there! Didn't you pop in to see Mr. Scrooge once before? Of course, you're his nephew! In the summer, I believe it was—yes! God bless you, sir, and may you have a merry Christmas!"

"The same to you, Bob. Is my uncle in?"

Cratchit smiled wryly. "And where else would he be?"

"Splendid, then I'll go on in," I said, and pushed by the clerk with a will, despite his objection, remembering fondly how my uncle had received me before and how we'd drunk claret together on that warmer day.

But when he caught sight of me, Uncle Ebenezer jumped to his feet in alarm, as if he had seen a ghost. I don't know why I thought that, but prior to my arrival he must have been agitated about some matter and was put out to see me at that moment.

"Steady, Uncle. It is only I, your nephew."

He sat down again, his hand going to his heart. "Heavens, you gave me a fright! I thought you were someone else come to annoy me. My Lord, Fred, what are you doing here on such a miserable day?"

"I want to ask you to my home for Christmas dinner. Didn't you get my letter?"

"My boy, please run along. I'm much too busy for such diversions. Dear God, what else can happen on this dreadful day!"

"I see I've come at a bad time. What is the matter?"

"Never you mind. You'd best go. We're closing early tonight—very soon. So you must get along."

I smiled and winked at him. "I shall not go until you promise you'll join us on Christmas Day," I said with a light heart. "My darling wife so wants to meet you!"

"Bah!" he grumbled and scowled in his usual way. "Impossible."

I did not yet budge. "Uncle, please. I am terribly desirous for you to come."

There was a pause. He cocked his head as if in thought. Then he began to usher me out with a feigned smile. As he did so, he said things I knew he didn't mean.

"Well, perhaps I can, Fred, perhaps I can! Yes! But please run along now, and I'll give the matter serious thought. Serious! Of course I will consider it. Christmas Day! Just as in the old days."

After I exited the building I heard the old man loudly castigating Cratchit for letting me trespass into his inner sanctum.

I sighed, for it was plain I'd failed in my mission to entice Scrooge into my home by appealing to him in person. I was now absolutely certain he would not come, and, indeed, he did not. That didn't bother me as much as his distraught manner, so changed from the summer visit. Whom was he expecting? Was his business in some sort of trouble? What else might be wrong—his health?

I turned these and other possibilities over in my mind as I walked home.

Once there, though, I put aside those dark ruminations. Instead, I gave myself over to the last of the planning of our first Christmas dinner, which, astoundingly, was less than two days hence. I meant to think on Scrooge later, to be sure, and I resolved to ask him again to come to our home for a visit in a rosier time.

As we drank our tea that night, Emily and I discussed what had yet to be done. She made a list. We often broke into spontaneous laughter, feeling silly that we were being so precise in our planning, as if, as Emily suggested, we were with Napoleon planning the Battle of Austerlitz. She emitted a glow I had not noticed in some time; and as she worked on her list she hummed under her breath, a habit recently misplaced.

I left most decisions about the food, the wine, and the games to my wife. More and more I was learning that she was a prodigious organizer. My duties consisted mostly of procuring food, drink, and coal and performing what other odd duties my logistics officer required, for we still had no domestic help. She did everything else, including decorating the room with holly, ivy, mistletoe, and the like.

Our little dinner was a smashing success. Although things did not proceed perfectly, every guest relished the food, drink, and revelry, to be sure. I do not think we ever hosted a better party, if only because all the guests—and ourselves—were elevated, if only for one day, out of the grip of the hard times that had befallen the country. It was a lesson for me that it is better to share one's good fortune with others. Having done so, I somehow multiplied my meager basket of loaves and fishes so as to feed the spirits of others.

Before year's end, I happened to bump into Bob Cratchit, of all people, in the markets of Covent Garden, where I had gone to buy a bouquet of flowers for Emily. It was a mild day for midwinter, late on a Saturday afternoon, and the place overflowed with a boisterous mixture of buyers and sellers of vegetables, flowers, and fruit. My, but there was a cornucopia of the last, including French plums and Spanish oranges. Seeing this bounty, one would have thought the hard times had vanished.

I bumped into Cratchit quite literally. We begged each other's pardon.

The little man clutched a bag of oranges and said he was on his way home, which he told me was in Camden Town. I was alarmed at his appearance, because the fellow looked to be dressed in tatters. I feared he might have lost his situation in my uncle's employ and that my unexpected visit caused his dismissal.

"Good evening, Mr. Cratchit," I said cautiously. "Was your Christmas a happy one?"

"Oh, it was ever so lovely, Mr. Fred," he answered gaily, smiling in quite a forthright fashion. Then he began to prate on about the joys of Christmas, his family of five children, and his "most excellent wife," as he phrased it, who, he said, was a formidable cook. I let him run on, deciding that he surely must still be earning a wage to be so cheerful—not that I reckoned my thrifty uncle paid him much of one.

Bob seemed quite buoyant away from his tiny office. Yet, by his clothes most people would deem the man rather poor. Obviously, he made tremendous sacrifices for the sake of his family, denying himself even the warmth of a greatcoat. Instead he still wore that shabby white comforter about his neck.

When he ran out of steam, I dared to ask after my uncle.

"And how is Mr. Scrooge?" I said. "When I saw him last, he seemed quite distressed over some matter or other."

Cratchit's smile vanished. His small round face contracted into a tight ball.

"Oh, sir," he said in a lowered tone, "your uncle is quite out of sorts since Mr. Marley's passing."

"What?" I said, startled. "Mr. Marley's *what?*"

"His passing, sir. Did you not know?"

"Marley has died? When was this?"

"Well, my goodness, it was early on Christmas Eve itself. Wasn't that the day you stopped in?"

"No. I came by the day before that, Bob—'twas two days before Christmas. You may recall my uncle was not happy to see me."

"Oh, right you are. I've gotten it muddled."

"What happened? How did Mr. Marley die?"

He glanced away from me, suddenly reluctant to spread bad news. In that moment the bell tower in St. Paul's rang for vespers. It was almost dark. A loud-voiced seller of figs was haggling with a woman to my left and in the course of it bellowing directly in my ear. I pulled Cratchit aside to a quieter spot by an empty stall.

He looked up to me with a worried look and said, "I'm afraid I must be on my way, Mr. Fred."

"First, tell me what happened. I was acquainted with Mr. Marley, you know."

He cocked his head. "Really. Well, I can only tell you that—that is, what I've heard on the street, as you might say. Mr. Scrooge told me and the other workers that Mr. Marley had suddenly taken ill and died. That was all he would say. Then he let us all go home early, even earlier than usual for Christmas Eve. He's always had a sore spot about letting us off on the holiday, you see."

"Yes, yes," I said impatiently.

He gave a chuckle and smiled. "So it *couldn't* have been Christmas Eve when you popped in, now could it?"

"What more did you learn, Bob? Please tell me."

"Only that the gentleman's heart seized up in the early morning. Mr. Scrooge went by his home to ask if he were coming in that day. You see, Mr. Marley had been, uh—well, he'd been taking too much time away from the office of late, much to Mr. Scrooge's displeasure."

"So it was a thrombosis . . . and Uncle discovered him that way, on the day before Christmas. Poor old Marley! May he rest in peace! When was the funeral?"

"Why, that very day," said Cratchit. "I understand from reliable sources that your uncle was able to prevail upon some vicar he knew, and that the man made no objection—everybody being of a mind to get such an unpleasant obligation over and done with before the feast day, you see. So Mr. Scrooge called upon a bailiff or governor in the district about the legalities, and poof! All was accomplished lickety-split."

"What an awful thing," I observed. "One day a man's alive, and the next he's in the ground. With no time for anyone to hear of it. God bless us! Did he have a family, Bob?"

"Oh, no," he replied, "not Mr. Marley. Nor any friends I know of, excepting your uncle. If we'd knowed about a funeral, I'm sure some of us in the firm would have attended it, to show our respect. Of course, Mr. Scrooge would have to grant us the time off for that."

"Not likely, eh?"

"No, sir." He tipped his hat and turned to go.

"Wait a minute," I asked, touching his arm. "What of his legacy? I mean, surely he had a living relative on whom he could bestow his estate."

Cratchit assumed a pose of someone deep in thought, with his head tilted and his eyes narrowed. "Might be he did, Mr. Fred, such things being likely as not." Then he came closer. "But you must have heard—and if not, mind, this is general knowledge—that your uncle and Mr. Marley put in their business charter a clause, by which, in the event of one of 'em passing on, the other was to inherit his share of the company. Not only that, but all the other's worldly possessions to boot."

"Good Lord!" I exclaimed. "How extraordinary!"

"Yes, sir," he agreed. "Mind you, I don't think either of the two gentlemen ever considered taking a wife or having a family. Or giving anything to charity, either, eh? With them it was always business, business, business."

I tried to digest this information. It would mean my uncle never planned to leave a farthing to me or my family, not that I'd given the possibility any thought. Yet would he bequeath nothing at all, not even a token sum, to the poor hirelings who had toiled under him? Those like Bob, who worked hard and yet remained poor? Apparently not.

"This is a wretched turn of events," I said. "I assume, then, with all the haste with which Mr. Marley was dispatched, that nobody at all, excepting the clergyman, attended the poor man's funeral."

"Not so. Mr. Scrooge himself attended," said Cratchit. "He did, verily. But he was alone in doin' it, so I heard. In addition to being sole executor, sole beneficiary, and sole friend, your uncle was the sole mourner."

With that he gave me a respectful nod of his head and hurried off to his most excellent wife and five children.

## CHAPTER 3

## THE TRUTH ABOUT MARLEY

For days I was troubled by this news. Not out of affection for Jacob Marley, a man whom I remembered as a talkative fellow who jested with me when I was a child; as a grown man I never once spoke to him, except on that summer day I hailed him in the street. No, it was the dark bargain between the two business partners that seized my imagination. How could those two men, both in their primes, have no other aim in life but to accumulate wealth? I recalled the time I suggested my uncle take a wife. Had he rejected the notion out of hand because it would reduce the bottom line in his personal ledger? Perhaps the proviso Cratchit mentioned was not there originally but added when the two men reached a certain age—that is, after their prospects for a rewarding private life had diminished.

But whether the bargain was made in youth or middle age, there was a whiff of Marlowe's *Doctor Faustus* in it. It was as though the two wagered to see who could live the longer. The winner got the money, the loser the grave. It may not have been the usual "bargain with the devil" but certainly the devil brokered the arrangement.

I thought back to my recent visit to Scrooge & Marley—that foggy winter day when my uncle jumped to his feet when I barged into his office. He was as jittery as a cat on a hot anvil. What was it all about? Perhaps he'd been granted a grain of foreknowledge, for I now knew his partner died suddenly the very next day.

Many speculations and fears about the matter continued to plague my thoughts. Eventually I cast them away, lest brooding on the matter drive me to strong drink. The new year brought change, as it usually does, and for myself all the changes were good. Living costs moderated, and it was generally bruited about that the hard times were coming to an end. Perhaps the bounty I'd seen at Covent Garden was a harbinger of this. My career at the law firm continued to blossom, and I received a promotion. Most importantly, my wife now carried a child. Her knitting now was done with a view to baby clothes.

A daughter was born to us in late September. Alice was a healthy child and soon became the delight of our lives. How I regretted that my departed parents were denied the joy of a grandchild to dandle on their knees! But I'm thankful to say that I did not dwell on this sentiment, for Emily and I now busied ourselves with the many changes that a child brings, immersed in the wonder of this blessing.

As the time drew nigh to Christmas, I thought again of my Uncle Ebenezer, who hadn't crossed my mind for many a month. I remembered my resolve to ask him once more to feast with us on Christmas Day.

*This time he'll join us,* I thought. *Surely he will come to see my child.*

Was I so proud and vain a father as to assume he would be completely enchanted by this newborn creature? Of course I was.

This time I forwent writing him. I decided to approach him directly, but not at his place of business. That had not gone well last time. Instead I decided to visit him on a Sunday afternoon at his lodgings. I deemed he might be more amenable to my invitation away from the dismal trappings of the warehouse.

The day was cold but clear and sunny, which cheered me and gave me hope that this year he might visit us. After suffering the loss of his friend Marley, perhaps he'd want to reestablish ties with his family. Surely he'd be delighted to learn he had a great-niece living in this impersonal and indifferent metropolis, and I was certainly anxious to tell him.

I don't think I ever visited his lodgings as a child. If my mother ever brought me to them, I must have been quite small. But in due course I found the place, a handsome brick building, encompassing three or four suites of rooms, from the look of it. I knocked briskly on its bright green door.

An attractive woman with gray hair soon opened it.

"Beg pardon," I said. "I've come to visit my uncle, Ebenezer Scrooge."

"Oh, dear," she said, "you don't look a bit like him. I'm afraid he's not here, young man. But do come in out of the cold." She shivered and bade me enter. I noticed the woman was smartly dressed, either preparing to leave or recently returned.

I introduced myself as we stood in the hallway, a place I judged to be only slightly warmer than the outside stoop.

She began to tell me about herself. In a short time I learned that her name was Mrs. Abernathy, that she was a widow, that she owned the house, had lately come from church, and was about to prepare luncheon.

"If you don't mind," I said, interrupting gently, "may I go to my uncle's rooms and wait for him there?"

"But he's not here!"

"So you said."

"You don't understand, sir. He moved out—now when was it? February? No, not during Lent. I believe it was earlier in the year. That's right! Fifteenth of January, it was. Yes! You should know I have a good head for dates."

"Then he no longer lodges here?"

"No, sir, though he did so for twenty years. That's how long he rented and lived under my roof. Or was it only nineteen years?

But never mind. A quiet man of business, your uncle, though I know not what sort of business he conducts. He told me his office was a short walk from here."

"I apologize, for I knew nothing about his leaving. Have you a forwarding address?"

"Indeed I have," she said. Her eyes narrowed, and she took a moment to scrutinize my face. "Have you been abroad, young man? How is it you don't know your uncle's new address?"

"We are a scattered family, ma'am, and my retiring uncle has for a long time been rather distant, so to speak, from the rest of us. What I mean to say is—"

"Say no more," she interjected with a wry grin. "I haven't spoken to my sister Agnes for ten years. Now, let me fetch you that address."

It turned out Mrs. Abernathy's head for dates was much better than her head for scraps of paper. I stood in the drafty hall shivering for a quarter of an hour, wishing I were outside in the sun. Finally she returned and read me the address.

I thanked her.

"It's a wonder I even found this note," she said. "I've had no call to produce his new address before today. Not once! No mail has come for your uncle here—not that much ever did—and you're the first person to visit him in, uh—goodness, how many years has it been? Let me see."

"I'm forever in your debt, Mrs. Abernathy," I said and hastily departed.

At the corner I asked a policeman where the street might lie, and he pointed me in that way. As soon as I began to stride forward in earnest, enjoying the embrace of the sun on my back again, I noticed familiar shops and coffeehouses here and there and concluded that I was again in the vicinity of Scrooge & Marley. I recalled Mrs. Abernathy's remark that my uncle's place of business was a short walk from her house. Typical of him, I thought. It exemplified my uncle's nature, which was defined by an everlasting frugality

The policeman had told me I had not far to go and he was correct. I soon found the street, which was a narrow one off the main thoroughfare. He'd also told me the street would come to a premature end. In other words, it led nowhere. Once I turned into it, I tempered my energetic gait, finding I did not like this shadowy byway. It was nearly deserted. The shops were not swept up in front and their windows were coated with coal dust. Some were abandoned. An idle wind blew dirt and debris around and whined softly under the eaves.

I had to walk the entire distance of that street to reach my destination. The way ended in a tired heap of a decaying house that stood squarely at the terminus, bridging both sides of the street. A short yard paved with bricks lay before it. It was evidently now in part a commercial building; its left and right wings were converted to shops for a stationer and a tobacconist, respectively. The entrance to the residence lay in between, where steps led up to a massive door. Most of the paint had peeled off it—though not from the sun's doing, I judged, for surely little sunlight ever warmed this narrow, desolate street.

After bounding up the steps I took hold of the large brass knocker and rapped smartly three times. The knocker made a raucous sound, whose echoes died away in a somber cadence.

I waited for a minute. No one came to answer the door. I imagined that my uncle, if at home, might well be ignoring the outside world and would not disturb himself. So I knocked again.

And again.

I was disappointed to have gone to this much trouble and not be admitted. I didn't care that I was making a dreadful racket in this gloomy place. I preferred that noise to the moan of swirling dust. Though I could hear a few sounds from the bright world I'd left, they were so distant that they sounded mournful and lost. I was about to knock a seventh or eighth time when the door suddenly opened a crack.

"Who is it?" demanded a hoarse and surly voice.

"Frederick Truelock, at your service," I said, trying to imbue my voice with cheerfulness.

The door opened wider, but I could not yet see into the darkness of the place. Then the questioner stepped out and said, "Good Lord, Fred! You do have a way of popping up at the oddest times!"

"Uncle!" I responded, for by this time I could see him in the light of the street. He had changed in appearance these last twelve months. His hair, which used to be only partially gray, now favored that hue. He seemed to have lost an inch of his height. I knew he was no more than fifty-five years of age, but he appeared much older.

"What can the matter be now?" he demanded.

"Nothing is the matter," I said. "You have been in my thoughts of late, so I decided to pay you a call."

He sighed heavily. "I suppose you want to come in," he said.

"Thank you, Uncle."

He stepped aside so I could enter, closed the door, locked it, and began to shuffle down the hall. I followed, noticing he moved rather slowly. The hall was dark, lighted only by a few weak rays that crept in from a sidelight of the door.

He took me to his drawing room, which was illuminated slightly better. Then I noticed he wore a dressing-gown and slippers.

"Were you asleep, Uncle? I hope I didn't wake you."

"How could you not? I wonder you didn't wake the dead!"

"Sorry. You were in bed, then? Have you taken ill?"

"I was merely taking my weekly nap, the reward of person of my years who works diligently six days a week. Sit down there— that chair is the least bothersome. I don't normally keep wine at home, I'm afraid, so I have little to offer a guest. I've never had one before."

I took a seat and realized how cold it was in the room. "Oh, that's all right," I said. "A spot of tea suits me better anyway."

He stared at me vacantly, then said, "My word! Well, sit there awhile and I'll produce some."

He left the room. There was coal in the fireplace as well as tinder and matches nearby, so I lit a fire. I think he was happy to see it when he returned with a small tea service. "I have no biscuits," he said.

"That's quite all right."

I offered to pour.

"I believe I know your mission," he said as I filled the teacups.

"You do?"

"Another Christmas Day bears down upon us, and once again you want to invite me to dine with you on that day. Isn't that it?"

"That much is true," I said.

"You are persistent, young Fred, if not stubborn. I do believe that's a family trait we both share." He chuckled.

The remark, as well as the chuckle, was the first indication his mood was improving. Perhaps it was due to the fire in the hearth. I had to think back to the day we shared wine in his office to recall anything to suggest he ever shed the heavy mantle he displayed to the world at large.

"You are correct in that," I agreed. "At least as it applies to myself. I cannot say if stubbornness was ever rampant in the rest of the family. But as to the matter of Christmas: you may recall that last year you promised to dine with us. Yet when the holiday came, I looked for you in vain."

He regarded me strangely. "I promised, you say? That I do not recollect."

"Ah, but perhaps you were making sport of me," I said, "because the day I called on you—late in the day, it was, and two days before Christmas—something apparently had upset you before I arrived at your office. You were exceedingly anxious that I not tarry long."

His mouth twitched and his eyes flicked to the side. "Oh, yes . . . I remember now."

"Not that you signed a legal contract to come," I said quickly, trying to keep the tenor of my words light. "It's always a gentleman's right to cancel a dinner engagement."

"Yes, but it's not good form." He rose and went to the fireplace, holding out his hands to warm them. Then he turned back to me. "Fred, a sequence of events had reached a crisis when you burst into my office that day." He paused a moment. "An extremely nasty day it was."

I nodded. "A blanket of fog smothered the entire city."

"I do not refer to the weather," he said. "Certain matters—business, personal, and legal—had come to the fore. I was in a quandary."

He looked away from me, as if in thought.

His words piqued my curiosity. But I looked at him steadily, keeping my expression blank, projecting neither interest nor a wish to change the topic of our dialogue. This was a mannerism that I, as a solicitor, had developed to deal with certain clients, men who wavered between the poles of a decision. I had found that taking no part in their internal dickering was the best way to avoid a complete dismissal of the subject at hand. In this case I sensed my uncle was on the verge of explaining himself, and I didn't wish to mar this inclination by expressing an opinion.

Several minutes passed. A longcase clock struck the half hour. At that signal my uncle returned to his wing chair and drained his teacup.

I kept quiet. So did he, and for a long while we sat there without speaking. The silence weighed heavy in the room. I could now hear the faint tick of the clock's pendulum marking time.

"I have likely said too much already," he began. "But perhaps I should explain a few things to you. Even though you are a trusted relation, I must have an unqualified vow that you will keep confidentiality."

"You have it," I said.

"Please be sure. You must not share this information with anyone, not even your wife."

"Uncle, I am a solicitor. I trade in confidences."

He considered this, then nodded. "I suppose you do," he said. There was still tea in the pot, so he poured us both another cup, then sat back in his chair, thinking. Or delaying.

I ventured to prompt him. "By any chance would this pertain to your friend Jacob Marley?"

He jerked his head toward me. "How did you know that?"

"A while back I learned that he passed away. Never mind how I discovered this." I thought it best not to drag poor Bob Cratchit into the conversation. "It must have been a trying time for you, losing a partner and friend. Did his death affect the business?"

He snorted. "What happened *did* affect the business, verily. It made it better." Then he drank some of his tea.

"What? Surely his absence puts more of a burden on you," I said.

"You have hit upon it, nephew. I now run the firm alone and work harder than I ever did. On the other hand, I run things as I see fit."

"Ah, I see."

"You do not see. As I said, many things were going on that day, the day you blundered in. Oh, bother! Maybe I err in thinking you need to know any of them."

"I can give no opinion on that," I said. "But I pledge my complete discretion as to anything you may tell me. I must say, however, that I was later vexed to know that after he died I was not contacted. I would have attended the man's funeral."

He gave me a mysterious look, shook his head, but said nothing.

"Why didn't you inform me of his passing?" I continued. "Did you not remember how amusing I found Mr. Marley when I was a small child?"

"Do not wax sentimental, Fred. That failing is a pitfall for a man of business, and I daresay for a young solicitor as well."

I wanted to contradict that notion but held my tongue.

"No," said my uncle, "I saw no earthly reason to tell you that Marley died." His tone was dismissive. There was a strange spark in his eye.

I felt my blood rise. "Very well, then," I blurted out. "What is it that you do want to tell me?"

"I'm getting to that. And believe me, it has much to do with the habits of Mr. Marley. Yet it rankles me that you attach so much significance to the man."

I set down my cup rather smartly. "How can you speak so ill of the dead?"

His brow furrowed and his steely eyes bored into mine. "Because Jacob Marley is *not* dead, nephew. Now you may understand why there was no reason to tell you he was."

⊰◈⊱

This was how I first learned the strange truth about Jacob Marley. At least, the crux of it. At the time, though, I merely thought I'd misheard.

"I don't understand," I said. "You mean he did not die on Christmas Eve last?"

"No, he did not."

"Then I was misinformed."

"So you were."

"When did he die, if I may ask?"

"I told you, nephew, he is not dead! I don't know how to say it any plainer."

Now I was truly in a state of confusion. "But the funeral . . ."

"There was no funeral, not really. And since there was no church rite, I did not think to inform you of one, for I did not reckon with your sentimentality, nor your curiosity in the matter. Tell me, how is it you heard that he died? Does your law firm routinely cull the register of the dead to see if there might be a spot of business to be had?"

"No," I shot back, finding his jape insulting. "I discovered it quite by chance. But I was sure to find out, Uncle. After all, I planned to come and see you again—as indeed I've done today—if only to invite you to my home for Christmas dinner."

He gave me a rather crooked smile. "Perhaps you'd like to reconsider your invitation."

I had to hold my tongue; I knew not whether my uncle nettled me on purpose, or whether his plain, stubborn reluctance to explain the matter was the thing galling me.

"Is this some kind of elaborate jest, Uncle? Please tell me if I'm the butt of it, and I shall laugh heartily."

Then Scrooge himself laughed. I don't think I'd ever heard that sound before, not in all the years I'd known him. It was a warm, baritone sound.

"My nephew," he said, "it *is* a jest, and quite an elaborate one—a jest which my friend Marley has played on the entire world. I admit I was having a bit of fun with you just now. And you're correct: I expected you would learn of his so-called death sooner or later. I thought it would be later. And I didn't expect it would matter to you so much."

"Most certainly it does," I said.

"I see that now," he continued. "It's unsettling to me because, apart from a few exceptions, every soul in the kingdom has accepted his demise without question."

"Really? Why do you think that is so?"

"Because the fellow is not missed! He left no wife, child, nephew, or niece. He had no close romantic attachments. No one cared about the man! The only person who did is you, Fred, because you remember him fondly from childhood. And since you might unwittingly make mischief, I think I must share the full story with you."

"By all means, do," I said, now completely absorbed in speculation and wondering what sort of fellow Marley really was.

Then he sighed. "I can see that my Sunday nap has flown away as swift as thought."

"I can brew more tea if you like," I said, smiling and rising from my chair.

He also stood. "I wonder if I might find a bottle of wine if I scoured the cellar sufficiently. Come with me. I may need your help in decanting it."

Puzzled, I said, "But you said you didn't normally keep wine in the house."

"I don't," he answered as he shuffled off, "but there might be a few bottles which were left behind by the former owner of this house."

"How odd," I said as I followed him. "What kind of person would abandon a portion of his wine cellar?"

"One eager to depart. Jacob Marley, for instance."

## CHAPTER 4

## TWO APPRENTICES

When we returned to the drawing room, we brought with us a bottle of sherry from Andalusia. I poured us each a glass. Uncle at first ignored the wine, seemingly more interested in taking up his pipe. In the meantime I added coal to the fire whilst he made himself comfortable in his wing chair, draping a shawl over his shoulders and then lighting his tobacco.

I waited patiently for him to begin. But now he seemed reticent.

"If I might inquire, Uncle, did you yourself help Mr. Marley carry out this—this fraud? For that is what I must call it. Surely you know it's a crime to falsify public documents, including death certificates."

"I do know," he said. "However, by the time he proposed the scheme, I was relieved to get rid of the man as a partner. We both had worked hard for many years to further our business, but of late he'd become a liability. So much so that I worried about the very survival of the firm."

"But why did Marley want to arrange this 'jest'? What drove him to it?"

He hesitated a moment. "Let me think a minute," he answered. Then he puffed on his pipe, no doubt earnestly arranging his thoughts. Finally his face brightened, and he said: "Yes, yes, that's the way I'll begin, for you must first learn the nature of the man's character and our relationship. Thus, I must start my narrative at the very beginning."

I merely nodded, sat back, and sipped my sherry.

"Jacob and I met when we were both apprenticed to the same accounting firm, one that lies in Shoreditch. I had recently arrived in London with references and a modest nest egg—money I saved up when I lived in the north of England."

"In Lancashire?" I asked.

He smiled and nodded. "You know that, I suppose, since you are my sister's son. Ah, little Fan, how I miss her! As for Jacob, he came from Liverpool and had even less money than I, partly because he'd been in London longer. Neither of us had relations in the city and we felt quite alone. We were close to the same age and soon became boon companions.

"We were alike in our ambitious spirit, for we were young and bright and keen to set the world ablaze. Those were heady years, Fred. The power of steam harnessed! Iron produced cheaply and in great quantity! Because of these and other advances, giant textile mills were rolling out cloth in great quantities, and railways were extending their iron tendrils throughout the country, creating a royal road for the marketing of goods. Jacob once said if a man cannot make his fortune in such times as these, he has no pluck at all."

I nodded in agreement but was unsure he was correct in so lavishly praising those developments.

"In other ways we were not alike. The first thing I noticed about Jacob was that he dressed fashionably and braided his hair into a pigtail, a popular conceit at the time. The second thing was that he was as smart as the dickens. He could add a column of numbers in his head faster than anyone else in the office and twice as fast as plodders such as I, who must touch pen to paper to cipher. I was ever the slow, steady worker; Jacob liked to impress people with his mathematical tricks. He was shrewd too, already a man of the world, whereas I myself was a bumpkin. I felt rather like the country mouse who came to visit his city cousin. He was fond of stout and porter. I drank only plain beer and not often, my parsimonious habits having been ingrained in me by an early life of poverty. You may find it strange, then, that we undertook a friendship or even a loose association."

"The match does seem peculiar," I agreed.

He drew on his pipe. "It was the loneliness, I fancy. And something else: we both aspired to success. We wanted to be rich. And that being the case, each of us saw in the other a trait lacking in himself, one necessary to prosper. Marley had quickness and daring. As for me, to be immodest, I had a depth of mind he did not possess. In matters of business I saw the details, the pitfalls, and the deceptions."

I had never heard my uncle speak so long and with such clarity. In fact it rather disturbed me I had never given any thought to his intelligence or business acumen. I'd only reacted to his superficial mannerisms. How thoughtless I'd been!

"Though I was shy, Jacob was an outgoing chap," he continued. "But when he wasn't flitting around, we would often tarry together in a tavern of an evening, conspiring to change our fortunes. Ha! Youth! There's nothing like it, eh? In our dreaming and plotting we finally hit upon what seemed a practical endeavor certain to succeed. Jacob had built up many business friendships, for he was a loquacious fellow whom nobody shunned. "Hail fellow well met"—that sort of man. And I, lately come from the north, could claim acquaintance with several men of standing in the textile factories there. So we wondered, could we possibly become traffickers in cloth? There was much demand for it. At length it was decided upon: we would found our own wholesale business! We would bring fine cloth to London and distribute it to the many eager tailors, cloth merchants, and manufacturers in need of the commodity."

My uncle went on at great length about the inception of Scrooge & Marley and the early struggles to make it successful. This part was of scant interest to me, though my uncle enjoyed telling it. I pass over it here. At length I felt I'd learned enough about the early days of the firm and how he viewed the young Marley, so I asked if he would not elaborate on more recent times and explain how his partner had become a "liability."

"I'll come to that directly," he answered, his voice weakening. as if strained by holding forth for so long. He coughed several times, and I wondered if the pipe smoke irritated his throat. He drank of his sherry for the first time. Though he did not seem to care for it, the wine refreshed his voice.

"Mind you, I never said Jacob was a bad man. But he was often a foolish one, in my estimation. When his mind was directed firmly on a goal, he was extraordinarily adept. It was he who who built up our sales; there is no doubt of it. As for me, I worked with our suppliers, kept the books, and oversaw day-to-day operations.

"I believe there dwelt something restless in the man's heart. He tended to give in to certain vices—to drink too much, visit the bawdy house, eat food that was over-rich. When we were still in our youth, I thought these propensities were nothing but expressions of the boundless energy in a young man's fiber. But for Jacob they outlasted his early days."

He cleared this throat and took another drink of the sherry.

In the interval I said, "I've often wondered why neither of you married." Then I smiled at him. "Say, do you remember when I put to you a similar question?"

He laughed. "Indeed I do! 'You were but a lad. And I believe I gave you a facetious answer in return. In my own case it was partly due to my reticent nature around women. Also, I was devoted to the business and rarely had the opportunity to meet young ladies. Jacob had many women on his arm over the years—none of them the retiring type, I assure you—but he never wanted to settle down and abandon his frivolous ways. He was always in search of something new. Even when he passed the span of thirty years, he was always gadding about at night, haunting the theater, the tavern, the brothel, any place that would entertain him for a few hours.

"These expensive pursuits took their toll. For one thing, he grew fat with all the fancy eating and drinking. I'm sure that's the man you remember from your childhood, eh? I jested with him about his paunchiness, but he never seemed to care about how he looked. The other consequence was that he never seemed to keep enough money. I put my share of the profits in good investments, among them certain rail lines. Jacob acquired this teetering pile of stone and brick in which we sit. Why he wanted a large house is beyond my ken; at the time I thought he might be planning to marry, but when I broached that idea, he fell into a fit of laughter. He also purchased an expensive phaeton and a horse with which to pull it, to better facilitate his nocturnal wanderings. I do not know how else he spent his money, but I'm sure he spent more than he invested."

Scrooge clucked his tongue a few times as a sad comment.

I waited a moment, then said, "I'm not sure I understand why you removed from your rooms at Mrs. Abernathy's house. I thought the place quite cheerful." I could tell I had touched on a sore point, for he clasped his hands and rolled his eyes.

"Lad, I've asked myself the same question all year long. I was happy enough there, except that Mrs. Abernathy has a tendency to run on—that is, if she can corner you. You've probably guessed that I 'inherited' this property, so to speak, upon Jacob's ostensible death. I might have sold it, but it is even closer to the office than were my old rooms. So I moved in. But there are certain expenses, including taxes, that make it odious. You may have noticed I lease out two rooms of the house to shopkeepers."

"I did notice."

"The leases bring in very little. And I must pay a charwoman, Mrs. Dilber, to clean the entire place. It's altogether a losing proposition. But let me continue my narrative."

I poured more sherry.

"Permit me to go back a bit further, to the year your parents moved to town. I was exceedingly glad of this event, because I had sorely missed your mother. Oh, I did so cherish your ma! She was the only one in my family I truly cared for. I say that with regret, for I have ever been adrift in life, alone. And one never feels as alone as he does in the bosom of a great city, surrounded by strangers—for then he must admit that he *is* alone. Her presence, then, gave me a shining light toward which I could occasionally turn my melancholy mind and heart.

"But it turned out that your father and I never got on. I will not elaborate on that point, except to say he was a good man and a good provider for his family. And of course I still visited at various times of the year, as you well recall.

"I dragged Marley along when he would come, though it was far from the kind of social gathering the fellow was accustomed to. I nurtured a small hope that perhaps in witnessing scenes of a genial domestic life, he might calm his restless urges, that he would see another path, so to speak. But this did not happen. For it was in those years when you were growing up tall and straight that he began to eat opium."

I was not prepared for this thunderbolt. I hastily set down my glass, nearly spilling its contents. "What did you say?"

"It's quite true."

I shook my head. "Did I hear aright? You did not mean to say 'laudanum'?"

"No, I did not," he said, adding tobacco to his pipe. "All of us take laudanum occasionally for aches and pains. What other remedy is there? I take it and I'm told women take it exceedingly often. The population of our country has come to rely on opium in many forms."

"I will grant you that," I said. "But *eating* it!"

"Do not be shocked," he continued. "Jacob Marley, in the insatiable quest for novel excitement, took to ingesting the drug in its native form, not in the liquid mode of laudanum. I know not how often he partook of it in this way, but it was enough so that in time he lost interest in our business.

"He had an office next to mine, as you may have surmised. Now, mind you, at that time it was not unusual for him to come in late, or leave early, or not come in at all—these were acceptable occurrences, because he was often away, combing the city for prospective clients. That was his great faculty, the ability to interest people in our products, people he'd never before met until, say, he bought them a pint. But now—well, my Lord, he stayed away for days!

"After many weeks of this, I noted that he did not look the same. His skin had turned sallow. Even stranger, he lost the belly which he had slowly built into a great protuberance. I do not know if the drug caused this loss of weight or whether he was so preoccupied by the activity itself that he neglected to eat properly."

"How terrible! I assume you berated him for this behavior?"

"Of course I did. And he in turn made excuses. At first he denied using the drug; and later, after he admitted he'd done so, he asserted—many times—that he was finished with it. He'd ingest it no more! And I must say he did resume his duties for a time. But there were still occasional days when he would go missing. I would sometimes stop by this house on my way to work, trying to roust him out. I was not, however, as persistent as you were today, and I soon departed if he did not readily answer the door.

"As a friend, I worried about his health. If in a drugged condition he saw visions and heard strange sounds, mightn't he become so deluded as to injure himself? And if he did so, who would know of it? Who would render aid? Following a long period of his not coming in, I demanded he give me a key to his house, so I might look in on him sometimes. After much resistance, he gave me the key. I think he was ashamed that his troubles had brought him to this pass."

"So," I said, "this was when he became a burden to you. And why you wanted to dissolve the partnership."

"No," my uncle said. "Not yet."

He stood up and stretched his arms. "There is much more to the story," he said, "but I wonder, Fred, if you haven't heard enough to satisfy your curiosity."

"No, not nearly enough," I quickly rejoined. "You promised to tell me what was afoot on that foggy day when I came to your office last year."

He sighed. "So I did. But is it not enough for you to know that Jacob decided to disappear? And did?"

"No," I said flatly. "I cannot fathom why the man would take such a drastic measure."

He cleared his throat. "Well, then, I can see I must entertain you even longer. But, in overtaxing my voice box this afternoon, I seem to have grown terribly hungry. Before I continue I would like to take some food. I suggest we visit a nearby tavern I frequent. It's only a little way from here, on the main thoroughfare."

As if to second this suggestion the clock began to toll the hour of five.

"Good heavens!" I exclaimed. "It cannot be so late!" Even though I had marked the clock's occasional outbursts during our time, its rough monotony had deterred me from paying close attention to the actual time of day.

"I'm afraid we have whiled away the afternoon," he said. "But see here, why not dine with me, eh? Then I'll gladly give you the rest of my account."

"No, I must go home," I said. "The light is waning. Emily will be worried."

"I see," he said setting down his pipe with a smug expression.

"You must dance to *her* tune."

I gave him a cold look.

"Perhaps you can visit another time," he said.

"'Twould be easier, Uncle, if you would simply join us on Christmas Day."

"I shall consider doing so, young Fred, as always. But there will be neither time nor opportunity to discuss these gloomy events in the setting of a jolly party—for I assume that is the nature of your dinner? A gay gathering of friends and relations?"

"Exactly."

"Then I suggest we delay this history for another occasion. Next time, if you please, be so kind as to write me so your visit may be more convenient."

It seemed to me that my uncle's tone had taken on an edge, that he was mocking my natural desire to return to my own hearth and home. Perhaps he was inwardly congratulating himself that he had never married, owning that the drawbacks of the institution outweighed its benefits. Or perhaps he was merely disappointed that the spell of his story was not sufficient to detain me, for I believe that he had begun to relish the telling of it.

"Very, well," I said curtly, anxious to be off. " As you say, another time."

I put on my greatcoat. Scrooge lit a candle and then escorted me down the dark corridor to the front door. Outside, that sinister little street lay in shadow, and I hastened out of it.

Only when I came close to home and was reviewing the day in the twilight gloom, did I comprehend I had forgotten to inform my uncle of the birth of my daughter.

## CHAPTER 5

A DIFFICULT PARTNERSHIP

Uncle did not come to our dinner that Christmas. This time, however, he wrote me to express his regret and to say how much he enjoyed my visit. He also sent warmest regards to his "niece," by whom he meant my wife. That was all. This left me to wonder when I might hear the rest of his story.

Our dinner was again a success, for having more to spend on it, we increased the amount of provisions, especially the quantity of punch. Once again we behaved rather childishly in playing the games (forfeits, blind man's buff, and the like). There was much merriment and talking and imbibing.

I intended to send a brief letter to him immediately after Christmas, but in a short while I was burdened by work and put off the task. The end of the year is a time when many obligations come due. There is an effort to eliminate one's debts or collect what one is owed. Mergers are made or dissolved. Lawsuits are contemplated.

Being preoccupied, I did not write to my uncle until Twelfth Night. We took down our holiday decorations that day now that Christmastide was over, and I thought back to Scrooge's absence at our party. Then I recalled my failure to respond to his note. I hurriedly wrote him a short letter, asking if we could set a date when I might visit him or he visit me. In closing, I told him, at long last, of Alice's birth and apologized for neglecting to inform him of the event.

I was relieved to have finally dashed off the missive, yet I almost forgot to post it. It was a busy day, for Emily and I careened about in a state of flustered excitement to prepare ourselves for a rare night out. That evening we left Alice with a nursemaid and went to a ball.

I did not expect to hear from Scrooge until February, in which month I'd suggested we meet. In only a few days, however, I received a parcel from him. Inside were expensive baby clothes, but no correspondence of any kind. I felt honored that he had sent a nativity gift, even though Alice had long outgrown the size of the garments.

Emily was pleased to receive his generous gift nonetheless.

February passed without my hearing a word from my uncle. I did not press him as I still remained busy. Still I remained curious about Jacob Marley and found myself posing questions at odd moments, for instance upon first awakening or when walking in the street. *Did the man succumb to his addiction? Did he overcome it? What drove him to counterfeit his own death?*

Scrooge eventually wrote me in March and suggested I come and see him the following Sunday afternoon. I accepted. This time I brought along a basket of sandwiches and teacakes—a means of satisfying our appetites without leaving his home. Uncle seemed amused by this tactic.

"Thankee kindly," he said, "but today I doubt we shall be nattering into the night."

"Oh, it's nothing," I replied. "A mere bite or two."

He was properly dressed on this occasion, having decided to willingly forgo his customary Sunday nap. I noticed there was more light in the drawing room. Either the sun shone more brightly this day or his charwoman had cleaned the windows. On a side table he placed a bottle of claret. He told me he preferred it to the sweetness of the sherry, which stood next to it.

Yet we again started with a cup of tea. He'd laid out biscuits aplenty. It was as though he were rediscovering an old habit long forgotten—as well as the pleasantness of common comforts.

"I've been quite busy," he remarked.

I said that I had also, and this led to a discussion of our respective labors. He said he was still doing the work of two men, and I, smiling, remarked that sometimes I felt that way myself. But I daresay this was no idle grumble of his. He complained he could not keep the books, oversee the warehouse, and also run about town in search of new customers.

"Surely, Uncle, you can hire someone to replace Marley. A salesman or two?"

"That I have tried to do, Fred. I hired many salesmen and dismissed almost as many as I hired. None lasted long. These fellows relish the chase but almost never subdue the quarry. Good-for-nothings, all of them! I must say that last year was a bad one for my business."

"It appears," I observed, "that your former partner was irreplaceable."

He did not respond to that. I poured out more tea.

In this small interval a pleasant feeling welled up in my bosom, so glad was I that my kinsman—the only one I knew of—had today taken pains to play the proper host.

"Yet I feel that matters will take a better turn in the coming months," he said. "There were other troubles last year not related to my partner's departure. For example, the hard times at the beginning of it, as you must remember. More to my specific detriment, the factory of one of my suppliers, a large mill in Manchester, was vandalized by the Luddites, and for many months they could send us no cloth."

"How appalling!" I exclaimed, outraged by the crime.

"Do not overexcite yourself, nephew. Violence cannot deter the march of progress. Repairs to the machines were made, and the firm has resumed shipping their products. Their cloth is of the finest quality, and I am altogether sanguine at the prospect of making a profit again. But now, unless I'm mistaken, you're keen to hear more about my former partner."

"I am, truly," I said and then sat back to listen.

---

"Though Jacob was my good friend, I never approved of his manner of living. He indulged in too many vices, as I told you. But his opium consumption was a habit that was new to me. I tried to understand it. In his defense, I must say he took laudanum for many ailments—back pain, toothaches, and so on—and perhaps even as a remedy for that woeful malady which is engendered by the consumption of too much wine the previous night, eh?"

Here my uncle chuckled. I think he was trying to make a joke.

"It may be," he continued, "that Jacob gradually increased his dosage in response to the pains brought on by aging and thus found himself taking far too much of it."

"A dangerous practice," I said, for I knew this excess was all too common.

"As you may know, laudanum is a diluted form of the drug—a tincture. But Jacob discovered that one may buy the drug in its crude state, in pellets or sticks. What a customer may want with these solid forms is not asked by the chemist. What is it to him? Nor is it costly. One may buy a grain of the stuff for a penny! The chemist assumes, I imagine, that the purchaser will sprinkle it as a powder on food or concoct his own liquid solutions.

"But Jacob simply took the drug directly, as many people do—but he took a staggering amount, up to fifty grains of it a day. One grain of the solid form works out to something like twenty-five drops of laudanum."

I shook my head. "I wonder the man did not destroy his innards."

Uncle nodded in agreement and finished his tea.

Though I found this information interesting, I did not see how it bore on the man's disappearance. I think my uncle read this thought in my countenance.

"Perhaps I digress," he said. "See here! Would you care for some claret?"

I indicated that I would, and he poured for the both of us. Uncle took a sip of the wine and continued his narrative.

"Now, as I said last time, Jacob recovered to some degree and resumed his duties—with occasional lapses. But he never regained his old spirit, for I'm certain he never completely gave up that vile habit. Then, about four years ago, something new got hold of him. Once again his attitude changed. This time his spirit was completely revitalized. It was as if the old Jacob had returned."

"My word!" I said.

My uncle then reached for his pipe.

I could not imagine what new drug might have evoked such a transformation. It occurred to me that, being a serious, hard-working young man—perhaps a dull one—I myself had failed to keep abreast of the sensual temptations of my times and therefore had lived most of my life under a veil of beneficent ignorance.

"Fred," he said after lighting the pipe, "have you heard of the 'hells'?"

"I have heard of the One Hell," I shot back gaily. "And I devoutly wish not to go to the place. Or do you refer, perhaps, to the nine circles of hell in Dante's poem?"

"No, I mean the hells men have created in this city: the silver hells and the copper hells. For no matter which metal one uses to characterize them, they are all damnable."

"Oh, yes," I said, now catching his meaning. "Certainly I have heard of these establishments. Do you mean to say this was Marley's new interest?"

"Indeed it was," said my uncle. "You know, Fred, gambling was ever the province of the upper classes, with certain exceptions. For example, any man may legally bet on a horse race if he goes in person to the racecourse and lays his money down at the post."

Here I interrupted. "Yes, Uncle, but haven't working men always bet money in the pubs? As an adjunct of playing darts or quoits, say?"

He dismissed that with a wave of the hand. "That is mere wagering, not betting. I do not think the Crown has ever worried much about such activities. I am speaking about the kind of gambling done in fine clubs established for the idle rich—clubs like Crockford's, whose members include the Duke of Wellington. It is a respectable establishment in which a peer may amuse himself with many games—and in so doing perhaps lose his inheritance. But the government cares little about that and allows it to continue. What does it matter if an earl or two loses his estate? But, mind you, if there are no coachmen to carry the rich to their silver hells—nor farmers, cooks, mariners, and so forth, to do the daily labor—the country would stop breathing and quickly expire. Therefore, it is only for the *common people* that it prohibits gambling in its worst forms."

"Uncle, you sound like a political reformist."

He set down the pipe and took a sip of claret. "I am nothing of the sort. I am a man of business. But the lure of something for nothing is not limited to the rich. How could it be? Eventually the substance of the clubs was translated to the so-called copper hells. It was bound to happen. Such a vice 'trickles down,' legal or not.

"Marley in his youth tried out these crude, working-class gambling parlors—wretched places, full of vile people from every corner of the kingdom. Many of the games they play are found at Crockford's, except that the stakes are lower—shillings instead of guineas. Fortunately, Jacob was not then infatuated with gaming, not even with the game of hazard, which is as ruinous as it is popular."

"Did you ever go with him to one of those places?" I asked, fascinated, for he seemed to know whereof he spoke.

"I did go once to one of these crude establishments, out of curiosity."

"What was it like?"

He paused a moment to recollect, then said, "We went into a part of town I shall not name. Marley assured me that the club was respectable, at least for a lower-class house. It was called the Thames Club. Its location was in a plain, drab building down a side street, with no marking of any kind. Marley pulled a bell cord at the door. A burly man opened it, ushered us into a vestibule, and quickly shut the door. The man said nothing but rang a hand bell. Marley, knowing the protocol, approached an iron-clad inner door and waited. A small aperture slid open in this imposing barrier, and a pair of eyes considered us as we stood there. I suppose we looked acceptable, for the door then opened, and we were admitted.

"The main room of the house was given over to several tables, the largest for the game of hazard. At that table, the players looked like respectable men—I even recognized a merchant I knew, and this surprised me, since I had expected the lowest sort of guttersnipe to dominate the play. Still, I could not believe how rashly those fellows bet on every throw of the dice.

"There were quieter games in progress, and I watched Marley bet on *rouge et noir*, a game played with several decks of cards. There was little skill in any game I saw, and after Marley had amused himself, we left. He told me later, over a pint of beer, that he had no appetite to risk money at these pastimes for the chances of winning were slim."

"What drew him to it later in life, then?"

He puffed on his pipe. "I think it was a reaction to his other vice, the opium-taking. Or rather, to the *reduction* in the fearful amount he formerly ingested. As I mentioned, he was not the ebullient fellow he once was. He plodded through his days, all the time fighting his desire for the drug, sometimes failing in that, always miserable. He languished, then, in his own kind of hell for many months. He needed something else with which to beguile himself."

"Gambling," I said.

"Yes, but remember, he had tried the copper hells in his younger days. He knew there was no way he could profit in them, especially since cheating was rampant in those places. He was certainly not a person to throw away money merely to partake of the free food and drink they provided. It happened that Jacob had a friend of many years—a gentleman whose name I would rather not mention—who had joined one of the newer clubs—Gillingham's, to be exact. Marley went there as his guest. It's a silver hell, to be sure, but membership was open to any wealthy and respectable man, regardless of whether he was titled, a member of parliament, a military officer, or a diplomatist. They did, however, require that new members be sponsored by a current member in good standing. The annual subscription was an exorbitant £25. When Marley's friend offered to sponsor him, he joined."

"Wait, Uncle. Why would the odds be any better in a refined club?"

"You are correct; they are not, at least for games that rely solely on luck, such as hazard. To be sure, those games are also popular in the better houses, where there is less chance of one being cheated. But clubs like Gillingham's offer other games that a gentleman might play with better chance of success."

"How is that possible?"

"Well, there are a few games in which skill plays a larger part—quieter games, such as piquet and backgammon. At any rate, Jacob found one that he already knew and liked. It is a genteel pastime, one played in all the great homes of England as a diversion after dinner."

"I am hard put to guess what game that might be," I said.

"I'm certain you've played it, Fred," he said with a smile.

"For it is whist."

"Whist! Surely you're not serious."

"But I am. Mind you, when a man plays it in a silver hell, he can win or lose a fortune in a single night. It is said that one famous noble once lost 100,000 pounds at whist in his youth. Thereafter he gave up gambling altogether."

"Yet like any card game, it relies on chance, does it not?" I asked, not quite understanding how it could be otherwise.

"To a certain degree. There is luck in the draw and distribution of the cards. However, whist requires intelligence and strategy. For example, one must keep track of the cards and tricks played, finesse the honors, and defend against the other side. If one is skillful, he can do quite well. Jacob Marley, when sober and lucid, had the perfect mind for the game."

"You seem to know quite a bit about the game of whist yourself, Uncle."

"I do, verily, for I played it quite a bit when I was apprenticed to old Fezziwig in my youth. It's an engaging pastime, but never did I bet money on the outcome."

"I imagine they do so at Gillingham's, eh?"

"Exceedingly," he said with a knowing smile.

"I must acknowledge their clubhouse is a beautiful building," I remarked. "I have had occasion to pass by there."

"See that you continue to pass by, nephew. The high-class clubs are all beautiful. But if you take up the forbidden sports in these houses, you will, in time, face utter ruin."

"Does that mean that you yourself have ventured inside such a club?"

"I was Marley's guest several times at Gillingham's. This was about a year and a half ago, after he'd regained his old zest and *savoir-faire*. One day I pressed him for the reason for the transformation. I expected to hear of his complete liberation from the god Opium, but instead he told me he had found a new pursuit that brought him much pleasure and gave him new friendships in the upper echelons of society."

"Indeed," I mused. "No doubt his brilliant mind made him a cavalier of the card room."

"He did well," said Scrooge. "And my curiosity led me to follow him to the place, mainly to see if it was peopled with as many lords and ministers of Parliament as he reported. There was a small rise in our sales, you know, and I thought his hobnobbing with such company might be good for business."

"What was it like?" I asked, now curious.

"Unlike the copper hell, the house flaunted the glitter and finery of the aristocracy. The staff wore livery. But the arrangement of rooms was not so different. The large front room contained a buffet with wine and food free of cost, whilst in the center of it stood the green baize hazard table. On each side, a croupier sat holding a rake and wearing a green shade over his eyes to protect him from the strong light of the chandelier. The players crowded round where they could, and unlike their plebeian counterparts, all were sedate and well-mannered whether they lost or won."

"My word," I said. "It sounds to me like a place that belongs in the lower regions of the earth. For what pleasure could a man take in winning when he must also pretend not to care?"

"I agree. I sometimes wonder if our betters live such boring lives that they need the jolt of a great victory or a great reversal to feel any emotion at all. Of the two, perhaps it is the latter—in the form of a staggering loss of money—that makes them more aware of their proper place in God's creation."

"But Marley did well, you say?"

"To be sure. He had begun his membership at Gillingham's Club several weeks before I ever set foot on its plush carpets and he kept at it for many months more. I watched him play once and noted that, unlike some other games, whist there was played quietly, with little of the chatter and falderal that accompanies more lively games. Lately it has occurred to me that the main reason Marley was able to wriggle free of the grasp of opium was his determination to excel at whist."

"A worthy juxtaposition in the focus of his mind, I would

say."

"No doubt this new obsession ensured his continued abstinence. The worst thing to happen at this time was this: he kept winning. Not every night but more often than not. And when a man wins that often, he assumes he will go on winning forever."

"I don't follow you," I said. "Why shouldn't he expect to win? Wasn't he merely displaying the skills you spoke of—that is, his keen mind for numbers and his quickness?"

"Yet one never knows when a shrewder opponent might enter the fray or when the cards will turn against him in a cruel fashion." Uncle paused and sat holding his glass of claret for a moment. "Dame Fortune," he said finally, "is no more constant than Demon Opium."

"If you please, continue," I said. "I would like to hear the whole thing out. Though I don't relish what I know must come, I would like to have done with it."

"Very well," he said and took a drink of wine.

## CHAPTER 6

## THE WHIMS OF FORTUNE

"Marley continued to visit Gillingham's frequently. Even though he didn't always win, he achieved such a level of self-confidence in his play that he didn't fret when he lost. He felt he would recoup his losses and extend his overall winnings in short order. He became, then, a steady player, a regular, a man who was there night after night.

"As one might guess, whist is not the best game to reward a player with a fortune in a single sitting. If a man is that desperate, hazard or *rouge et noir* will have to be his choice. Marley aimed to increase his winnings in an orderly progression, week by week. He was in no hurry.

"So dedicated was he to this strategy that he sought to better his chances in every conceivable way. For instance, he thought to modify his diet. Unlike many opponents, who gorged themselves on exotic delicacies at the club's dinner table, Jacob ate very little that could possibly disturb his digestion and hence cloud his mind. He told me he kept mainly to boiled chicken and toast, washed down by water. Only at the card table did he drink wine and then only in moderation. He would have left it out altogether but to do so might have aroused suspicion or vexation among his opponents. He spoke louder as play progressed, to give the impression of imbibing more than he actually had.

"After my last visit to Gillingham's, I heard only a little from Jacob about his further exploits at the table. We did not speak of it during the business day, for neither he nor I was of a mind to spread it about that he spent so many hours at a fashionable gaming club. Our clerks and warehousemen knew only that Marley had been restored in some way and that our business once again sailed straight and true. He and I would occasionally sup together at a nearby tavern—the one to which I invited you December last—and there he would regale me with anecdotes of the card room. So hale and hearty did he seem at that time, I was truly convinced his hours at the club were beneficial for him. I now feared he would amass such a fortune that he would leave Scrooge & Marley to devote all his energy to his newfound passion."

Here my uncle paused a moment, and I, suddenly feeling restless, rose to my feet.

"How did it happen, then?" I asked gravely, impatient to hear of Marley's downfall, for I was cocksure I knew to what terrible end his narrative was leading.

"Beg pardon?"

"How did Marley's luck desert him? For I assume that soon you mean to tell me that he lost all his money."

Scrooge sighed. "You are correct to say he lost all his money, Fred. But it was not due to bad luck—nor bad play on his part either."

I sat back down. "Then I am truly mystified."

Uncle closed one eye and peered at me strangely. "What would you say if I told you that he was waylaid by highwaymen with drawn pistols?"

I felt an itchiness on the back of my neck, a physical sign of my irritation at his circuitous, drawn-out manner of relating his story. I did not reply, for I knew he expected docile patience on my part. Nevertheless I think I clenched my teeth.

"Now, Fred," he chided, "don't look at me that way."

"How can I not look at you askance when you indulge yourself in hyperbole and improbable fancies?"

"You must forgive me that figure of speech. I only meant to draw a parallel to the extreme nature of his predicament. For the truth is, Jacob was swindled, plain and simple."

"Swindled? You mean someone cheated him at the card table?"

"I do."

I heard the big clock toll four. I took a drink of my claret. "Are we perhaps getting to the end of the tale?"

"Not yet," he answered. "Can it be that although the days grow longer with the season, you again feel the pull of, uh, your domestic tether?"

"On the contrary," I answered firmly. "I have set aside the entire day for my visit. I informed my wife that my visit might continue past sunset and into the night, and therefore she should have no concern about me, even if the time of my return were to touch upon the tenth hour."

"Goodness," he said, "let us pray fervently we do not go as late as that."

The truth was that I had told Emily not to worry until darkness fell. I was still rather put out by Uncle Ebenezer, though for reasons I didn't understand. I am not normally an impatient man, yet somehow he managed to nettle me with the slightest effort. Then he coughed several times, and I could see he was tired of speaking and needed a respite.

"Shall we visit that tavern you spoke of?" I asked. "We can sup there, if you like."

"I am a trifle hungry," he answered, "but not as hungry as that. Instead why don't we eat some of the food you brought?"

I'd forgotten about the Emily's basket. So we buttered some teacakes and had another round of tea. During this interval I spoke at length about my daughter, Alice. He showed a real interest in his great-niece. Yet there is not a lot one can really say about a six-month-old infant, and it dawned on me that most of my giddy comments fell on deaf ears. I felt a bit foolish. "My invitation to you still stands," I said. "I would be honored if someday you were to come visit me and my family. Then you might judge for yourself whether Alice resembles my mother, as I fancy she does."

"Hmm," he said, and his tone seemed neither positive nor negative. "I suppose you expect me to keep up the family ties, eh?"

I did not comment on this remark. At such moments my uncle confounded me, for he never said the expected thing. I wondered if I would ever understand him.

I wanted to steer our conversation away from family matters awhile since he was not easy in discussing them. So I changed the subject to general topics of the day. We spoke of King William's failing health and the consequent prospect of a new queen in the person of his niece, Princess Victoria of Kent. What would that be like? Of course, he had an opinion on the matter and enlightened me to matters of the royal succession. An avid reader of the *Times,* my uncle knew more of the goings-on in the government than I did.

There were two roast beef sandwiches in the basket, and we ate them. My uncle seemed to enjoy the food.

"Did you know," he said, "that the Fourth Earl of Sandwich, the man who outfitted Captain Cook for his voyage around the world, invented these clever tidbits?"

"Seems to me I have heard something of the sort," I said dryly. "Or else I have misconstrued the origin of the name."

"The story goes," he continued, "that the earl was in the habit of asking for meat between two slices of bread so that he need not leave the gaming table to take a proper meal. You see, the earl was also devoted to gambling at whist!"

I studied him carefully to see if he was having me on. I was not certain one way or the other, so I said, "My, it seems the whole world loves the blasted game."

After our impromptu meal was finished, he said he was refreshed and would like to continue. I was more than ready for that.

———◆———

"The first I knew that Jacob was in trouble came toward the end of the summer before last. This was on the very day you popped into my office the first time. Remember? You told me you'd seen him in the street, hailed him, but had been unable to get his attention. Part of my consternation in seeing you arose from the conversation I'd had with Jacob immediately before he stormed out of the office.

"You see, Fred, he'd asked me for a loan of £40,000."

"My word!" I exclaimed. "One could buy himself a small estate for such a sum."

"It's quite shocking indeed, especially since he had recently boasted of making a large profit after a year's play at Gillingham's. He didn't say why he needed this amount, only that his own money was tied up in bank securities and the like and that it would take him a fair amount of time to convert those assets into cash. Hence, the loan would be temporary.

"I asked the reason for his haste although I already had a suspicion. He would not answer. But of course I would not let it pass, even for an old friend. He finally admitted that he'd lost quite a bit of money—more than he asked for now—in the card room at the club. He'd signed a promissory note for the amount he could not cover."

"But Uncle, that sort of note is a debt of honor and not legally binding."

"That is exactly what I said to Marley. He replied that, though that might be the case, he was bound to pay it or be expelled from the club. Not only would his reputation be ruined, but he would no longer be able to play whist in that club.

"'See here,' I told him, 'you mustn't chase after your losses, Jacob. That is extreme folly.' Then I asked him how long it had taken to lose such an immense amount.

"'Ah, Ebenezer!' he said to my horror, his face drooping, 'it was all in a single session of play. We sat down last Friday evening, and for the first time in playing there, I lost steadily and heavily. I thought I had a bad partner. Even though he departed at midnight, his replacement was no better.'

"I asked him who the winners were.

"He shook his head, then he said, 'Viscount Thornsbury and the Earl of Archwood. I could not understand how these lords became so damnably proficient in such a short time, for I had observed their play in the past. I beat them on those occasions— separately, however, never together. That troubles me, for I think the partnership rather odd. The viscount is young, and the earl quite his senior. Seeing the two playing together, I thought I would have an easy night of it. But from the very first hand, I felt the breath of the three-headed dog of Hell breathing down my neck.'

"'And no doubt meaning to drag you to Hades,' I replied. 'Was it bad cards?'

"'The cards were unrelenting,' he admitted.

"But then he added that there was more to it. There were so many clever turns of play, so many times a trick was lost which he might have won, that he felt that the goddess of luck meant to destroy him.

"'Then why didn't you get the blazes out of there?' I demanded.

"'I truly believed the cards would eventually change,' he said, downcast. 'They had to sometime! So I agreed to raise the stakes. At two a.m. the club closed their doors. But the four of us kept on playing till daybreak.'"

"Hold on, Uncle! A moment ago you said he was swindled; surely you can't mean he was swindled by these two lords."

"I can and do mean it, Fred. Absolutely."

My jaw dropped upon hearing this. Uncle Ebenezer did not seem to notice.

"Jacob kept on speaking of that evening, needlessly supplying me further details of his disastrous Waterloo. But I ceased listening. It's been my experience that those who want money from me—or who owe me money and don't have it—are the most loquacious people on the face of the earth. Evidently they believe if they spew enough words in my direction, their argument will become cogent and as clear as glass."

I had to smile, for I knew my uncle well enough by then to appreciate his peculiar line of reasoning. "I hope you did not make a loan to Mr. Marley for such a fantastic amount."

"Nor for a lesser one. I was angry with him and refused to consider a loan of any sort."

"That was wise of you," I said.

He regarded me with a slight smile. "You think so? Is that really what you believe, Fred? Didn't you tell me how kindly you regarded Mr. Marley as a favorite memory of your childhood?"

"That is true," I agreed. "But childhood memories do not necessarily indicate the mettle of a man's character."

"Well, then, I must say you have less humbug about you than most men I deal with."

"Tell me," I said, "what did Marley do when he learned he'd been swindled?"

"Oh, Fred, that is the most terrible thing of all: *he did not know he'd been swindled!* And he never did find out the truth. Jacob was many things, but he was never a cheat, and therefore could not fathom that two peers of the realm would conspire to swindle an honest man. He was ever wary of playing in the copper hells, but not in Gillingham's—goodness, not there! That was the reason he joined the club, to gamble with gentlemen who are honest."

"Now I'm completely at sea! If Marley himself never learned the truth, how is it you know he was swindled?"

"I am certain he was. But there is no direct proof. You will have to hear the rest of the story to see if you agree with my conclusion."

Another thought occurred to me. "Was there collusion between the club proprietors and the men who fleeced him?"

"Not likely. Jacob once told me the proprietors at Gillingham's make very little money from the whist players, only a small fee for games played. They do not bank the game, as they do in hazard or faro. They look to the more popular tables for their profit. In the card and backgammon rooms, the betting is solely between the players themselves, and debts incurred there are considered only debts of honor, as you pointed out. They are secured only by the debtor's moral integrity."

*Moral integrity.* My stomach took a sickly turn. I thought that "moral integrity" was the last thing I would look for in a gaming house, no matter in which elegant room the game might be played.

Scrooge continued: "And apparently in the card rooms of that club there had never been a hint of cheating, not a shadow of it. Therefore, I doubt there was collusion. The management was far more concerned about cheating at the hazard table. There players must purchase counters to use in their betting—this way the house has no worries about payment.

"At the whist table the players themselves must agree beforehand how they shall settle up after the final rubber. Some insist on a cash settlement in bank notes. Others agree to accept a promissory note for all or a portion of the debt."

"An IOU."

"Yes. The latter is generally in effect if not explicitly stated."

" How strange Marley never found out he was duped. Well, what did he do after you refused to lend him money?"

"On that day you saw him in the street, Fred, he was setting out to ask other friends for loans. He bragged he had friends in every quarter."

"Was he successful in raising the money he needed?"

"I'm coming to that. Because I declined to help him, Jacob did not speak to me for weeks. Our relationship in the office cooled— all the men saw it. He continued to make sales, but he did not let me know of new prospects nor any details of what he was about. Nor did I ask. I carried on, keeping to my own work, hoping that somehow he would solve his problem."

"It sounds like the former situation, when he was eating raw opium."

"Yes, and for a while I thought he might regress to that terrible habit. In the month of October, however, I heard a rumor that he had settled his debt with the lords—completely! I profoundly hoped the rumor was true."

My uncle was silent a moment, and his face took on a sorrowful look. I asked if he was too tired to continue. He shook his head. "I'm fine," he said. But he was silent a moment longer before he continued.

CHAPTER 7

DEBTS OF HONOR

"The rumor proved to be true, and matters improved in the company offices after that. Jacob came in every day or informed me where he would be. I never questioned Jacob about what had happened—I was content that he'd resolved his problem. We gained customers. Our sales rose. For a period in autumn, then, Scrooge & Marley was again a promising enterprise.

"But in late December he came into my office near closing time to ask if I would have dinner with him at the tavern we frequented. I had not seen him for several days. Now I recoiled, for his face was haggard, unshaven, worn. Obviously he was in some new difficulty. I knew at once I must go with him, and so I instructed Cratchit to shutter the office and go home. I felt intuitively that Marley would not ask for money this time but for help of another sort, perhaps advice. A strange color haunted his eyes, and inner turmoil caused his fingers to tremble. I quickly donned my greatcoat, and we departed.

"An ugly mist greeted us on the street—cold, wet, and discouraging. We cut through it without speaking, walking smartly till we reached the tavern door. They knew us well there, and soon we were seated at a table in the corner, away from the general hubbub of the place. The girl brought us our usual pints. I ordered bangers and mash to eat, Jacob some sort of fish. But he ate little.

"I waited patiently for him to speak.

"'Well, Ebenezer, I'm done for,' he said when he could refrain from speaking no longer.

"'Did you not gather all the money you needed?' I said, thinking to myself that now, at long last, I should help him make up whatever the difference might be. After all, Jacob was my oldest friend. I did not approve of his style of living, but we had weathered many storms together. We were partners. I decided I must help him this time if I were to ever sleep soundly again.

"But my intuition about his not asking me for money was correct; he did not do that. He said, 'I did finally raise the money, yes—but not as you may suppose from the good will of my friends.' He emitted a plaintive little laugh, a sound that chilled my spine. 'I have learned something about my situation. It is this: I have almost no friends in this vast city.'

"'That is utter nonsense,' I countered at once. 'Why, you are the most convivial and popular man I ever met. We would have no business at all if it were not for your ability to charm the most aloof stranger in a trice.'

"'Thank you,' he answered, 'but when a man makes friends so easily, it is not often that the friendship is of a lasting sort. Even so, I felt that certain comrades of mine in the business world were my friends, that various acquaintances in the theaters and music halls were my friends, that members of the families who so often asked me to join them in their homes for dinner were my friends and, lastly, that my fellow card players were my friends. Even if those of this last group were down on their luck—a situation which I understood—I expected a few of them would be able to help me out and would do so. After all, they knew I am honorable and would pay them back, not to mention that I remained a businessman with a steady income.'

"I asked him how many of these so-called friends loaned him money.

"'A paltry number, Ebenezer. And when I tell you who did, you'll see why I raised so little. I was disappointed to find that none of our associates in the cloth trade would advance me a farthing—not one of them! They sneered at the very idea of loaning money to pay a gambling debt, despite doing business with us for many years.'"

My uncle coughed and took a sip of tea.

I used the opportunity to ask a question: "Uncle, what of those people who so often asked him to dinner parties? Surely they would help. He was a sought-after guest, was he not?"

"That he was!" my uncle replied. "Here's what Marley said: 'Perhaps I overvalued my connection to those gentlemen. People like to entertain, you know, and often they need someone to make an even number. This gave an old bachelor like me a chance to view another side of life—in much the same way as I was able to do when you invited me to your sister's years ago. I enjoyed those dinners and always felt I was valued as a guest. Yet only one of these gentlemen, a Mr. Higginbottom, was disposed to help me. He loaned me a hundred pounds without batting an eye.'

"'My word, Jacob,' I responded.

"'I met that gentleman years ago and I've been to his home many times. He turned out to be a true friend. I suppose the others never considered me part of their circle, even though I brought gifts to their children for years. I was merely the fellow who made six for dinner. I daresay they appreciated my lively conversation, but it seems they judged they owed me nothing more than the food and drink I consumed at their table.'

"I could tell Marley was extremely distraught. His voice grew raspy and broke several times as he spoke more and more forcefully.

"'Of all the disappointments nothing was worse than the

refusals from those at the club,' he said. 'In those halls, nothing debases one's esteem more than a losing streak. I must say, I was utterly downcast that not a single person came to my aid, not even gentlemen I'd helped out in similar situations. One of them, the fellow who sponsored me, remarked that he thought it was in rather bad taste to request financial assistance from those who might be playing from a shallow purse themselves.

"'Only two other people were kind enough to loan me money. One is a chorister at the music hall, and the other is an actor. Surprising, eh? Most of those types don't have two pence to rub together, yet these two didn't question my sincerity or propriety, but merely dipped into their modest savings to help a person in need.'

"'Well, then,' I remarked to him, 'it seems you have at least three friends in this city other than myself.'

"I did not mean to wound him with those words, Fred, but my careless remark caused him to lose his composure utterly, for now tears raced down his cheeks. For the first time in my life, I saw Jacob Marley break down under the weight of heavy emotion. He sobbed silently, his fist over his mouth, his eyes shut tight, his chest heaving.

"But after a long moment, he righted himself and brushed away the tears. Then he drained his tankard. 'Yes, only three friends besides yourself—that's the hard truth of it.'

"'Ah, but Jacob,' I told him, 'you and I are much alike. Neither of us is given to the extended cultivation of friends, now are we? We look to numbers and goods and ideas to occupy our minds. In that regard you've been a great success. You were always a good man of business.'

"'Business!' he cried. 'Where is the comfort in it, Ebenezer? After fifty years on this earth I have nothing—or rather *had* nothing—to comfort me but my banker's book. And now I no longer have even that! Business? Mankind was my business. At least it should have been.'

"I took hold of his arm. 'Let us not yield to sentimentality,

Jacob,' I said. 'We must avoid that quagmire.' This admonition seemed to sober him, for then he reined in his sense of ruefulness and sorrow.

"We rested for a time, not speaking but merely eating our food. I soon finished my meal and ordered two more pints of beer, for I could see that my friend was caught up in a great crisis and needed someone to listen to him.

"Marley began speaking again in a normal tone of voice. He told me that during the late summer—when he had yet to raise the money—the two lords caused untold misery for him. They hounded him to pay the IOU, even to the extent of requesting he be barred from Gillingham's until the debt was satisfied.

"That sounds a bit harsh," I said.

"It's pure arrogance!" Uncle cried. "Those two lords, like most of their class, seldom settle quickly when they incur a gambling debt, I've heard. What they do is scribble notes and let them build up until someone embarrasses them over it. And yet when money was owed to *them* by a person of a lesser station, they demand recompense at once. If it is not forthcoming, they call down the wrath of heaven on the debtor, invoking Nemesis and the furies themselves to exact punishment!"

At times I do believe my uncle showed a flair for the poetic.

"Last summer Jacob was not intimidated by the hounding as much as he was determined to prove his own skill and win back the money. Jacob was ever a fighter, and more than anything else, he hated losing in a contest. He liquidated his holdings in the Stock Exchange and sold property he owned in Sussex in an effort to pay off his debt. This amount did not completely cover the shortage, however, and so, regrettably, he solicited the help of a money-lender."

I must have flinched to hear that term.

"Yes, Fred," he continued, "I see you're aware of the huge risk he took. Money-lenders are nothing but cutthroats and a blight upon the kingdom. Nevertheless Jacob finally raised the money to nullify his gambling debt. So the rumor I'd heard back in October was true.

"He then told me that he borrowed not only an amount to settle the debt with the lords, but more. He said he needed a goodly stake, a war chest, to use in recovering his losses by again returning to the whist table. He was bent on this desperate course, for better or worse."

⊱◈⊰

I could scarcely bear to continue listening, sickened as I was to hear step by step the details of a man's complete ruin. Jacob Marley might have chosen to leave the gambling debt unpaid, for the lords had no legal means to collect it. Of course, then he would have had to give up gambling at Gillingham's. So the man went to perilous lengths, not only to pay off the debt, but to secure the means to win it back.

My uncle continued. "When he was sufficiently capitalized, Marley returned to the club and assailed the whist table with vigor. At first he did well, playing for modest stakes. But he could not quickly build up his winnings because he now had to satisfy his money-lender. Interest had to be paid to the blackguard each and every week.

"He avoided playing with the nobility, but one night he noticed that the Duke of Devonshire was losing heavily. After a position opened, Marley managed to join the table. The duke continued to lose. Finally, after swearing an oath, the duke quickly rose to depart. Marley and his partner demanded he settle his debt, which only irritated the fellow even more. He hastily scrawled a promissory note and stormed out.

"So Marley had little to show for his trouble that evening, despite having won all the rubbers. God only knew when the duke might settle his debt. Jacob was now extremely vexed, owning that he'd wasted most of the evening."

My uncle lit his pipe and sat still a moment.

"It was then that the Earl of Archwood appeared in the room," he said at last.

For a moment neither of us spoke.

"I assume," I said with a straight face but drooping eyelids, "that Marley left the club and went home immediately."

"I'm afraid not, Fred. For Viscount Thornsbury was not far behind the earl, and after acknowledging Marley and treating him with respect—after all, he had delivered to them an enormous sum of money—they were happy to sit down with him to play a friendly game or two."

I clucked my tongue in despair. "I can guess the outcome of this reunion," I said. "In fact, Uncle, I'll wager I can complete the story for you."

"Well, by all means, young Fred, do go ahead,," he said with a smile.

"It's quite simple. They played all night, and in the end, Marley lost his entire gambling stake—everything he had. Actually more than he had, for he still owed a sizable amount to the money-lender. But, being a good loser, he showed coolness and perhaps even levity, joking he'd once again been seared by the hot flame of the goddess of bad luck. Then they all laughed and had a drink together to show there were no hard feelings between them."

I shall never know if those men had a drink or laughed, but my uncle certainly laughed, a sound that was still quite foreign to my ear.

"Upon my word, Fred, you tell it better than I. You have an imagination I lack. All I can do is convey in my own stiff manner what Marley told me."

"You've told the story well enough," I said. "But am I correct in the main?"

"That you are, but for a detail or two. Before they began play the Earl of Archwood stipulated that they play a cash game. He said he'd been gravely troubled by Marley's predicament after their last engagement and that he could not in good conscience allow it to happen again to the poor man."

"The effrontery!" I cried.

"It does seem that way to you and me. But perhaps the earl was only expressing a typical nobleman's viewpoint. I doubt, however, he was 'troubled' on Jacob's account. He was certain he would win but wanted bank notes rather than another debt of honor."

"What did Marley say to the earl's comment?"

"He told me he nearly lost his temper. But he discussed the proposition with his partner, who had played well with him against the Duke. The man thought it a capital idea, and Jacob agreed with him; he too needed bank notes instead of an IOU."

"Was I correct in supposing Marley lost his entire stake?" I asked.

"Yes. But you were wrong to say they played all night. It did not take nearly that long for Marley and his partner to be crushed."

I picked up my teacup and found it empty.

My uncle continued. "It's puzzling to me he never realized the two lords were swindling him. Perhaps he couldn't conceive that either one was smart enough to hoodwink him."

"But how the devil do you know they really did cheat him? You weren't there yourself."

"Ah, but I tell you, Fred, upon my honor, I suspected it from the first. Maybe because I have less respect for human nature than did Jacob, especially for the variety that calls itself aristocratic."

"Granted," I said, "but surely, if it's only a suspicion—"

"'Tis more than a suspicion! Tell me, have you kept up with the newspapers of late?"

"No. I admit I take only time enough to scan my *Observer* and my *Times.*"

"Ah, well, there is really no reason you should have followed this particular scandal. It has come to light only during the last month or two. I was on the watch for something of this sort, and once I got wind of the news, I endeavored to learn everything I could about the matter. That's what I meant in saying I'd drawn a conclusion but had no direct proof the two swindled him."

"Go on."

"The first whiff of it was seeing in the *Times* that Viscount Thornsbury had brought an action against a Mr. John Edmonds for libel. The latter accused him of cheating at cards."

"The viscount, you say. And it was for libel, not slander?"

"According to the *Times,* Edmonds made the accusation in a public forum, a weekly newspaper called *The Satirist.* An accusation in print draws more attention."

"And you believe Mr. Edmonds was swindled by the same men who swindled Marley?"

"I do, and I wondered if the item appeared in the newspaper by chance or was inserted deliberately, as a challenge to the viscount."

"What do you mean? Why would Edmonds do that?"

"It goes back to those so-called 'debts of honor.'"

"How so?"

"As you pointed out, Fred, they are not enforceable by law. The courts could not possibly handle the volume of cases that would be brought if gamblers could use the courts to recover their money. And I remind you that gambling is still held to be illegal for the lower classes. So the only thing a wronged man, especially a commoner, can do is expose the cheater publicly, as Mr. Edmonds did in *The Satirist* newspaper. Such a move has the possibility of ruining the reputation of the swindler, which of course is the object. It's the only legal recourse available to a victim of cheating. The accused man must then respond if he wishes to save his reputation, and this is what the viscount did. He sued."

"I see."

"This creates a situation where the defense must prove the plaintiff guilty of cheating. And apparently cheating is a hard thing to prove in court. But if one can prove it, the defendant is not held to be libelous."

"You seem to know quite a lot of civil law," I said with a chuckle.

My uncle puffed on his pipe. "I only know what I read in the news reports. To continue, the trial commenced, and witnesses were called for both sides. Those for the plaintiff, including the Earl of Archwood, testified as to the viscount's character and claimed never to have seen any impropriety whatsoever. But witnesses for the defendant described in detail how the cards were manipulated. At the end of the trial the Chief Justice summed up the case with impartiality but apparently with sympathy for the viscount. No surprise there. However, the jury, shockingly, took less than fifteen minutes to deliver the verdict for the defendant, Mr. Edmonds. And with that stroke, the lord was forever branded a cheat. Despite commentary in the *Times* reviling the verdict, it's quite evident that the viscount, who was held to be a good whist player, could not resist enhancing his play by subterfuge."

"My word, how did he do it, Uncle? What was the *modus operandi*?"

"Two methods were mentioned in court. One was a trick called *sauter la coupe*—'slipping the cards,' as some have it. This trick was mentioned in the *Times,* and later I read a better description of it in *Fraser's Magazine*. Tell me, nephew, by any chance do you recall any details about the game of whist?"

"I do," I responded, "though I'm a terrible player. I never learned the finer points of the game."

"Do you recall how trump is determined?"

"Of course. It is the suit of the last card dealt, which means the dealer gets it. It is dealt face up for all to see. Though it belongs to him, the dealer leaves it on the table, if memory serves, until the first trick is played."

"Correct," said Scrooge. "Now, consider how lucky for the dealer and his partner it would be should a high honor turn up as the trump card."

"It would be helpful, I suppose."

"What if, before he shuffled, the dealer put the card he wanted on the bottom of the deck? Maybe the ace? That's fairly easy to do. Players would be talking and drinking as he gathered up the cards."

"But Uncle, the player to the dealer's right cuts the deck, does he not? Then the ace would end up in the middle. That's the entire reason for cutting the cards."

"Absolutely. Ah, but that's where the trick comes in. It can be done several ways. One way is to simply reverse the cut by picking up the wrong stack first as if by accident. That's not as easily done as you might think. It requires a bit of dexterity to deceive the opponents into believing their cut was adopted. A truly skilled cheat *does* adopt their cut, but at the same time he takes care to slide his chosen card to the bottom of the recombined deck. This requires considerable skill and is rather dangerous for an amateur."

"Surely this lord was not a prodigy in sleight of hand," I said. "I find it hard to believe he'd attempt either of those things."

"As it turned out, he took a rather low road. What he would do is instigate some distraction—usually a fit of coughing—and then take his hands off the table momentarily and reverse the cut."

"Good Lord! No one noticed?"

"Not at first. But eventually somebody did, and Mr. Edmonds exposed the cheat for the world to see. Poor Marley, alas, never caught on to the deception. He had never been assaulted by such turpitude in a silver hell before."

I thought this over a moment as my uncle took a sip of water to cool his throat. Then I said, "I'm no expert at the game, but it seems an awfully small thing—that is, the misappropriation of a single card—to cause the loss of so many rubbers of whist."

"It does, doesn't it? But suppose twenty rubbers are played in the course of an evening. Viscount Thornsbury and his partner would get to deal the cards ten times. If the ace was slipped six times, it would give them a significant advantage over the honest players."

"I'll have to take your word on that," I said.

"I only quote from an article I read. And do you not remember that I said *two* methods of cheating were mentioned in court?"

"Oh, yes. What was the other?"

"It's more incriminating, I would say. And far more deadly."

I was unable to conceive what this might be.

He raised an eyebrow. "They marked the cards."

"Good heavens!" I exclaimed. "How did they accomplish such a fraud? I was assuming the packs of cards were supplied by the club."

"They are, and there was nothing wrong with them. As the hands were dealt and played, however, the cheaters surreptitiously marked the cards by cuts of the fingernail. Usually they marked only the aces and kings, along with the suit. At crucial points in the play of the hand those marks assisted each of the two conspirators, by showing critical cards either in the opponents' hands or in the hand of his partner across the table."

I nodded. "I can't believe they were so bold. I must say that method seems safer to use than the other."

"Neither is safe to use with experienced players. These are not new devices, apparently. The mistake the two peers made was to use them in high-stakes games in the view of gentlemen who are true men of the world and have observed those and many other tricks time and again. So you can see now why I'm convinced Jacob Marley was swindled in the same fashion."

I did see but still found it hard to believe respected members of the peerage would stoop to such base crimes. Yet there it was, as adjudicated by a court of law.

"What happened after that?" I asked. "Both men, I take it, were implicated."

"Not so. Only the viscount officially. The Earl of Archwood was never alleged to have performed those acts of legerdemain himself. Nevertheless the earl retired from the public arena of gaming and no longer frequents the clubs."

"And the other?"

"He left for the Continent the day after the verdict—went to Rotterdam, they say. He is not expected to return. The man is completely disgraced and dishonored."

## CHAPTER 8

THE FLAME OF ADVENTURE

The room was still, the tea cold. Outside, the spring day was quickly waning. Yet I had no inclination to depart, though Emily would soon be expecting me. I couldn't leave until I'd heard the last there was to hear about Marley.

I indulged myself in a sherry.

"Uncle, you still haven't explained why Mr. Marley dragged you to the tavern that night. You've only described a desperate man who wanted to confess his mistakes."

"He was more than desperate. He was defeated. Isn't it plain enough what he wanted?"

"I can hazard a guess."

He rose and went to the hearth, where earlier he started a small fire to ward off the gathering chill. "That night in the tavern," he continued, "was Jacob's final attempt to save his hide, for he could pay neither principal nor interest on the loan made by the 'financier' who agreed to help him. 'Help him'— rubbish! Those men seldom fail to exact their pound of flesh in the end. Now Jacob would lose everything he owned. And more."

"What do you mean by that?" I asked, struck by his harsh

tone of voice.

"His freedom. Forgive me, I've neglected to relate a detail or two in my narration. Tell me, how do you think he managed to get a loan from the money-lender?"

"I have no idea."

"Let me put it another way. What do these Shylocks require from a borrower? Think, solicitor!"

"Hmm . . . well, of course they require collateral."

"Correct. Collateral. And at this point what collateral could Jacob offer?"

"Nothing much, I suspect. You said he'd already sold his stocks and his property in Sussex. What else remained?"

"This house, of course, which he had to keep as a place to live. But he also owned another building in this part of town. I do not recall exactly where it sits, though he showed it to me once. The structure encompasses eight or nine flats. He bought the property a few years back on a whim, as an investment only; and though he got income from it, he never raised the rent nor took pains to keep it up. In the process of liquidating his assets, he was disappointed to learn that the sale of that building wouldn't help him much. He would remain short of the mark he sought, for, as I said, he wanted to build up a war chest.

"It happened that he had an old friend who was an appraiser, and by enlisting this fellow to help him—and employing a few tricks I'll not mention—he was able to convince a certain money-lender that the building was worth far more than its true value. And so it was, nephew, that this ill-kept building became his collateral."

I merely shook my head in disbelief at this.

"It's a grim tale, I'll warrant. Though it was not lawful of Jacob to do it, you should not grieve for Shylocks. The money-lenders ruin countless lives, mostly those of young men of high social standing whom they separate from their fortunes. This particular fellow was as vicious and callous as any of them. Luckily for Jacob—or perhaps unluckily—he was not as vigilant as the rest.

"And so, after the lords cheated him the second time, Jacob knew he was done for. He could not pay the money-lender even the next weekly payment of interest. It was yet another Waterloo—nay, worse, it was his doomsday. If he defaulted on the loan, the lender would then foreclose and quickly discover that the building's value was not as high as made out to be. He then would prefer charges and likely succeed in having Jacob thrown into debtor's prison."

I shuddered. "His predicament was worse than I imagined," I said. "If only he'd been content to sell the building, rather than seek this extra money for his damnable 'war chest.' At least he might have got out of debt."

"Yes, poor fellow. And he never knew he'd been swindled. But when I ponder the matter, Fred—and I have given it much consideration—he was bound to lose all his money at some time in the future; not because of marked cards or nimble fingers, but because of better players and bad luck. That is the true fate of the gambler. I hope you will take heed."

"Do not worry about me," I said. "I'm of the same mind entirely."

"Good, nephew, good!" He sat down, smiled, and asked me to pour him a sherry as well. "I'm glad to hear that."

I poured his sherry and refilled my own glass. For a moment we said nothing, only partaking of our wine in silence. I felt exhausted, completely drained from hearing the wretched history of Jacob Marley. Yet questions remained.

"Uncle?"

"Yes?"

"You still have not answered a question I put to you many weeks ago, the day you first informed me that Marley was not dead."

"Which question was that?"

"I asked whether you helped him counterfeit his death. The truth can scarcely be otherwise. He appeared on that misty evening to ask for your advice and aid. You've told me how you advised him. Now you must explain what exactly you did for him."

He did not reply but instead stared into the weak light emanating from the window.

"Remember, Uncle, I've given you an unqualified pledge never to speak of anything you tell me about Marley."

"Even to your wife?" he asked.

"Even to her. I suppose he might have asked you to help him flee to the Continent, as that disgraced and deceitful viscount has now done. And of course he would have asked you for traveling money. As to anything else, I'm afraid to guess, so grotesque are the various pictures that run through my mind."

He turned to face me, his jaw set firm. "You are correct in saying he wanted to flee the country. But for Jacob it was not enough. In the face of financial ruin and prison, he devised a far more radical plan. Radical? Nay, it was preposterous."

"He could convince the world that he had suddenly died."

"Yes, Fred, and he considered this absurd ruse a better tack than simply absconding. Marley's obligation to the money-lender was not a debt of honor. It was, rather, legal and enforceable since he had signed a document promising to repay the loan at an exorbitant rate of interest. He reasoned it was safer to be dead than a criminal at large. Therefore he arranged the whole charade down to the last detail, including securing the services of a physician, an undertaker, and a priest. The only other person he needed to help him . . . was me."

"What exactly did he ask of you?"

"As you suggested, he needed traveling money. But he also needed my good will and assistance in giving credence to the fraud. Someone had to attend the funeral and see to other legalities. If he merely disappeared, the money-lender might sue to collect Marley's share of our business. I did not like that prospect. And so I became a willing partner in the deception."

"I understand, Uncle. But in addition to his share of Scrooge & Marley, you knew you would inherit anything else he left behind . . . for instance, this house. Isn't that so?"

He frowned. "And a phaeton that sits in the carriage house—a luxury I'll never use." My uncle flicked his eyes toward me in a strange look I could not decipher. "I gather," he continued, "you're aware of the wills we signed years ago, each partner endowing the one who outlived him?"

"Uh, yes, Uncle, I did hear of it . . . I forget how."

I clearly remembered it was Bob Cratchit who told me of their wills at the Covent Garden market, but I did not want to cause any difficulty for the little man. I'm terrible at dissembling, though, and I may have flushed a bit. At any rate, he didn't seem to care and went on.

"Then you should be able to see there was no need for me to buy him out. By means of the ruse he proposed, I would inherit his share of the company, and there would be no need to resort to a contract or a bill of sale. If instead he had chosen to merely slip out of the country in the dead of night, then the money-lender would have taken me to court, I'm sure. He may have thought about doing so anyway. But given the uncertainties of the law and the attendant legal fees, the man was content to lay claim to the building used for collateral."

"I see now why 'twas safer he were dead," I said, trying to sound a note of humor.

My uncle did not smile. "It was enough for me that I would have the business intact. But I did not agree to the scheme because of any gain that would come to me but rather because Jacob was my dear friend. He was anxious to get out of the country and start a new life. The whole affair may be called sordid, but my conscience is clear on the matter."

I was sure he meant it, for he was a man who obeyed his conscience. I wondered if he himself ever wanted to start a new life, or if he was so mired in his bachelor ways and love of capital, he could never do so.

"There is not much else I can relate about Marley," said my uncle. "I told Jacob in the tavern I would help him arrange his sham death and would give him enough seed money that he might start life again somewhere. The next day I withdrew the money from the bank.

"Not only did I give Marley the money he needed to start anew, I also arranged to repay the three people who had loaned him money: the chorister, the actor, and Mr. Higginbottom. I felt they should be recompensed for their kindness.

"The last time I saw Jacob was two days later in my office. He was sailing from England in the morning. We shook hands, and he thanked for me for my steadfast friendship. I nearly faltered by giving into sentiment; for we had once been a superlative team. But Jacob did not falter. He had regained his strength of purpose and was resolute in beginning a new life on foreign shores. I wished him good fortune, and he soon disappeared into the fog.

"Not long afterward, my bothersome nephew came trotting out of the same fog that still hung about the city and proceeded to invade my office. Completely unannounced, I might add. You were on a single-minded mission to invite me to Christmas dinner. Seeing you there after such a short interval unnerved me, for at first I thought you were Jacob returning because of some trouble."

"Ah," I said, "now I understand."

Scrooge stood, looking somewhat weary, I thought.

"There is a little more I must tell you," he said. "After that night he was gone for good. But my part was not finished.

"The next day, Christmas Eve, I deliberately went to the office later than usual—some two hours later. This was part of our plan. For the past fortnight, I had railed often about Marley being absent in the office. They now informed me he had not yet come to work, and so I pretended to emulate a proper tirade. I must say that I was a little disappointed the clerks did not seem appalled or even surprised by my play-acting; that gave me a clue as to how common those lapses of temper have become to my employees, eh?"

He laughed.

"This time," he continued, "my little tempest did not blow over so quickly. I told my clerks in no uncertain terms I was going to go fetch Marley in, even if I had to drag him down the thoroughfare by his pigtail. I made sure that all of them heard me. You'll remember that I already possessed a key to the house, given to me during the days when he was a slave to opium. You were still a lad back then."

"Yes, you told me of the key last time I was here," I said. "You wanted to look in on him, make sure he hadn't injured himself."

"Quite so," he answered. "In my little pantomime I rummaged noisily in my desk searching for the key. When I had it, I stalked off, telling Cratchit he was in charge. I must say the poor fellow looked as if he were being put in charge of the exchequer.

"I walked fast and hard, stamping the pavements heavily and muttering under my breath, impressing passers-by with my anger. At least I'm vain enough to believe that was the case. But I grew tired of the game and took up a softer gait after a while. When I came to the house—this house, of course—I rapped that giant, ungainly knocker several times, hoping to attract attention from casual onlookers. What a racket it made! Then I inserted the key and entered."

Here my uncle paused, evidently collecting his thoughts.

"What is it, Uncle?" I asked.

He looked me in the eye. "I hesitate to tell you this part, Fred. You see, I felt the touch of death in the house. There was no sound to be heard in the place; and, owing to its position at the terminus of a bleak and silent street, none penetrated the walls from the outside. The dead air felt puffy in my ears, as if heavy vapor were cloaking any sound that might reach me. There was a palpable eeriness in that dark hallway. Maybe that was caused by the mission I was embarked on, for I came there to pretend to discover Jacob Marley dead of a heart attack. To accomplish that I only needed to stand in the hall a few minutes, then run out the door to summon the physician we had engaged. That was all. Yet the brooding stillness of the house drew me inward, down the hallway now familiar to me, up the creaking stairs, and finally to the master bedchamber, where Marley would have last slept. For what reason, do you suppose? Did I think my footsteps needed to imprint the dust to prove I intended to roust him out of bed, my stated purpose in being there? No. The public would soon believe that Marley was dead as a door-nail, and nobody would ever say nay to that idea. 'He was dead to begin with,' the doctor would tell the constable. There was no need for me to actually go to the room where he reportedly died.

"But, Fred, that is exactly whence I went."

I kept very still, alert in anticipation.

"I had some sort of premonition, a dread of what I might find in that room," said Scrooge. "My mind began to devise various states of affairs. Perhaps Jacob was loath to embark on a ship, having never before done so. He suggested to me that he might travel to Edinburgh instead, an option I advised against. In that case he might postpone his disappearance, which would complicate matters.

"Worse, he might have wrestled with deep despair—despondent as he was over his ruined career—taken opium, and fallen into a stupor the previous night. If so I would find him unconscious, and our plans would be in disarray. Or . . ."

"Yes? Go on."

"Or perhaps he had taken his own life."

Scrooge turned away from me and ambled toward the fire.

"The house itself made me go to that room, Fred. I had see for myself. That's what I believe. We arranged for the whole world to think that Marley had died, and when such an audacious thing is done well—down to the last detail—it often succeeds. Perhaps the house itself had already gleaned from the vibrations in the air, from our talk, from our whispering, that its master had died and now lay as a corpse in his bed."

I quickly poured myself another sherry.

He continued: "As I walked down the last few steps of the hallway I became certain in my agitated mind that he was truly dead. I swear to you, my hand was trembling as I turned the knob and entered the room. My heart almost gave out when I perceived a figure in the bed."

"A figure?" I cried.

Uncle laid a hand on my shoulder. "Calm yourself, Fred. It was not so. The figure was nothing but a heap of twisted bedding, upon which an old, unwanted greatcoat had been tossed. It turned out Jacob left quite a few items of clothing. He needed to travel light."

I shuddered. "I am not sure why you still reside in this horrible dwelling," I said as I wiped away a bit of perspiration.

"It matches me in many ways," he said quietly. "Perhaps that's the reason." Then he returned and sat down in his chair.

"Do you think he made it safely to his destination?" I asked.

"I have no way of knowing. He is gone; that is all we can say. He told me he could never write me. It would be too dangerous. Ah, Jacob, Jacob, what a terrible mess you made of your life!"

"I doubt he fled to Scotland," I said. "He must have eloped to the Continent. I shall keep the secret, of course. And yet it seems to me you were incorrect when you told me that I was the only person who cared about him."

"Who else was there?"

"Why, yourself, of course. There was not enough monetary incentive for you to take part in such a dangerous and illegal scheme, Uncle. No, that was not the reason. You have also told me you did it out of friendship, and that I believe."

"Yes, he was my friend. But do you remember that I once told you that I agreed to help him because he had become a liability to the firm? And how I worried about its very survival?"

"I do," I said.

"Good, because that is also true. His behavior over the last twenty years drove me to wish many times that he would stop creating so many problems. But that was impossible. His personality was firmly set; he would never change. Therefore, I began to wish he would go away, simply vanish. I did so, many times. And when at last he begged me to *help* him go away, I found it impossible to refuse. Fred, I did it for both reasons."

I did not reply at first. My head was turning over the notion that one may choose a course of action for both pure and impure reasons.

"I am curious about one thing," I said at last.

"What is that?"

"Will he ever return?"

My uncle smiled. "We argued about this matter in the tavern. He seemed to think that after a few years he might be able to come back to England. I maintained that such a move would endanger both of us. You would know more of the legal problems than I. He would still owe the debt—that seems clear. Jacob thought that he might make a fortune for himself abroad and buy his way back into society."

"Both ideas are absurd," I said. "Even if he grew rich, he would still have to pay off the money-lender. Think of all the interest that would have accrued—it would be enormous! More serious would be the falsifying of public records, to which you were also a party."

"Yes. That is ever on my mind," Scrooge replied and gave a heavy, regretful sigh.

"How much money did you give him? Was it substantial?"

"I gave him enough to perhaps set up a small shop, something to sustain him in his exile."

I nodded. "Then it's doubtful he will amass a fortune. Think of it: he is now adrift in a strange land, dealing with odd ways, having to learn a foreign language."

"Well, no," my uncle said, interrupting me. "He would still be speaking English."

I could not think whither the man had taken himself. "How's that?" I asked, searching my uncle's face.

"He's not gone to the Continent, Fred, as you assumed. Marley has gone to America. He booked passage to New York."

This stunned me at first, but then I deemed it might be a

wiser strategy. "Then perhaps he *will* become rich," I exclaimed and laughed.

"I doubt it. Despite what you read in novels, one does not necessarily become rich simply by immigrating to America."

"Yet it must be a fascinating place," I said. "On the one hand, there is quite a civilized region along the eastern coast; but going westward, one encounters, by degrees, an unforgiving wilderness stretching to the great Mississippi. At least, so I've heard. I assume Mr. Marley will reside in the civilized area."

"I don't know. He did express an interest in a place called Texas."

"Texas? I've never heard of such a place. Where does it lie?"

"I'm not precisely sure. It is a province of Mexico, lately settled by Americans with the permission of the Mexican government. But according to the *Times* there has been much dissatisfaction on the part of the Texians, so they have declared their independence. Some sort of war is now afoot."

"Good gracious! The Americans do like to declare independence and break away, I must say. What is there about the western hemisphere that so affects them?"

Scrooge cocked his head as if taking me seriously. "It is the abundance of land that intoxicates them. An adventurous man can get a bit of land there if he is willing to sacrifice and brave the dangers. That is not possible in our country, nor anywhere that I know of in Europe. Land is a shining lure to the pioneer."

"Surely not for Marley, he of the keen mind for numbers and gallivanting ways." I chuckled. Then I said, "Will he open a pub, do you think?"

Uncle rose again, rather slowly, arched his back to stretch it, and yawned. "I do not know." He appeared weary, and in that moment I thought Uncle looked quite old.

"He is only a few years your junior," I pointed out. "What I mean is—if you'll excuse my saying it—he is no longer a young man. Surely a man of his years would not fling himself into the wildest regions of the frontier."

"We are not so feeble, he and I," was the stony reply. "The flame of adventure flickers in the hearts of all men, whatever their age may be."

"Well said, Uncle, well said!" I rose to my feet and also stretched. "'Tis getting late. It's high time this young man embarked on the adventure of finding his way home."

He arched an eyebrow. "Oh?" he said. "Are you as tired as all that? It is only eight o'clock or thereabouts. I thought we might nip out to the tavern and have a pint."

I knew at this juncture my uncle was only teasing me. It was part and parcel of his colloquial manner. Strangely, I now liked that he did so, for it was a sure sign we had reached a certain level of trust. "No, no, I must go home," I said. "My custodian will send out the hounds if I do not soon cross the moat."

"Is she so very anxious to lock you up for the night?"

"I'm afraid she is. I am let out only on special occasions."

He put his left hand on my shoulder and shook my hand with his right. "Farewell, Fred. I had not thought I would ever share the truth about Jacob Marley with any living soul. Now that I have done it, I feel a pleasing sense of relief. Of all the men on earth, you are the only one I trust without reservation."

"That's as it should be," I replied, "for we are blood kin."

I gathered up my things, including the basket. We had eaten everything in it.

He lit a small candle and led me down the entry hall to the door. He offered me the candle to take with me, and I took it, imagining how bleak and dark the little cul-de-sac would be. I struggled to think of something more meaningful than "good-bye," but could not. Nor did I think prattling on in a meaningless way would ease my transition into the night.

Neither did he.

After a handshake, the door swung shut behind me.

Now that I was alone on the stoop, I saw that there was precious little light around, other than the aureole of the small candle I held. A single streetlight guttered rapidly twenty yards away—

the sole source of illumination ahead. I stepped carefully down the stair to the yard and picked my way along in the darkness. All was silent, save for the persistent barks of a faraway dog. I took pains to restrain myself from walking briskly, lest I trip over a crate or loose bit of rock.

When at last I reached the thoroughfare, I sighed in relief, grateful to be out of the sinister byway. I extinguished the candle and put it in the basket. A vision of Emily came to mind. A short time ago I'd made light of her concerns, but I knew she was a woman who worried excessively. I disliked being the cause of her concern and began to hurry along. By a stroke of good fortune, I spotted an empty hackney cab rattling by. I hailed it and soon was riding toward home in comfort, out of the cool night air. The driver kept a slow, steady pace that jostled me little, and the repetition of the clip-clopping hooves lulled me into a doze. Or perhaps my eyes closed because I had drunk too much sherry.

My head was ajumble with feelings and ideas.

In the main, my thoughts ran to Scrooge. I wasn't sure yet if I understood him, nor if I ever would. He was a strange brew of a person. Yet all the little steps, forward and back, that had brought us closer now seemed worth the trouble. Very much so.

I also dwelt a bit upon Jacob Marley and the story of his downfall. The man was obviously a rake and sometimes a scoundrel. And yet, as I slipped into sleep, his daring gambit in setting off for America thrilled me so much that I felt envious of him, for I knew that I would never go there myself. I mused that perhaps America was only for the penniless, unlucky, or disgraced—a destination for someone who had nothing left to lose.

The most persistent thought of all was *Where in God's name is this "Texas"?*

## CHAPTER 9

## THE SIGN ABOVE THE DOOR

Spring and summer sped by. As usual, my labors at the law office commanded the better part of my days as well as many evenings. I sometimes felt that home was a place I visited only to catch my breath and rest briefly before reentering the fray. Emily was also busy, taking care of the baby, still arranging the household to her taste, and constantly involving herself in the affairs of her mother, sisters, and cousins.

In September, we celebrated Alice's first birthday. We had postponed the christening of the child, mainly because other matters always intruded. The occasion of her birthday prompted us to take action in the matter. Emily's mother was especially anxious we do so. Thus my wife began to make the arrangements. She promised me that I need do nothing in connection with the rite except to help send out a few notes.

Then one morning, as I made preparation to leave for the office, she said:

"Fred? You do know that we require another godparent, don't you?"

"Eh?" I said, being somewhat distracted. "I thought you

enlisted your Aunt Matilda and one of your cousins."

"I have. They joined the ranks quite willingly."

My mind turned this over a few seconds. I said, "And you need a third?"

"Of course we need a third," she said wryly. "Sometimes I wonder if you were born and raised under a cabbage leaf."

"I do recall, vaguely, that sometimes three are required," I said, instantly wary for what might come next.

"The third must be of the opposite sex, you know."

"Ah, yes, I recall that as well. You must make allowances for me, dearest, since I never attended a christening nor participated in one. Excepting, of course, my own." I laughed, but she didn't seem amused at the remark.

"I was thinking, dear, we might enlist one of *your* relatives in our endeavor."

"But darling, I have only one such relative in all the world."

"Yes, I know. Your Uncle Ebenezer."

I shook my head in the negative. "I doubt my uncle would agree to participate in a christening," I said. "He's not one for ceremony."

"He never goes to church, does he?"

"I don't know. But whether he goes or not, I'm sure he has no desire to play a role in church business."

"Bosh," she said. "God-parenting is a mere ceremonial duty. It will cost him no money, only a little time. All he must do is repeat some words when prompted."

"I shall be late, my love." Then I stepped toward her, meaning to kiss her on the cheek.

She put a gentle hand on my chest to halt me. "Please speak with him, dear," she said. "Will you?" Her gray eyes bore into mine.

"Very well," I said, with a regretful sigh, then hastily departed.

That small conversation was a harbinger of change between us—as it was between myself and my uncle.

On the day Emily entreated me to ask Scrooge to become a godparent, I still regarded the two of us as a rather young couple. We were but four years married and four and twenty years of age. God had already given us a child, but in my eyes we had taken only a few steps together in the journey of our marriage. To tell the truth, I did not yet feel fully acclimated to my role as a husband. She felt differently, as soon would become plain.

I wonder now, in old age, whether this disparity in perception is common in marriages, especially in the modern milieu of the city. The husband, plunging into his chosen profession, experiences a fleeting alternation of day and night, immersed as he is in the details of his work. Time passes swiftly for him. The wife, however, has more time to consider the passage of days and to notice the small changes that affect the underpinnings of their marriage. She has her nose to the wind, so to speak, whereas her mate often cannot understand her chosen direction and resists going that way, content as he is with the *status quo*.

Also wives are generally quite adamant in dealing with the changes they perceive and, verily, dealing with them as they see fit. In this case, Emily had firmly decided that one of my kinsmen should stand as godfather to Alice, and nothing short of Napoleon's *Grande Armée* would deter her from the notion.

I considered other candidates besides my Uncle Ebenezer. First, I wrote to a cousin in Leeds, the only relative whose address I could unearth. He was a second cousin once removed, or some such relation, and, like my uncle, he carried the surname of Scrooge. I was saddened to hear back from his widow that he passed away some ten years ago. My father had left me the names of a few of my Truelock kin, but I knew not how to contact a single one of them.

Facing the hard truth, I wrote at last to my uncle, trying to keep the tenor of the message light and emphasizing the joy of the coming event. I asked him to kindly grant me this special favor and pledged to never again ask another like it. That was all I said. I hoped he would not regard the request as a clumsy way to draw him into my family circle, for he had shown no desire for that, not even in simply making the acquaintance of my wife. He had refused three times to come to dinner at my home. Yet I dared hope he would grant this latest request.

There was no reply.

I wrote again, and again received no answer. I knew I must act, for the christening was scheduled in two weeks' time. Since I had to perform an errand in the vicinity of his business, I decided to visit the office unannounced and make my case in person. I pondered whether getting down on my knees would do any good.

I did not relish the task. I had not forgotten how adversely he received me the last time I popped in without warning. But that visit was on a cold, foggy evening, and, as I now knew, he was extremely agitated at the time due to Jacob Marley's surreptitious departure. Today I hoped things would be different.

It was a fine afternoon in October, and I walked amid abundant sunshine. As I came upon the warehouse, which seemed even smaller than the last time I'd seen it, I noticed the tersely worded sign was unchanged. He had not bothered to paint out Marley's name. Nor, for that matter, to add any paint at all. I resolved to mention that a faded sign did not reflect well on his firm.

Inside I found Cratchit earnestly at work.

"My word, if it isn't Mr. Truelock!" he exclaimed upon seeing me come in. Rising from his chair, he wrung his hands and wrists, a habit I had previously noticed.

"How are you, Bob? And how is your family?"

At the word "family" he began enumerating all manner of details of his wife and their children, one of whom had been sick of late. I listened to him patiently for as long as I could.

Then I said: "And, uh, how are things here in the office? How is the firm doing?"

"Not so good, for, as you know, Mr. Scrooge carries the load of two men now."

"I hope he does not overwork himself."

He twisted his lips and knit his brow, as if deeply pondering the question. "'Tis hard to say, sir. I suppose he does more than he ought. More than he's used to, that's for certain. He generally opens and closes the place himself these days, often leaves the office to have midday meals with the clients, and usually writes letters into the night. I know, because I must copy them in the morning." He chuckled good-naturedly.

"Goodness," I said. "The workload sounds quite taxing to me."

"Oh, I suppose it is," he said, nodding, "but he's never been one to shirk, now has he?"

Keeping to protocol, I asked him to announce me. I dared not chance bursting into his office again.

This time my uncle seemed pleased to see me. "What an unexpected pleasure!" he exclaimed. "Sit down, nephew, sit down!" He reached for the bottle of claret, and likewise produced sherry and brandy for my consideration. "The clients come to my own office now, if they drop in at all. I have to coddle them as best I'm able."

"What of Marley's office? Does it remain empty?"

"We have converted his office into a little storeroom for the clerks. Thus they need not go into the warehouse for paper, ink, and the like."

Then he asked about my family, and I told him we were extremely healthy. He was pleased to hear it.

"You seem to be quite healthy yourself, Uncle," I observed. "Even though Bob tells me you carry a heavy load these days."

"A bit heavier, I suppose," he said. "Hard work never hurt a man, in my estimation."

We toasted with our claret, and then he said, "Let us get down to the matter, shall we? I can guess the reason you've come. And

I regret to say I am much too busy to play godfather to your daughter . . . uh—"

"Alice," I supplied.

"Alice, yes. Lovely name! She is now thirteen months, is she not?"

"Correct," I said, "but, Uncle, I implore you, I beg you, to attend the ceremony. I promise it will take only a tiny amount of time out of your busy day." I handed him a scrap of paper upon which I'd written the place, date, and time of the christening.

He stared fixedly at the information and said, "I will see if it can be managed." He did not sound hopeful; nor did he look me in the eye when he said it.

"And will you repeat the words as the priest recites them? That would please my wife exceedingly."

He sighed. "Do not ask me that, Fred. Perhaps I can attend the christening as an onlooker, but nothing more."

"Please understand, Uncle, if you can, how few choices are open to me in the way of family connections. You and I may be the last bearers of two ancient family names—Truelock and Scrooge—and there is no other person in the world for me to call upon."

"Truly unfortunate," he answered. "But over the years I have conceived many ill feelings regarding the Church of England. Most of what they proclaim is nothing but humbug."

"Can you not put aside your quibbles for one day?" I remonstrated.

"I cannot, Fred. It's not in my nature to go through empty motions, especially one of the Church's rites. I promise you this: I will be a better benefactor to young Alice than any godparent you choose in my stead. You'll see."

The thought came to me that, contrary to his statement, not so long ago he chose to go through the empty motion of Marley's sham funeral rite. I did not mention that, however. And since I could think of nothing else to say or do, I drank the wine.

"At any rate," he added lamely, perhaps to allay the

disappointment that must have shown in my face, "I am overjoyed to hear that everything is satisfactory in your household."

*Satisfactory?* I smiled to hear him say that, for I knew my failure to secure a godfather would certainly not please my wife. But then, suddenly, out of the depths of memory—perhaps because I at last judged his answer was immutable—another possible godfather appeared in my mind's eye, whom I hoped would be a solution to the problem. Having seen that glimmer of hope, I put aside my current disappointment, sighed, and poured myself another glass of his claret.

Then I put to him the same question about the firm I had put to Cratchit.

He scowled. "Business lately is only fair," he said glumly. "In general, the textile trade is weak, as are many others. Money to borrow is scarce. Also, the King is said to be in ill health, and that irrelevant fact has affected all manner of things."

"Uncle, if I may," I began haltingly, "I would like to bring something to your attention. It's the condition of the sign that marks your front door."

"The sign, you say? What of it, lad?"

"It's terribly faded and dreary-looking. It needs fresh paint. In its present condition it might cause a client to doubt your company's solvency, don't you think? Why not have it painted anew? And whilst that is being accomplished, you can remove Marley's name."

He paused, then said, "Does the sign appear to you as repulsive as all that?"

I nodded and tried to smile.

"Then I shall consider your suggestion, though the thing merely denotes our location on this crowded street. Heavens, it's only a sign! Well, I don't relish any further expense at the moment, however. And as for Marley's name, it shall remain there."

"Why?"

"Mainly because I do not want to pay a solicitor to legally

change the name of the firm. What's in a name? as the Bard says. Why rename it simply because the man is . . . gone. Customers might not understand. Changing the name would cause confusion. They might think some new company had arisen or that the old one had gone into bankruptcy or—"

"Very well, Uncle," I interrupted somewhat peevishly. "Feel free to leave the old reprobate's name up there as long as you like. Keep it there till hell freezes over!"

He laughed.

"But mind," I continued, "someday a customer will come in off the street and expect to have an interview with your erstwhile partner."

"It has already happened, my boy!" he shot back merrily and laughed. "One day, when I'd barely returned to the office, a young man breezed in and asked to see Mr. Marley. 'What can I do for you?' I asked him, and he said he worked for a tailor on Fleet Street, needed some cloth, and would like to get it wholesale. We had a pleasant conversation. The fellow was polite and kept calling me Mr. Marley the whole time. He ordered several bolts."

"So from now on you answer to Marley as well as Scrooge?"

"Why not? It's all the same to me."

Then I had to laugh myself, for it was so like him to say such a thing. Finally I said, "Your practicality overwhelms me."

"Business, my boy. It's all part of running a business."

"But wait!" I said. "Mightn't that money-lender who had his hooks into Marley get wind of your impersonation? Then he might drop in sometime and demand payment from you."

"Bah! Let him try. Behind you, on the wall, is a framed obituary cut from the newspaper. If that ain't enough to convince him, I'll direct him to the churchyard where Jacob's headstone sits gathering moss."

We laughed again.

"I do sometimes wonder where old Marley has got to," I mused aloud.

At that careless remark, he put a finger to his lips and rose from his chair. He slipped noiselessly to the door, opened it a crack, then closed it again. "You must keep your voice low when speaking of that matter. Sometimes I suspect Cratchit snoops at my door, pressing his ear to the crack."

"Sorry," I answered in a softer tone. "I don't suppose you've heard from the fugitive."

"No, nor do I expect to. I wrote to the shipping line and found out that the vessel on which he sailed made it safely to the New York City harbor. That's all I know. I have no idea whither he wandered after he disembarked."

"Do you suppose he traveled to this Texas province you spoke of? I've heard nothing about the place."

"Oh, Fred, I sincerely hope he did not," he answered gravely. "There was a much-delayed item in the *Times* concerning the war for independence there. The Mexicans laid siege to an old Spanish outpost where the Texians were holed up. Eventually they stormed it and massacred the lot of them."

"My Lord! Massacred, you say?" I repeated, not sure I heard it right.

"They say it was a complete slaughter." He averted his eyes and gazed elsewhere in that windowless office of his. "Wars are seldom pleasant topics of conversation," he added with a sigh.

On that somber note, Uncle said he had much work to do. I nodded and, observing the protocol, departed forthwith, sensing he had expended his allotted social time for the day.

Since he was unwilling to serve as Alice's godfather, I went to see a man I knew from my boyhood days, a colleague of my father at the wine purveyors. I remembered Mr. Evans as a genial and kind person. Indeed, he had sent me congratulations on both my marriage and the birth of my daughter. I hoped he would speak for Alice in the christening ceremony.

He did.

My uncle, on the other hand, never appeared that day.

## CHAPTER 10

## A NEW MONARCH

After my uncle told me Mr. Marley had safely reached America, I deemed this would be the last I would ever hear of the gentleman, if such he may be called. Even so, his spectacular downfall loomed large in my imagination for a long time. Perhaps that was due to my childhood memories of him when he seemed a clever and important man. Or perhaps I dwelt on his fate because his true history was a dark secret I shared with my uncle. And yet, to be truthful, I still regarded the man more a victim than a criminal and harbored more than a little admiration that he engineered such a monumental fraud. I hoped he would succeed in the New World.

It turned out that his arrival in America was not to be the last word of Jacob Marley that reached my ears. There would be more. But these further revelations did not come to light for several years.

In the meantime, Uncle Ebenezer and I both continued to deal with the adversities and rewards of everyday life, only occasionally interacting with each other. Yet it is undeniable that some of our setbacks were caused or influenced by the vanished

Marley. His very absence proved trying for my uncle, and the story of the deceit and deception by which he lost his money would affect my own career in a profound way.

My wife was satisfied with Mr. Evans as godfather, although she made a deprecating comment one morning at breakfast about my complete failure to convince my uncle to own up to his responsibility. I let it pass.

With the christening over, my life, both professional and personal, settled back into a humdrum course. I became quite bored with it. For the first time, I found myself indifferent about my work as a solicitor. No longer did I look forward to the morning walk to the office. My profession now seemed routine and dull. In December Emily and I discussed arrangements for Christmas. I should say, rather, that we argued about them. I felt we should forgo hosting dinner that year and let someone else take the responsibility. I was a bit tired of the whole business. She disagreed, saying that since we had begun it, we should continue. After all, our friends looked forward to it. In the end I gave into her wishes.

I tried to adopt the spirit of the season as best I could though it felt as though I were merely plodding along in the footsteps of my former self. As for Uncle Ebenezer, I decided to send him his invitation by the post, as there seemed to be no great advantage in my personally speaking with him. He never chose to attend anyway.

Nor did he come this time.

All went well with the dinner, though. It cheered me that our guests were taken with our beautiful child, who was then only beginning to walk. Emily's mother played nursemaid that day, keeping the baby in the nursery most of the time. The food was better than ever. I drank too much punch and fell asleep in my chair as one of our guests amused the others with a ghost story.

Of the following year, I have little to say about my own situation. During that year King William died, and Princess Victoria ascended the throne. The girl was barely eighteen, yet she bore promise as a unifying figure for the government and the people. At year's end Emily and I once again hosted our now-traditional Christmas dinner. I had no thought to dissuade her this time, for the event had become the highlight of her role as a matron, or so it seemed to me. I did less to help with preparations than ever. Apparently my efforts were not needed or wanted. As before, I wrote to Uncle Ebenezer, asking him to join us, and he again chose to avoid the inconvenience of human contact. I am sure he preferred to make use of the holiday to nap and catch up on his reading.

This boring existence of mine followed roughly this pattern for the following two years. I cared little for the work I was doing though I took care that it measured up to professional standards. It was my livelihood, after all. At home things were much the same, and I performed the ceremonial duties of a thoroughly domesticated husband. I didn't grumble about it, but neither did I show any enthusiasm. Emily had by this time made the acquaintance of several other married women. She participated with her lady friends in various activities, political, charitable, and social. These kept her busy, and she seemed happy.

My sole delight lay in seeing my daughter grow and thrive, even as my own life remained changeless.

The following year took a more propitious turn. Our Queen decided to marry a German prince, Albert of Saxe-Coburg and Gotha, who had been courting her for several years. Naturally it was she who proposed. They were wed in February. Despite my own indifference to this event, I observed it had an invigorating effect on public life. The Queen was popular and her Prince quite dashing. The newspapers could not print enough about the young couple, nor could ordinary people in the street, tea shops, and pubs stop talking about them.

Later that year I was assigned to an important case, a lawsuit concerning a business contract whose terms had been violated—at least so our client maintained. To my surprise I was made lead solicitor in the case. It gave me a chance to work with one of the most esteemed barristers then practicing, the man who would plead the case in court. It was my job, however, to prepare the case for trial, and in that capacity I worked tirelessly with my associates to assemble the evidence. I drew unexpected energy from my work on this difficult case, and for many weeks Emily and I got on well, each of us immersed in our own activities. My spirit soared higher than it had for years. I recalled what my Uncle Ebenezer once said, that in his estimation "hard work never hurt a man." I wondered if it might even uplift one, for it seemed I felt happier the harder I labored.

After the verdict was decided in favor of our client, I chanced upon Mr. Evans in the street outside the law courts. He himself had been drawn into the case in a minor way. Evans was a tall man, in good health, about the same age as my uncle. He made a trim figure for a man of his years, for his personal appearance was well cared for, his boots shining, and his suit immaculate.

"Hullo there, young Truelock," he said, a hint of merriment in his eye.

"Mr. Evans, how wonderful to see you again."

After shaking hands, we talked a bit about the case and shared our private opinions of it. He had been called by the other side, the defense, yet held no strong opinion of the verdict one way or the other. Then he changed the topic. "How is that goddaughter of mine?" he asked with a broad smile.

"Fine, sir. She'll be five years of age come September."

His mouth popped open in surprise. "As old as that? My, my! *Tempus fugit*. I hope I may see her again before she attains her majority!"

"You'd be most welcome to visit anytime," I said. We continued to talk of the child a few moments, then said our good-byes.

When I returned to the office, I felt my vitality sag unexpectedly. At first I thought it must be because Mr. Evans mentioned my father as we were chatting. "He would certainly be proud of you," he'd said. Sometimes an unexpected reference to my parents would put me in a certain mood, wherein I was prone to sulk and question the wisdom of Providence. But after I returned to my desk, it became clear that I was feeling that way because the big case was now over. Now there was nothing interesting to do. Certainly my colleagues and I were happy to get the victory, but I feared I would soon return to the horribly routine matters of wills, contracts, and the like, and thus sink into another stretch of gray tedium for months.

That was not what happened. Because the prior suit was successful, Mr. Chauncey assigned me to an even more important one, in which a charge of slander had been alleged between two members of Parliament. I would not lead this new effort, but I did not mind that. It was enough to be given stimulating work.

Life at home continued on a tolerable track. But not always.

As Alice's fifth birthday approached, several small parcels came in the mail, mostly from my wife's relatives. Then, as it happened, we received packages from my Uncle Ebenezer and Mr. Evans on the same day. The former sent a toy tea set, a very nice one made of faïence. Evans's gift was even more striking, a china doll made in Meissen, Germany. Emily told me these dolls were becoming the latest rage in toys for girls, at least for those who could afford them. This particular one was twelve inches high and had the face and dress of a proper lady. The doll was well-made; but the admixture of textures—that is, of porcelain and cloth—seemed an odd combination to me.

My wife, however, was delighted with this doll, more so than the tea set. "Alice's godfather seems to have taken an interest in her," she said.

"I told you about crossing paths with him. When I was speaking to him, I mentioned Alice's upcoming birthday."

"I see. Does Mr. Evans have a large family?"

"Two sons, but I do not believe he has any grandchildren."

"How would it be if we invited him and his wife for Christmas dinner this year?"

"That's a capital idea, dear, though I'm afraid Mr. Evans is widowed. Say, perhaps Uncle will come too. Since they are roughly of the same age, they might enjoy each other's company. They would have someone to converse with."

"Our friends are not as dull as all that," she said. "Or do you think so?"

"I did not say they were. But our friends are young, some even younger than are we. Some are prone to act frivolous after a sip of punch. I believe Uncle shies away from younger folk. Come to think of it, that may be the reason he never comes, thinking he'd feel ill at ease around them."

She gave a kind of snort. "Perhaps it would be best if we stopped inviting your uncle at all. Don't you think so? He's shown no interest in meeting your family in the least. It's really quite shameful."

"You must make allowances for him, dear. He's a singular old fellow."

"Eccentric and barmy is what he is," she retorted, color rushing to her face. Then she threw up her hands and walked away.

"Now, Emily, let's not have a row," I called after her.

"Very well, Frederick! We shan't. It doesn't matter to me whether you invite the old goat or not. He'll never come anyway. I simply hate to see you suffer from his repudiation year after year."

I quickly turned from her, feeling as though she had pierced me in a weak spot.

"What's the matter?" she asked in a softer tone.

"I hate to give up on him," I said at length. "I cannot say exactly the reason. Maybe it's because you have your mother, sisters, aunts, and cousins to invite, and I have no one but my uncle. I cannot stop inviting him, Emily. I will not."

With that I threw myself down in my favorite stuffed chair and took up the newspaper.

She came over and laid a hand on my shoulder—something of a wordless apology, I suppose. But she had stung me and I could not bear to look her in the eye.

⋙◆⋘

After that I began to wonder about Scrooge's health, for I hadn't seen him in four years. I wrote to thank him for the gift he sent Alice and used the opportunity to report to him several events, including my reacquaintance with Father's old friend Evans. I told him about his becoming Alice's godfather, the christening, my work on the lawsuit, and Alice's recent birthday. I heartily thanked him for the tea set. To me it seemed a splendid gift, something quite unexpected. At that time, I was not aware anyone produced such toys for children to play with. I omitted mention of the china doll, which everyone else praised so volubly. Finally I inquired as to his health.

I doubted I'd get a reply. However, I received one:

> *Dear Fred,*
> *I am pleased that young Alice likes*
> *her gift. I am also pleased that you are*
> *getting on in your career. My best to*
> *your family. Thank you for asking after*
> *my health. It is a sometime thing.*  *–S*

From his wording I was not certain if he meant his health was mostly good or mostly bad. My first thought was to visit the office and see for myself how he looked and sounded. But I had no pretext for such a visit and was busy besides. I decided to write to Bob Cratchit in care of Scrooge & Marley and ask him if anything was amiss.

The reply came in a few days' time. It was written in a beautiful hand, which I should have expected, since Cratchit had been a clerk for many years.

> *My Esteemed Mr. Truelock:*
>
> *I was honored to receive your letter. As you requested, I have made no mention to your uncle of said letter whatsoever. I must say I was surprised to receive correspondence in the office, as it is seldom, or even never, that a letter arrives hereto addressed to mine humble self. As to your uncle's health, I may say that he is strong as yet, tho some days he takes care to stay at home of a morning because of a cough he often endures. I hope this information may guide you. If I may interpose a personal note, I would like to announce to you that I am, by God's will, again a father, my wife, a most excellent woman, having delivered said baby on the fifth of this month. With that joyous news, I remain*
>
> *Your obedient servant,*
> *Robert Cratchit*

I was amused by this curious letter. As to the cough, I had no idea whether it was a serious matter or not. Yet the letter's writer did not seem overly concerned. I decided to wait until a time when I was able to visit the office and judge myself how Uncle Ebenezer appeared.

After I put away the letter, it struck me as passing strange that Cratchit did not mention whether his new child was a boy or girl. Thinking of the man, I could not help but contrast his situation to my own.

I had but one child and worked exceedingly hard to make a

good living, constantly fretting about income and expenses.

Cratchit now had *six* children! Yet the little clerk, who never seemed to worry about a thing, could not be earning more than fifteen shillings a week.

## CHAPTER 11

### THE SCENT OF PINE

As I had earlier feared, my work eventually became stale. Though I worked on the slander case, it was in a minor capacity. My labors were all routine, and I did not feel invigorated. A colleague named Edloe, who led the effort, was a pompous man who had "been at Eton" and his presence was a constant irritant. I took to stopping by a certain pub on my home in the evening to ease my frustrations. Thus I was frequently late in arriving at home of an evening.

When Emily began to complain of my tardiness, I retaliated by complaining of certain expenditures she had recently made. For example, she bought several sets of clothes for our child, some of them expensive. Alice was growing faster than a beanstalk, I said, and would outgrow them in short order, so it was foolish to buy so many clothes, especially fine ones. In addition, I told her I knew she often went to concerts and teas with her friends and that she'd lately shown very little restraint in spending money.

This brought her to tears. I had previously deduced, however, that her tears were not always as sincere as they appeared. And on this day, I would not be mollified.

And so began another period of hostility between us. It was the same as before: silent breakfasts, few words said in parting, little in the way of conversation in the evening. No intimacy at all. At length the silence became deafening. The unsaid things weighed on us like a mantle of iron.

After a fortnight, she confronted me one morning whilst I was drinking tea and eating a scone.

"Frederick, we must talk."

"We are talking at this moment, are we not?"

"You know what I mean," she said darkly.

I took a sip of tea, then said, "I suppose I do."

"Thank you," she said and quickly produced a large sheaf of paper.

"What have you got there?" I asked.

"This is the calendar. We are in Advent now, as you may have noticed."

I said nothing.

"We must set aside our—*difficulty* for a while," she continued. "I mean the difficulty between us at the moment."

"I'd be only too happy to," I answered.

She glanced over at me, paused. I think she was trying to see if I was mocking her. "Wonderful," she said. "Let's declare a truce, shall we?"

"Can we not have a full treaty?"

"Don't jest. We have plans to work out, and now is not the time to dally."

"What sort of plans?"

"Do you not see? Or do you merely pretend not to? It's time to plan our Christmas dinner."

I did not respond to that. I had already guessed this was the topic.

"Do not worry; my mother and I will take on the full brunt of the work, as we did last year. I only want to settle a few things, and then you can be on your way."

That struck me as impertinent. Did I need her permission to

leave for the office? "I'm afraid I must be going," I said. "I must not be late."

"Very well. We'll talk about it when you come home, then."

I rose to my feet and took up my greatcoat. "That won't be necessary," I said, "because there is nothing we must settle. We're not having the party this year."

She smiled wanly. "Not that again . . ."

"No, dear, we're short of money. It's time we had a quiet, simple Christmas, only the three of us. Oh! And, of course, your mother, if you wish—absolutely. Perhaps next year we can resume this 'tradition' of ours."

"Darling, I never see my cousins during the year. Nor many of our friends. Everyone does so very much look forward to the event, don't you know. And it's always fun to hear what they have been up to during the past twelve months, as well as to celebrate—"

"I must be off," I said curtly and strode into the hall.

I caught the sound of a soft, plaintiff wail when I shut the door behind me. Possibly she shed a few real tears that morning.

Outside, the cold air soothed my heated brow. As I walked the pavement, I reflected on our little conversation. 'Twas odd, I thought, that over one cup of tea we said more words to each other than in the past two weeks. Of course, she only broke the barrier of silence because she needed approval to begin preparing for the annual event. Perhaps it was a good thing, as it gave me the chance to set the matter straight.

I am not sure why I decided to play the autocrat that day; perhaps it was only my long-simmering resentment at having no real say about the party. Or perhaps it was the certainty that this time she would spend more money than ever, if her recent conduct was any indication. Or it might have been that I was merely sick and tired of giving in to her.

During the next few days, we fenced with each other. She recovered herself and tried to act jolly, hoping to cajole me into a change of heart. *I was too bogged down in my profession,* she would say. *I needed to loosen my waistcoat. I needed to drink that extra cup of punch at least one day a year.* This was a formidable gambit, much more potent than further tears would have been. And I found myself acting playful in return, delivering spirited ripostes to each thrust.

Once she reminded me that we had planned to invite Mr. Evans to our dinner that year and that it was a shame he could not come and see his godchild.

"Since he does not know we were to have the dinner in the first place," I replied, "I do not think he will pine over the missed opportunity."

"And your uncle?"

"As you have pointed out, he never comes no matter how many times I ask him."

On another occasion she mentioned the name of a dear friend of mine, a boyhood chum who had attended all of our Christmas dinners and suggested that he, Arthur, would probably have nowhere to go to get a decent plum pudding.

"Let him marry, then, and consent to pay the price," I shot back. At the time I supposed my words were quite witty, but even then I knew I said them at a cost.

One afternoon, less than a week before Christmas Day, I came home early to find a large shrub lying on its side in our drawing room, in the corner, to be exact. I could not fathom why someone bothered to drag the nasty thing indoors. It was not even set in a pot of soil, as a flower or a fern, but was fastened to some sort of plank. I stared at it incredulously, then realized it must be Emily's latest offensive, though I knew not what it might signify. This made me laugh aloud, for though I didn't know the purpose of the vegetation, I truly appreciated this display of creativity on her part. I could hardly wait to hear the explanation.

"Doesn't it smell lovely?" She was standing in the doorway to the dining room, smiling. I supposed she thought my amusement showed approval.

"Smell?" I approached the bush and took a whiff. "Why, yes, very nice. Soothes the lungs. Almost as aromatic as that lilac bush we had in here last month." I had decided to pretend it was our normal practice to drag in large species of flora to perfume the fetid air.

Her face now contorted in disapproval at my making light of this alien thing.

Then Alice came running into the room and sprang into my arms.

"Hello, my dumpling!" I exclaimed, ruffling the little towhead's hair.

"Father, father!" she squealed. "Christmas is coming! There shall be candy and puddings and fun."

*Oh,* I thought, *perhaps this is her trump card.* I was mindful that this was the first Christmas Alice would fully appreciate.

I deflected the conversation to other questions, such as which of her dolls had come to tea that day and how was her china doll getting on with the stuffed pig. When Alice was in the room, Emily and I seldom argued.

Alice ran to the nursery to bring out a sketch or drawing she had done, and I turned to Emily and kissed her cheek.

"My," she said, "that was unexpected."

"So is that bush over there. And I may say, dearest, that I am delighted to find it in our drawing room. Absolutely thrilled!"

"Really? Why is that, husband?"

"Because I've had a dull day and cannot imagine to what purpose this thing has appeared. If I were the blustering sort, I should rant about it; but I find I do not care to rant, for I derive so much pleasure from the anticipation of your explanation that I almost wish to draw it out."

"Good Lord, Fred, have you been imbibing?" she inquired.

"No, sweet, but if you'll fetch the sherry from the cabinet, I'll have a tot, and perhaps you'll join me as well, eh?"

She smiled again and went to retrieve the sherry and two glasses. Obviously she thought I was on the verge of changing my mind about the party. In reality I was not. I only felt, madly, that I wanted to enjoy a rare moment of mirth with her. For who knew what lay ahead?

After we took our sips, she giggled and complained that her head had begun to spin.

"Perhaps we should both sit down," I said. "For I may become befuddled myself when I hear the purpose of the new household item, whatever the purpose may be."

She tittered. "Goodness," she said, "it's not meant to be permanent, you know."

"That's welcome news. Unless it's the latest custom to make composts in the drawing room."

At that she whooped and nearly spilled her wine. Then Alice back ran in with her "sketch," a disorganized series of lines and circles purported to represent her china doll. I praised it, but she herself thought it could bear improving, so she sat down on the floor with a charcoal stick and began to draw.

"Well, then," I said to Emily, "shall we at last get down to the story of the bush?"

"It's not a bush!" cried Alice from the floor. "It's a tree!"

"A tree!" I echoed, confused. "Even stranger."

"A Christmas tree," Alice elaborated, not looking up, for she was absorbed in her artwork.

"Let me have a go at this," I said. "Instead of bringing holly and ivy into the house for Christmas, the new craze is to import an entire tree, an evergreen from the look of it."

"That is very nearly the truth," Emily said gaily. "Oh, Fred! You are so far removed from the times! Have you never heard how the nobility have long celebrated the season by bringing inside specimens of firs or yews? They've done so for years."

"No, I'm afraid I don't keep up with the nobility."

"Some say it is a German custom begun by Martin Luther. Families decorate the trees and place presents round them for the children. And don't think it's so foreign, for the country folk in England often obtain a yew branch, bring it inside, and decorate it. 'Tis a very old custom."

"All well and good," I said, "but I don't see why we, in the bosom of London, need imitate either the country folk or the Germans."

"It is the latest mania! As you likely do not know, Prince Albert surprised the Queen recently by secretly importing spruce trees all the way from his native country to the palace. She was enchanted by them, they say. The magazines reported all of this in lavish detail."

"So now we must imitate the royal family?"

She smirked. "I bought the tree from a gardener for a pittance, dear. It's only a little pine sapling. We will decorate it with paper and tinsel."

"I want to decorate too," said Alice loudly.

"And so you shall," I said, then rose and paced about, having lost my fascination with the invader in our drawing room.

My wife was correct; I truly was removed from the times, from the fads and nonsense that seemed to bubble up from newsprint and gossip and not least from Emily's tea parties. My mother and father had been plain-acting in the way they did things, and I, a sheltered child, never knew much falderal in this season. Christmas as a holiday was not that prominent in our calendar. I did not remember ever seeing holly or ivy or mistletoe in our home; Mother only set out colored candles and candy during the season, and I would receive a gift on Boxing Day. All very plain. *Why must customs change?* I thought. Life was difficult enough without reinventing everything.

I had another sherry before dinner and tried to enjoy my daughter's infectious energy.

Perhaps I ignored shifting social customs because I was continually mired in my work, I thought. Rarely did I scan a newspaper or pay attention to idle chatter. Rather I was devoted in trying to improve my career—without much success, it seemed to me.

The next day a verdict in the slander suit was handed down,

and this time we were on the losing side, which did nothing to help my prospects. I soon found myself again relegated to even smaller tasks.

It was a black day for the firm. Our client who lost the suit, a baron of one of the oldest families in the country, decided to take his legal business elsewhere. He was thereafter quite vocal in berating our handling of the case. Rumors swirled about saying other clients might follow. Several senior solicitors, including Edloe, resigned all at once and joined other firms—an unprecedented event.

My own status remained unchanged; I was neither promoted nor reassigned. I could only pray that my situation was secure, and so I carried on as circumspectly as I could, even though a new rumor spread that the firm itself might soon founder.

At home Emily persisted in badgering me about the Christmas dinner. Time was growing short, she asserted, and it would soon be too late to make preparations. Without raising my voice or posturing, I continued calmly to refuse.

"Not this year," I would say to her.

So determined was she to prevail, that one morning she suggested that, since I was clearly in no mood for celebration, I might prefer to take a short holiday on Christmas so that she and the guests could carry on without me. I was at first shocked by this but soon realized it was only a bitter jape. The remark only made me more determined than ever to maintain my stance.

Yet in no way did I enjoy the last several days leading up to Christmas that year. It had never been my custom to be inflexible, and I cannot say even at this late date exactly what drove me to act at variance with my true nature. At any rate, my self-contradictory behavior wore me to a frazzle. I slept badly, suffered lapses of concentration, and hardly ate a thing. After my day at the law office I stopped in my "refuge pub," the public house whose fire warmed me. There I would fortify myself before going the rest of the way home.

On Christmas Eve I stopped there again and this time I

remained longer than usual. Remorse for my stubbornness had slowly worn me down. *Why am I so intransigent?* I asked of myself. I had made a thorough hash of things. Emily had not spoken to me in two days; I would now have no diversion from my dismal routine; and little Alice would not comprehend why she could not revel in the promised merriment. Because of my stubbornness, we would have to grimly soldier on.

By common standards it was a wise decision to cancel the party. We needed to conserve money. Who knew what might happen? The firm might go under, leaving me without an income. If unchecked, Emily might spend us into the poorhouse. Furthermore, if I had given in to her wishes after all my refusals, she would have never again heeded my words in a serious way. But standing at the bar that evening, drinking my ale, I reflected that the struggle had not been worth the price. I had accomplished little and only made things worse.

Now it was Christmas Eve, and nothing could be done about it. It was too late.

No wonder I lingered and drank more than I usually did. Other men were also drinking, and some of them were laughing and playing at darts. To me the laughter sounded as thin and as light as the frost on the windowpanes. These men seemed not so much merry as they were skittish. Perhaps they had no families, or perhaps they did not care a farthing about Christmas. They felt at home only in a pub.

Finally I decided I could delay no longer. I wished the barman a happy Christmas, shook his hand, and departed.

On the walk home I continued to ruminate, this time trying to see the brighter side of my present situation. For one thing, I should be thankful I had a home to go to on this night and that I was excused from work tomorrow—not everyone could boast of the latter. At the law firm, matters were bound to get better, for all things ran in cycles, after all. Emily and I would reconcile once this dreadful season was behind us. Alice would blossom and give us much joy. It seemed clear to me that I need only make my family see we must stand together as a unit, act as one, that we had much to look forward to and would surely prosper in the new year—and that our traditional Christmas festivities would resume next year on schedule. I would take a solemn oath on it.

I also conjured before my eyes another way we might celebrate the current holiday, one that would be less noisy and giddy, but perhaps more memorable. We could still decorate the tree, drink punch, eat our plum pudding, and even play games. Then I could read to my daughter from Perrault's *Mother Goose* in front of the fire. We would have a quiet, cozy Christmas. It would make a welcome change—a happy time we might fondly recall someday.

This vision of a different sort of Christmas warmed me as I took the last few steps to the house in which we lived, walked up, and entered our flat. A small lamp on a side table glowed dimly. It was nearly out of oil. As was the case of late, Emily had not waited up. I wondered if I should wake her, then decided not to. We would talk in the morning, when all would be new again. Tomorrow we would draw closer as a family. I was sure of it.

I decided to go straight to bed.

When I went over to turn down the lamp, I noticed an envelope lying there. I opened it and found a letter addressed to me.

> *Dear Fred,*
>
> *I have decided to go to my mother's for Christmas. Today Alice and I will embark on the new elevated rail line to Greenwich. We are sure to enjoy this novel mode of transportation. Mother is quite lonely this time of year, as you know. Since she cannot visit us this year, I thought it best to stay at her house a few days and cheer her up. I am taking only a few gifts, the ones I obtained for Alice at the Christmas market. I leave behind the alphabet bricks you were saving for her. They will make a nice surprise when we return.*
>
> *Dearest, I hope you will not be angry. I truly*

*believe we need to spend some time apart, so we both may think on our situation. I am concerned for you. You work so hard and constantly worry over so many things. We shall talk over the matter later. And I shall write to you after we arrive in Greenwich.*

I read it three times. Then I groped in the half-lit room for the bottle of sherry.

CHAPTER 12

AT LOW TIDE

I slept on the divan that night, which was something of a surprise when I woke up in the morning. Most likely I merely fell asleep after I sat drinking sherry in the half-darkness, praying the elevated locomotive had not toppled off its rails as it passed over an unsteady arch.

After two cups of tea, I regained most of my composure. Knowing nothing else to do, I strolled about the flat, casually inspecting it as if I'd never before seen those rooms. Everything was in its proper place, but the furnishings looked foreign to me, sterile, as though I had wandered into a stranger's home, one I'd heard about but never seen. It was altogether an unsettling conceit. I concluded it was caused by the absence of those who were normally a part of the scene, those who bestowed life on the indifferent objects scattered throughout the rooms.

One object I regarded warily and with disdain: the Christmas tree. She had placed it on a small table near the fireplace and festooned it with two or three strands of shiny material. It looked rather drab and mournful there, and I inferred she had broken off the task of decorating the shrub, for it looked even uglier this way, belonging to neither the inside nor outside world. The only thing about the tree I liked was a small scrap of paper lodged in its lower branches, a charcoal drawing of something I could not fully apprehend—a cat, perhaps.

Then I reread the note she left for me. In it she said she would stay "a few days." I had no quarrel with their being gone for a day or two. Surely she would not stay the twelve full days of the season. If she did, I might go mad. As for Christmas Day itself, I could read a book. What an excellent idea! Read a book for pleasure only—the notion appealed to me. Or I could take a walk if the weather was nice. What else?

Then there came a knock at the door. In that house it was normal for visitors to make their way inside and proceed to the chosen flat directly. There was no bell. I was at a loss to guess who might be calling at this hour, on this day.

I opened the door and on the other side found my friend Arthur Trumbolt.

"Merry Christmas, Fred!" he thundered.

"Same to you, Topper," I replied after some hesitation, trying to read into his ample greeting a hidden message. I used his former nickname, which I had employed for many years, ever since we were at school together. Had he come by to make me feel regretful there was no dinner to enjoy this year? Possibly— though generally he was not one to use sarcasm as a weapon.

My friend said nothing else, but merely stood there beaming like an overgrown idiot child, his expression playful as he brandished a bottle of wine or spirits. He looked the same as he always did—trusting, artless.

I remained puzzled, though, and waited for him to say something else.

"Well, old boy," he said at last, "aren't you going to invite me in?"

"Of course, of course," I answered and moved back, thinking perhaps he'd come to cheer me up. But how could he know the situation?

"By Jove!" he sang out after he stepped inside. "You've set up a Christmas tree!"

"Very astute of you, Topper. I am pleased you recognize the decoration for what it is."

"I should hope so," he went on breathlessly. "But I never hoped to see one *here*. My word! How clever! I thought only the peerage and the wealthy were of a mind to erect such decorations." He went over to examine the tree.

"We follow the latest fashions," I said dryly. "The Queen and her Consort can do nothing that we ourselves cannot manage here in our humble flat."

He laughed. "Yes," he said looking round the room, "but, uh—oh, I say! I must be frightfully early."

"Early?"

"I do apologize for bounding in like this. Heavens! I'm like an eager first-termer, ain't I? Itching to impress the master by my punctuality."

"I find myself at a tremendous loss, Topper, because I don't quite follow your drift. What is that you have there, wine?"

"Sherry!" he exclaimed.

"Oh," I replied, feeling a touch queasy all over again. "Well then, why don't we have a spot of tea instead? As you point out, it's still early."

"You don't have to amuse me, Fred. No, no! Instead, make a worker out of me. I may as well pitch in. Let's get cracking! We can start with your little tree. The tinsel is lovely, but it wants something more, don't you think? What about paper stars? They're easy to make."

"Hold on, old boy. We don't need to decorate the tree. It's fine as it is."

"As you wish, Fred. It's your tree. But surely you'll want to put something on the mantelpiece, eh? Emily usually lays scads of holly and ivy up there, does she not?" He paused, and a blank look came over his bluff features. "By the way, where is Emily?"

"In Greenwich, visiting her mother."

"Eh? Come again?"

"She's not here, old friend. Neither is my child. At the moment I am bereft of both wife and daughter."

"You don't say," he uttered softly, confused, trying to comprehend the situation. "Is her mother . . . ill?"

"Not to my knowledge," I answered.

I went to the window and looked out. Profuse sunshine filled the street. Traffic was light. A handful of pedestrians hurried along. A large carriage noisily trundled by.

I turned back to him, saying, "How about that cup of tea?"

"By all means," he agreed.

I had him sit in the wing chair. I was glad everything in the room, with the exception of the divan upon which I'd slept, was neat and clean. Emily had a girl who came in to clean up and do whatever—a slavey, so-called—and it pleased me that everything was shipshape. No doubt my wife wanted to leave the place as tidy as possible, knowing I would likely do little for it myself in the day or two she was gone.

We drank our tea without saying much. I had no scones to offer.

"Would you like a bit of this sherry?" he asked, holding up the bottle.

I looked askance at the sherry. "I've a better notion. I have some Grant's in the kitchen. Let's have a touch of that."

He nodded.

I poured the whisky in two small glasses and we toasted the holiday. "And now what shall we do?" I asked him. "Do you fancy a game of chess?"

He made a dreadful scowl. "Fred, I am so very sorry to have stopped here today. I had no idea . . . oh, dear, I'm nothing but a royal muttonhead."

"Nonsense," I said. "There's nothing royal about you. You've cheered me up, Topper, and I am relishing your company."

"I merely *assumed*—I mean, it never *occurred* to me that you would not be having your usual Christmas dinner. For me it is has become . . ."

He tilted his head, searching for a word.

"A tradition?" I supplied.

"Yes, yes, exactly—that's the word. The same as going to church at midnight on Christmas Eve, which is my own family's particular tradition."

"But you do realize, don't you, that we never invited anyone to come this year, that accordingly the 'tradition' has been violated in a rather savage way, wounded in its middle age?"

His brow knitted in concern. "I say, old man. What's wrong, Fred? Have you and Emily quarreled? You said she's gone to her mother's. Is there to be a separation?"

"Heavens, no," I said, "I don't think so. Well, a short separation, at least, as you perceive, but it will not last long; at least that is my fervent hope. Yes, we quarreled. I think it can be put behind us nonetheless."

"How stupid of me to come round like this! It was the height of crassness to darken your door this day."

I laughed. "Don't be embarrassed that you darken a door here and there. Topper, a man of your size has no control over his shadow. If I were in half the good mood as you are, I should be tickled to death about your visit. For what does it indicate? That this celebration at my hearth has become a thing to look forward to with such certainty that we no longer need beseech friends to come but can rely on their attendance with no second thought. How wonderful! And next year, when we are all gathered again, I shall make it plain that we'll no longer burden the postal service with written invitations; that any of our friends and family may come to the feast without credentials or fear of ridicule; and yes, come again and again, each succeeding year thereafter, *ad infinitum!* Cheers!"

I held up my glass in a salute and quickly drank down the rest. Topper sipped his own whisky slowly, wondering, I conjectured, whether I had been kicked in the head by a horse.

In a way it felt to me that I had.

"See here," he said in a confidential tone. "Are you quite sober? Tell me, what's going on with you two? Why did you quarrel?"

I sighed. "I am not sure," I said. "I thought it was about whether we should have the dinner this year. Perhaps that's not the case. The true question is, who shall decide what we undertake as man and wife? Unfortunately, I picked the wrong matter to contest. It has affected too many others adversely, including yourself. Now do you understand?"

"Not in the least," he said with a dramatically sad face.

It was such a tragic expression that I was forced to laugh.

"Come, let's have another whisky," I suggested, feeling sorry for my friend's discomfort. I truly regretted I had let him down.

"No, no, I'll toddle on," he said and then drained his glass. "My sister invited me to dinner as she always does, so I'll nip over there this year and surprise her. It's a boring family dinner, but perhaps it's good policy to make an appearance once in a while. My father never understands why I choose to come here."

"Why do you?" I asked, truly curious.

"Can't you guess, Fred? It's because there is so much gaiety here. We do not have to wear long faces. No one reads solemn scripture. Here we may laugh and be silly! It's a celebration, after all. Ah, but you look cross, Fred. Do I sound inane? I do, don't I? I suppose I've grown too old to be permitted to be ridiculous."

*My word!* I did not know how to answer that, nor did the question seem at all frivolous. It sounded like a serious question to me. I tried to recollect how long it had been since I myself had taken the liberty to be inane.

"No, Topper. You have that god-given right. Please stay that way. I mean it."

He asked me if I would care to go with him to his sister's, and I replied in the negative. After he avowed that I could always rely on him and that we must meet again soon, he rose, shook my hand, and departed. He took his shadow with him.

After I shut the door, I wondered if Arthur would ever marry.

I had my doubts he could muster the courage, now that I'd frightened him by displaying the sea of matrimony at low tide, thus exposing its jagged rocks.

——⋙◆⋘——

No one else arrived to attend the party that was not to be held.

At length I decided I had to get out of the flat awhile. I plunged into the brisk air with relish, striking off nowhere in particular, enjoying the exercise and the warmth of the winter sun on my back. Foot traffic was a bit heavier now. People in small groups pattered along smartly, chatting among themselves. I surmised they were mostly flitting abroad to pay social calls, "keeping the holiday spirit alive," as was the catchphrase.

Midday approached. I still walked at a moderate pace, pretending I had a destination. I truly wished I did, as the thought of returning home did not please me in the least. I looked for a tavern or pub that might be open. Then another notion popped into my head, and without hesitation I altered my course and increased the pace.

It must be understood that I was in a queer mood and had been ever since I awakened on the divan. Arthur Trumbolt's visit had only exacerbated this capricious feeling. I was now detached from the ordinary routine of my life and consequently gained a certain freedom to act irrationally. My mind throbbed as if highly active, though I could not say what it was going on about.

Instead of truly thinking, I concentrated on the physical sensations, the sights and sounds of the street. This satisfied me all the way to my chosen destination.

The outsize knocker looked as it always had: tarnished and intimidating. I beat a steady rhythm with the device, not wanting to create a raucous, end-of-the-world sound, but rather a mildly annoying one—*mezzo forte,* if you will. In this way I hoped to avoid disturbing yuletide revelers in the neighborhood and yet impel the resident of the place into action.

He answered on the fifth or sixth rap and did not conceal his consternation in seeing me. He only pronounced my name and retreated, shaking his head in disbelief as was his wont. But he left the door ajar. I pulled it shut as I followed him inside.

"I shall never understand your maniacal obsession with this blasted holiday," he said after we reached the drawing room. He was smiling, though. His tone was not petulant; if anything, it was warmer than I expected.

"Apparently I have not been obsessed enough with it," I answered. I was about to ask for something to drink, but he was already pouring out glasses of claret. I had not seen him for several years and noticed he looked older—but then, he always looked older than he was. Otherwise, he moved with precision and without delay and seemed healthy enough in my view. He wore a smart dressing gown and slippers.

He looked at me oddly. "And how is that? For I have never encountered anyone as fervent about this day as yourself . . . unless it be Cratchit."

"How is Bob?" I asked, happy to change the topic.

"Near to starving, as far as I can tell. He has another child now, a sixth."

"Yes. I know."

"Oh, really?" An eyebrow was raised. "How's that?"

"I wrote him a few months ago, and in his reply, he mentioned his new addition."

"My, my! I am astonished. I had no idea you two were so comfortable together."

"I'll grant you it was an odd thing," I said. "I only wrote him to ask after your health. He said you had a persistent cough."

"Oh, that was weeks ago. A common cold is all it was."

"A cold may lead to worse things," I said, thinking of my

mother. "Far worse."

"Yes, I know," he said pensively. Then his mood changed to grumpiness. "Bah! Cratchit exaggerates my illness to you, yet he cannot deal with his own house."

"What do you mean?"

"I'm thinking of his son—Timothy is his Christian name, but they call him 'Tiny Tim.' Has he never told you of the lad?"

"No," I said, now curious. "Which child is it? The eldest?"

"Somewhere in the middle of the pack, I think. His growth is stunted and he cannot walk properly. Cratchit for much of the time carries him about on his shoulders, playing the draft horse, for otherwise the child can only go on crutches."

"How dreadful," I said. "What's wrong with him?"

"Nobody quite knows, least of all the quacks."

"Uncle, why do you make mention of this?"

"Because you remind me of Cratchit. It continually irks me that some men are so illogical as to miss the connection between income and expense. He earns only a few shillings a week, yet must house and feed a large family. He seems not to grasp the reason his money fails to last to the end of each week and constantly complains he is short."

"Prices are indeed rising," I said.

"Then we must adjust our behavior accordingly. Cratchit merely muddles on, making light of his circumstances, praying humorously for divine intervention. You would think he'd try to make every penny of his salary count. Instead, what does he do? He sires another child! My word, it's scandalous. I sometimes think—oh, never mind what I think."

"Surely his wife and the older children bring in a little money. Do you not think so?"

"Maybe they do, but it cannot be much."

"Well then, Uncle," I said. "mightn't you increase his salary a bit? Now, don't look at me as if I'm jesting with you."

"Out of the question. I cannot justify such a rise in his salary."

"What about his seniority and long service to you? Surely

that counts for something."

"What? Must I pay him more simply because I have not yet dismissed him? It is a mutual agreement we work under. He performs his work, and I pay him the agreed-upon amount. Nothing else."

His logic was impeccable. "You always entertain me when you hold forth with your views on business," I observed.

"Hmph. And yet you never take my words to heart."

I sat up in my chair. "Uncle, I must point out that clerks are indispensable. The modern world would collapse without them. True, there must be people to compose documents—people such as you and I—but we must employ others to legibly copy those documents, file them, mail them, and a hundred other tasks. My law firm employs an entire platoon of clerks. We would be lost without them."

"That may be true. But those skills are easily found. Clerks may be had for a farthing apiece."

"A good clerk is sometimes worth far more. We have a clerk named Wheelwright at the firm, and I swear the man knows more law than half the lawyers there employed."

"There are exceptions, I suppose, but I've seen none myself. Frankly, I pay what the market will bear. It's only good business. Honestly, Fred, tell me why you've come here today. Is it to debate economics?"

"I wish that was all there was to it."

"Have you determined at last to drag me forcibly to your annual carousal? I warn you, although I may look frail and weak, I have hidden strength and will fight you to the finish."

I laughed. "I will bear that in mind should I think to resort to violence. No, I cannot say why I came, except to hear you say amusing things." I reached for the glass of claret.

He stood up and moved over to where I sat. "Nephew, I sense something is amiss with you. This day and hour should find you scurrying about your home, preparing for the annual onslaught of merrymakers. Yes, you have told me you leave most of the work to your wife and mother-in-law; but you yourself should be overcoming last-minute stumbling-blocks and ensuring that all is in readiness—and that the liquor cabinet is full. At least, so I would think. Yet here you are, idling in my drawing room."

"For someone who never attends such gatherings, you are certainly well-acquainted with the preparations thereof."

"I was once the same age as you are now," he said, and then his lips curled into a smile.

"If by that you mean I am besotted with youth and have been misled by false gods . . . then I must agree with you. That is precisely the malady. But I believe I've survived the worst of it."

He sat down opposite me and picked up his pipe. Neither of us spoke for a while. In the interval he lit the tobacco and took a puff or two.

"Fred," he said at length, "you're agreeing with me. I must say that is alarming, nay, shocking and disturbing. In fact, there is nothing more alarming than to hear a man in the full bloom of his youth agree with an old geezer like myself."

"I am not as young as I seem. Not these days. Tell me, are you saying there is no wisdom to be learned from others? That only time itself can educate me?"

"No, but I find your attitude unnatural," he said. "Certainly you may learn from me when I talk of business or of character and so on, but by Pan's pipes it bothers me that a man as young and full of life as yourself should renounce his appetites, leave his home, and visit his reclusive uncle when there is a party to be found."

"Ah," I said mournfully, "alas, there is no party to be found this year."

"I see. Well, I thought it odd I did not receive my yearly summons," he said. "What happened?"

"As head of my household, I decreed we should not have a Christmas dinner this year. I felt it was time to enjoy a respite from the expense and bother of it. My work has suffered of late. As a result my position at the firm is precarious—as is the health of the firm itself. The cost of living has increased. That is the sum of it. But my sentimental wife did not understand. One may say she has a way of looking at life similar to Cratchit's: Keep the colors flying high and carry on, no matter what! At any rate, since there was to be no celebration in our home this year, she decided, on her own initiative, to take Alice and go to her mother's house in Greenwich for the holiday. Therefore I find myself quite alone."

Uncle nodded sagely and not without sympathy. After puffing a bit more he said, "I see. But why did you come to *my* house?"

I cast my eyes about the room, searching for an answer, for I did not know how to answer him. His bookshelves were overflowing.

"I came to borrow a book," I said. "I am in desperate need of something to read."

CHAPTER 13

A NEW MODE OF TRAVEL

My wife and child did not return in one or two days as promised. The two days became three, then four, then five. Even though I was disappointed, I did not go mad, though. Instead, I adjusted accordingly and adopted a new mode of living, a much simpler one, hoping it would not endure long. I rose in the morning, ate a piece of bread, and went to the office. On the way home, I stopped in a tavern that served decent food, ate, and drank a few glasses of ale before continuing the rest of the way. I read a bit before going to sleep, though on many nights I felt too tired to read more than a paragraph or two of the weighty book my uncle had lent me. It was a very ordered and lonely existence.

Fortunately, Emily wrote to me several times.

The first letter gave details of her journey on the world's first elevated railway, the London and Greenwich, which ran from a stop near London Bridge to the newly completed Greenwich station. She reported that Alice was thrilled by this aerial adventure. Upon their arrival she discovered her mother had decorated the house exactly as she remembered it as a child.

Her sisters, who still lived at home, received her warmly, and they all agreed it was wonderful to celebrate the holiday again in the family home. Emily had two sisters, one older than she and one younger. The older one was plump yet attractive, whilst the younger was still girlish and slim as a reed. In my opinion, Emily had inherited most of the beneficial family traits, for there was no doubt she was the loveliest.

Her letter was long, and the first time I read it I did so hastily, not caring to dwell on the details of the dinner itself—that is, which cousins joined them on the feast day and what they ate. I was looking to see when she would return but did not find that information. I replied tersely, mentioning Arthur's visit and my call upon my uncle. I kept the tone of it factual and did not speak of my shock and disappointment to find the flat empty when I came home Christmas Eve.

Our correspondence continued in that vein. Each wrote about what he or she was doing, or what others said, all plainly and without much comment.

Emily wrote that her sisters were amused to hear that Topper appeared unexpectedly—they owned it was exactly like him to do such a thing—and both said they missed seeing him and the others who usually came to our affair. In one letter she related that Alice missed me and inquired of her if I was "happy." For my part there was little of interest I could relate, so I inserted office anecdotes, even though she normally did not find them very amusing, and items I gleaned from the newspaper or heard at the tavern. I even told her I was engrossed with Gibbon's *Decline and Fall* and commented on what I thought of the book thus far.

I was grateful we kept open a line of communication. But in our correspondence neither of us mentioned the rift that had opened between us. We only alluded to it indirectly.

It seemed she was in no hurry to return. When New Year's Eve approached, she told me she and her sisters were to go to a cousin's house for a small dinner party. There was no mention of a possible date when she would return. When Twelfth Night, the official end of the season, passed I could not help but remember wistfully the ball we attended when Alice was a baby and things had been so good between us.

What was I to make of this extended stay? It was as though she and Alice were away for a month in the country. That was how I preferred to regard it, for I knew this habit was common in many families—the wife and children vacationing somewhere whilst the husband remained in town and worked until he could join them in the holiday. However, such an arrangement was usually planned for the summer, not the middle of winter.

I disposed of the tree and made sure there was no trace of Christmas left in the flat. The servant girl, Doris, came round, and I had her tidy up the place. With the holiday over and the new year afoot, I began to simmer with a growing resentment. When in God's name were they coming home? Would they stay in Greenwich until Easter?

It struck me as foolish not to discuss our marital problems in our correspondence. In fact, it seemed the height of folly. She was not away in the country waiting for me to join her—not at all. We had to stop pretending and bring our problems into the clear light of day if ever we were to resolve them.

Since it was my turn to answer her last letter, I resolved to write a serious and frank one and so set about it with a will. I said flatly we must come to an understanding, that it was outrageous for her to remain at her mother's house so long and give no thought to her wifely duties here, that Alice was my child as well as hers. I demanded she bring her home. I listed several other demands.

But after reading what I'd written, I tore up the letter, for I knew I would gain nothing by such assertions. Though I had certain rights, some legal, it would do no good to sling them at her in that way. I had tried to act the autocrat before and what had it gotten me? I did not want a relationship based on fear. In my heart I yearned for some ideal form of marriage, one that possibly did not exist. As my uncle had observed, I was still young enough to have a healthy appetite for such longings.

So I began a new letter trying to explain my actions to her. This one was apologetic. I related my troubles at work, holding nothing back, even the possibility of losing my position. I hoped to make her understand the reason I was so concerned about conserving money. I apologized for canceling the Christmas dinner and promised I would never do it again.

I crumpled up this letter as well. She would never take it seriously. Moreover, it sounded fawning and weak. It would avail neither of us if she were to feel she'd won the battle by leaving me.

I got to my feet and began to pace around the room, sick in heart to think we were never to be close and loving again. And that it was my own fault.

Finally, amid my pacing and brain-wracking, I impulsively dashed off a third letter. I mailed it at once before I had time to reconsider. As it was brief, I attached only a one-penny adhesive stamp.

I mailed it late on Monday. After doing so I could only wait for her reply. I kept to my Spartan routine as before, but I was not as resigned to it as I was two weeks earlier. I balked like a mule in harness as I walked to the office and I never said a pleasant word to anyone. After work I went straight home, forgoing my boring tavern food, to see if I had received any mail.

Each evening I was disappointed. By Friday I was again a troubled man, wondering what to do next. I knew I had to do something, for I could not abide this eternal, torturous wait. It took only a day to send or receive a letter from Greenwich, which, after all, was not far. Nor was it expensive to mail a letter; a person need only affix a Penny Red stamp to a half-ounce letter to send it anywhere in the country. True, letters were occasionally lost, but my intuition told me she simply chose not to reply.

After much deliberation, I decided I must act. The next morning I took a small valise with me to work. In it I had packed a few personal items.

The office closed at noon on Saturday. In point of fact little work generally was done during that half-day. Conferences were held. Clerks caught up with their filing and tidying-up, and the rest of us planned for the coming week. Some senior solicitors never appeared at all, or came in late. It was a relaxed stretch of time, but for me on this particular day, this idle time played havoc with my nerves. I could hardly sit still and pretend to read my documents.

At precisely twelve o'clock, I bade farewell to my colleagues and left the office.

As the weather was mild, my intention was to walk all the way to Greenwich—I thought the exercise might do me good. But sitting in the office that morning, I changed my mind. Such a walk would take hours. It would not be polite to show up in a lather at her mother's house looking the worse for wear. No, walking would not do. I had to preserve what shreds of dignity I could.

Having decided on a different plan, I walked south from the office toward the river.

Soon I crossed London Bridge and located the train station on Tooley Street. It was a strange-looking affair, sitting up so high. To me it did not look completely finished. Uncle Ebenezer once waxed eloquent over the "heady years" in which we lived, the era he called the Age of Steam. He told me he was inspired to make his fortune by all the advances in science and transportation. I agreed with him that progress was a great thing—in principle. But now that I was about to embark on my first rail journey, I found I did not relish the view on the front lines of progress.

Everyone had read of this marvelous railway in the newspapers, and I imagined clearly how the journey would progress: a six-ton iron behemoth, belching smoke and steam, begins to move and powers its bulk atop a narrow viaduct that is supported by over 800 brick arches. The locomotive passes high over city streets, crosses a canal and a creek, and attains a speed (so they claimed) of nearly sixty miles per hour. Then, by the grace of God, it comes to a full stop in Greenwich station. I certainly prayed it would do so. This was not a journey for the faint of heart.

Yet Emily had done it, and so would I.

I purchased a ticket and was directed to go to the platform and wait. One must recall that this was the first rail station built in our capital, and there was not then those protocols and procedures to which we are now accustomed. For the many who flocked there on this day, steam-powered travel was *terra incognita.* They knew not how to behave. I noticed some men and boys crossed over to the opposite platform to have a visual inspection, hopping over the iron rails at will. This crowd of Saturday-afternoon daredevils milled about as if they were at a market. They were rowdy, eager for their outing, and quite impatient for a locomotive to appear.

Finally a train came into view, chugging from the east, the direction in which we would soon travel. I observed that the engine was reducing its speed as it approached. As it drew near, it slowed more and more, until finally the brake was applied and the wheels locked, which caused an agonizing banshee-like screech as metal scraped metal. Children covered their ears. I could not help but wonder if the convenience of getting quickly from one location to another was worth all this bother. Perhaps there would be a rise in the sale of earplugs. Still, the entire train managed to come to a final stop, producing a savage lurch that rippled throughout the cars.

At this the crowd on the platform cheered wildly.

We watched with rapt attention as the passengers of the incoming train slowly disembarked on the other side. I wondered if the cars held only sightseers on a day trip or if there were any passengers on board who actually had a good reason to travel from Greenwich to Southwark. Then a preposterous idea occurred to me. Perhaps someday, a man might live in Greenwich, or even Hackney and yet have employment in the City of London— and on a daily basis travel to his place of work by the means of locomotive—*and return home again in the evening!* It was almost too fantastic to imagine.

In watching the opposite platform fill with people, I discovered that at least two of the train's passengers were not sightseers at all but had in fact traveled this day on a one-directional trip. My heart beat rapidly as I stood gaping at them, not at first believing the evidence of my eyes. Then, afraid of losing them in the crowd, I sprang forward, sprinted over the tracks, and ran at them from behind.

"Emily!" I cried.

She turned around sharply, as if startled to be hailed in this place, then stopped walking and stood rooted to the spot, regarding me as I hastened forward.

I searched her face for a hint of her feelings, trying to discern in an instant what her heart might hold. Before I could make anything out, she rushed into my arms. Alice began to squeal with glee in an excruciatingly high register. I encircled them both and held them tightly. Some nearby onlookers applauded—I know not why, possibly because we were at that moment the picture of joy, a sundered family made whole again.

I gathered up their bags, hired a coach, and we soon started for home.

⟞◆⟝

Once inside the coach, Emily wept with relief and happiness and clutched my arm in both of hers, almost to the point of pain. As we rolled along I planted many kisses on her brow. Meanwhile Alice rolled about the seat, unable to remain still, sometimes tugging my other arm, sometimes peeping out the window.

"Fred, I'm dreadfully sorry I went away as I did," Emily said rapidly in the midst of her tears. "I hope you can forgive me."

"Never mind, dear," I answered. "Everything is set right again."

"I delayed to return so long because . . . because, well, I was afraid of what you would say when I finally did come home. My fear caused me to tarry longer than I ever intended. Oh, I should never have gone away in the first place!"

"There, there," I said and kissed her again.

But she would not be silenced. "It was sheer willfulness and it was wrong!"

"Emily, will you cease? We do not need to sort everything out, who was right and who was wrong. We were both in the wrong and each needs to make amends."

"Oh, Fred!" Then she blubbered something else I could not make out.

"In one of your letters," I continued, "you said we needed to spend some time apart, and perhaps you were correct. But now I want nothing more than to resume our life as it was before, only with more sympathy and frankness between us."

"Father!" cried Alice. "What is that man *doing* there?"

I glanced out the window and saw we were passing by a ragged vagrant who was urinating in the gutter. I reached for the blind and jerked it down. "Never you mind, Miss Truelove."

She giggled. "True*lock.*"

"Just so, but for me, you will always be 'Miss Truelove,' because you're my special darling."

She grinned at me with mirth but soon raised the blind again.

"Fred?" Emily said, for the first time sounding more herself, free of the grip of high emotion. "How did you know we were coming home on the train today?"

Looking away from her, I responded playfully: "Did you not write and tell me?"

"You know I did not!" she laughed. "Stop teasing!"

I kept silent a moment, still wondering why she hadn't answered my last letter.

Then she said, "Did Mother write you that I was coming? If

so, I shall be put out with her. Extremely."

"Why is that?"

"Because I wanted to surprise you! I wanted to come home without announcing it. I owned to tell you would invite bad luck, that it was better to come straight home and see if you would take us back again."

I chuckled, squeezed her hand.

"After all," she continued merrily, "if the two of us appeared on the doorstep you could hardly throw us out in the street."

I kissed her again. "Far from it, my love. I should have done a jig and embraced both of you at once."

"Oh, my dear husband," she sighed.

"It would have been a wonderful surprise." *Of course,* I thought, *I might not have been at home; I might have gone to a tavern, or worse. What would she have done then?*

"To be honest," I added, "I nearly gave up hope. You see, I waited the whole week hoping to get a reply to my last letter."

"Oh," she said. The syllable was barely audible.

"You did get my letter, didn't you?" I asked, wondering for the first time if my own short missive, as light as a feather, might have blown astray when in the custody of the new postal system.

She pulled me closer and whispered, "Of course I did, darling. That's what gave me the courage to return."

"Ah," I said, a bit puzzled. "I worried you might find my message deficient, or too slight—trivial, even. And I hoped you might send back a short reply."

"I'm sorry, then, that I did not," she said and kissed me on the mouth. Alice ignored us as she observed the ever-changing street life outside the window. "How could I not come home after I received your wonderful letter? Too slight? You could not have expressed your feelings any better had you written a thousand words or cast them in verse." Her eyes were moist. "Instead you simply wrote: *I miss you. Please come home.* I ask you, what more was there to say?"

I thought of the long, pensive letters I had written and

destroyed. Then I said, "It seemed necessary to speak directly from the heart."

"I am so thankful you did." Then she exhaled a long breath, as if to expel all her former fears, sat back, and laid her beautiful head upon my shoulder.

It was not until late in the evening that I explained why I went to the railway station. But it was a false explanation. I did not tell her that I had gone there determined to fly to Greenwich and wrest her from whatever entanglements kept her apart from me and reclaim her as my wife, no matter who might object. Instead, I told her that God sent me a sign I should go to the station and wait there until she and Alice returned.

She looked at me skeptically, smiled, and asked nothing more.

Next morning, as I woke from a dream, I wondered whether I should revisit London Bridge station and see if they would give me compensation for an unused ticket.

## CHAPTER 14

A MYSTERIOUS CALLER

O ur domestic life ran smoothly from that day forward. I do not mean that there were no disagreements, for those are endemic to any marriage, but there was never again a serious matter that we could not work out. This is not the case in all households. Friends and colleagues have told me they quarrel constantly with their wives for the pettiest of reasons. They usually complain that their women are too advanced in their deportment and know not how to accede to the wishes of their husbands, to whom God, they say, has given the right of rule in marriage.

"Love, cherish, and *obey,*" they recite.

I generally advise a fellow who references this section of the rite to reserve the "obey clause" of the contract for serious issues only and not remind his wife of it too often . . . if ever.

For a long time I thought, smugly, that I knew what marital devotion was. But in April something happened which showed the true scale of what it could be.

My wife and I were sitting at home, at our leisure, Alice having been put to bed. Emily was knitting something, and I was still plowing through the first volume of Gibbon's massive history of the fall of Rome, the book I borrowed from my uncle on Christmas Day. I interrupted myself to make an observation that occurred to me.

"This chapter is quite provocative," I said to her. "I understand now why my uncle, who praises this work, has taken issue with the Church."

"Oh?" she said, not looking up from her knitting. "Why does he, then?"

"The author asserts that the Church hastened the fall of Rome. And further, that it is guilty of many sins in the spreading of the faith."

She yawned. "Interesting." She still did not look up.

"No wonder he looks on the Church as 'humbug,' as he puts it. That's exactly what he told me, you may remember, when I asked him to come to the christening." I was about to say more when there came a soft knock at the door.

We looked at each other, surprised at this interruption. Visitors were infrequent, and unexpected visitors in the evening were passing rare, to say the least. I went to the door. Topper's Christmas visit briefly crossed my mind, but I doubted it was he. I soon discovered that it was not a man at all. When I opened the door I beheld a middling tall woman of perhaps forty-five years of age. A patch of gray colored her light-brown hair. She was dressed simply in a print dress, bonnet, and shawl. Although the face was rather sad in aspect, I felt somehow that this was not its usual state, for from her visage there emanated a foursquare optimism, partly due, I thought, to her lively blue eyes. I assumed at once that the lady had lost her way and was therefore in temporary distress.

"May I help you, madam?" I asked.

"Oh, I do hope so, sir," she said, her voice unsure. "I am seeking out someone."

"Aha," I said. "Perhaps I can point you in the right direction. Is it someone dwelling in this house?"

"Yes, sir, I believe so."

"And the name?"

"Truelock is the name. Frederick Truelock."

I stared at her dumbly, rather flummoxed.

"Would that be yourself, sir?" she asked.

By this time Emily had joined me at the door.

"Why, yes," I answered. "How is it, uh—I mean, how may I help you?"

A smidgen of relief seemed to relax her brow. "Oh, thank heaven! I have walked ever so far to get here. May I come inside for a bit, sir? I shall not linger."

I glanced at Emily. She nodded, and I stepped aside for the lady to enter.

"What a right cozy place this is," she remarked on coming inside, charmed out of her melancholy for a moment. I saw now that her shawl was moth-eaten and the dress faded.

"If I may ask, madam, who are you and what business might you have with me?"

"Why, bless my heart alive, I've forgotten to say who I am!"

"And exactly who would that be, if I may be so bold?" Emily said sharply.

"Why, I'm Mrs. Robert Cratchit, at your service."

Emily looked at me questioningly. She evidently recollected the surname but could not sort out its proper place.

"Dear," I said to my wife, "why don't you make a pot of tea? Mrs. Cratchit has walked all the way from Camden Town, I believe. She must be exhausted."

"Please do not trouble yourself on my account," said Mrs. Cratchit, though her sparkling eyes belied her words.

Emily merely smiled and went to the kitchen.

"Please sit down, Mrs. Cratchit, and tell me how I may be of service."

Though she seemed anxious not to impose, she did not refuse to sit. "Very well, sir, I'll just rest a tiny bit," she said as she took a chair. She looked about her, apparently admiring the room. "I cannot stay any length of time, for Martha—that's my eldest—she will not long be able to keep my Bob convinced I have gone to visit a sick friend."

I knew not what to say. So I waited patiently for Emily to bring in the tea. Meanwhile Mrs. Cratchit praised our modest furnishings with a string of compliments.

Then I realized my silence was making her uncomfortable.

"May I ask how you found us? I'm only curious. We're delighted to receive you, of course."

"Well, you see, my Bob was so proud that you wrote a letter to him awhile back. I believe it was to inquire as to your uncle's health. Anyhow, I noticed there was a return address on it."

"I see."

Emily entered with the tray.

"I hope I have not overstepped," she continued. "My husband showed me your letter and asked me to keep it with our other mementos."

Emily poured the tea and sat down next to me. I noticed Mrs. Cratchit took quite a bit of sugar.

"So, then," I said, "how *is* your husband?"

Her face suddenly contorted. "Alas," she wailed and then stifled a fit of sobbing.

"What is it, dear?" Emily asked, concerned.

"Mr. Scrooge has let Bob go. My husband has lost his position."

"What!" I cried, completely caught off balance. "What happened?"

"It seemed to me a small thing, really," Mrs. Cratchit went on. "He confused two letters he'd copied and mailed 'em to the wrong places."

"That sounds like a petty mistake," said Emily.

"Well," the lady continued, "one was a supplier and the other a customer, with the outcome that each was rather unhappy to learn—certain things, though I don't know exactly what it was all about. I have no head for business myself."

*And apparently neither does Bob,* I thought. Angry at my uncle's Draconian punishment, I began to pace around the room, fuming, as Emily comforted the woman. I thought back to my conversation with him last Christmas Day, when we discussed Cratchit, and I argued he should be given a rise in salary. Even though Scrooge would not hear of it, I thought at the time he was at least satisfied with his man's work. I never dreamed he would really sack the poor chap.

"When did this happen?" I asked after I regained my composure.

"It were over two weeks ago. Bob thought he might find a new position with little delay, but the times they've worsened, as you may know. My older children help out as they're able, but none has a sure situation, nor do they earn much. Some days we go without food." She choked up. "And me with the little ones, the youngest only a year old!"

She began to weep again, and Emily looked at me questioningly.

"I only came here out of despair, Mr. Truelock. I know Bob would never agree to it. But I thought maybe your law firm—for Bob mentioned you are a well-known solicitor—might have need of my husband's services. He's quite experienced, after all, and his mix-up with the letters seems to me a trifling thing."

I sighed. "I'm afraid my firm is not in the best health at the moment," I said. "They, too, have let a clerk go here and there. But first I will speak with my uncle about this. He may listen to reason."

"Fred," Emily said, "do not promise too much. Your uncle is not the most pliable of men."

"Oh, but it might help," said Mrs. Cratchit. "You never know. I thank you, sir. You are most kind." She finished her tea and rose to depart.

"Don't worry, dear," Emily said, "Fred will do his best to help you."

Next day I contrived to call on a client in the vicinity of Scrooge

& Marley—for the firm was still so called nearly seven years after the latter's "death." It was to my uncle's place of business I went first, sifting in my mind the arguments I would make to urge him to rehire the little clerk.

But when I entered the outer office from the street, I was shaken by what I encountered and felt befuddled, as though I had stepped into the headquarters of some other business. Instead of one or two clerks sitting quietly at their writing desks, I found three young men moving about the room, pressing and poking one another, tossing paper missiles, and arguing loudly as to correct rules. They stopped their antics at once and stared dumbly me. In that instant, they all three appeared to be impossibly young and callow.

One of the lads was bold enough to ask my business.

I cast upon him a baleful eye. "My name is Frederick Truelock," I said with gravity. "I'm Mr. Scrooge's nephew. Is my uncle in?"

They looked at each other, bewildered and frightened. Finally the tallest of them spoke up. "He is at luncheon, sir, with a client."

"Very well," I said. "I will wait for him in his, uh, inner sanctum."

I walked decisively to the door and entered my uncle's private office. I could hear them whispering amongst themselves, arguing and hissing at each other like children. As I sat there waiting, it occurred to me my mission might be easier than I imagined. In fact, my mood rose as I considered the mettle of the new clerical staff. To me they didn't seem like clerks at all but more like the proverbial three blind mice.

I had not long to wait, for I soon heard the outer door open and then the voice of my uncle, who'd returned from his midday meal. He barked at the clerks, clearly angry. One of them mentioned I was awaiting him, but Scrooge continued ranting, livid over some other matter—perhaps the residue of the paper missiles. Though I could not make out all the words, he was now engaged in a grand tirade. A few minutes later, I heard the outer door slam with great force. Then, very distinctly, I heard Scrooge say, "Get to work."

The inner office door knob rattled.

"Stuff and bother!" he sputtered as he entered his office. "Is there not a clerk in this city who has brain enough to cipher figures and make a fair copy of a letter?"

"I may know of one," I answered coyly. He ignored my comment.

"Fred, I am down to two clerks once again, for just this minute I sacked another indolent dimwit. He'd be well advised to find work as a muleteer or street cleaner, something that requires only a sliver of brain power."

"You seem to have a slight mess on your hands," I said, trying to refrain from smiling.

"Do not mock me, nephew; I'm in quite a dither." He retrieved the bottle of claret, poured, then lifted his glass and said, "Here's to Bedlam Hospital, whither I may shortly retire after I've been driven insane here."

After he'd made this rather depressing toast, I said, "Can you not guess why I have come to see you?"

"Eh? Well, it's still a few months until Christmas, so it can't be that. Or have you given up playing the host altogether?"

"On the contrary," I said, "I have decided to resume my duties this year, and of course you are urged to attend. But that is not why I came."

"Perhaps you've come to assess my health again."

"From what I have seen and heard so far, you are as robust as ever. I had no reason to feel otherwise, really; but in a way you touch upon the purpose of my visit. For had I wished to know the state of your health, I would merely"—I coughed—" have written to the person who informed me of it on the last occasion."

His black eyebrows—the last bit of his hair that remained that color—sagged low. "I *see* now. You have come to discuss Mr. Cratchit."

"Correct."

He shook his head. "If you had written to him again, he

would have likely told you I was at death's door—or some other bit of humbug. The man is a simpleton."

"Well," I said, drinking a bit of the claret, "if I *had* written to him, he could hardly have replied anything at all, could he? Since he's no longer employed within these walls."

"You never cease to amaze me, Fred. As I recall, we discussed the fool at length on Christmas Day last."

"We did, yes. It was you who brought up the topic."

"Only because he is a prime example of ignorance and financial mismanagement." He paused briefly. "That's not why I dismissed him, however."

"I know the reason. He confused two separate letters, I believe."

"At least he told you the truth. Did you know that his thoughtless blunder cost me a valued client? I felt that severe punishment was justified. There are limits, after all."

"I found out about the incident by other means, for I have not seen Bob in several years. But Uncle, surely you have made an error in judgment this time. Think of his family, especially the new child. And then there is Tiny Tim,"

"Fred, Fred," he said and then turned away. "I need not mention his recklessness to you," he said grimly. "We went over the verge that last time."

"Consider the matter this way, Uncle. You have now punished him for his transgression. You have docked two or three weeks' worth of wages. Now take the fellow back, for goodness' sake! From the looks of your reception vestibule, your business is about to founder."

He stared at his glass, jaw set. I could not tell which way his thoughts ran.

In the intervening lull I heard through the wall contentious voices being raised. Then the sound of a tremendous crash issued from the outer room.

Uncle sprang up and hurried out. Through the open door I could see that one of the clerks had tipped over a writing desk, scattering a flood of papers across the floor. I gently drew the door shut, not caring to listen to the rush of invective then pouring from the firm's proprietor.

Once again the outer door slammed.

Scrooge rejoined me.

"I am now down to *one* clerk," he said with fire in his eyes. "And the remaining one had better dance to the tune double-time if he wishes to remain here a minute longer." He poured us another round of claret.

"Then you'd be left with no clerks at all."

"God save us!" he said in a miserable tone.

"It's fortunate that clerks can be had for a farthing apiece." I looked away and quickly took a sip of claret, knowing baleful eyes fell on me, for he surely recalled having made that remark himself.

I said nothing else but waited for him to speak first.

All was quiet in the outer office. Perhaps the remaining clerk, having no one with whom to contend, was actually performing a bit of work.

At last he spoke, quietly but with suppressed emotion. "It appears I am pushed to the limit of my endurance. Very well, I'll take Cratchit back. At least he has a splendid hand. I'll have the other one check his addresses from now on. What a world!"

I nodded and idly inspected my glass.

"What is it, Fred?" he said, annoyed. "Is this not the favor you sought from me?"

"It is, Uncle, but begging your pardon, it occurs to me that, hmm, you might see fit to increase the man's salary a little in view of—"

"Absolutely not!" he shot back at me, enraged, his color up. "The prior arrangement and salary will be adhered to. That is my final word!"

"Very well. At least the family will not starve."

"That remains to be seen," he said in disgust.

I stood up to leave. "I cannot stay, for I must pay a call on one of our clients. Afterwards I should be happy to notify Bob that his fortunes have changed if you will supply me with the address. All I know is he abides in Camden Town."

He sighed heavily. His bad temper seemed to have faded away. "No need," he answered with an air of resignation. "There is an errand boy who plies this street. I shall employ him to notify the fortunate Mr. Cratchit at once. What's a penny or two more?"

"Excellent," I said, feeling elated, but also a bit awkward, not accustomed to having gotten the better of him. "Well, then, Uncle, I suppose I must bid you good day."

"Good day," he responded as if from a pit of uttermost gloom.

I took a step toward the door, then turned back around to face him. "But I shall see you in a few months," I added, "when I call again on Christmas Eve."

He cast cynical eyes at me. "Must you do that, Fred? You know I will not attend your yearly fete."

"Hope springs eternal," I remarked with good cheer and quickly departed.

## CHAPTER 15

## THE CURSE OF THE BARON

L ater in the year I thought of the incident again when it became clear that hard times were truly descending on the nation again. The evening Mrs. Cratchit paid her call she already knew the process had begun. It quickly became evident to the rest of us. The price of bread rose, as did the prices of many other commodities. At the same time, a lot of men found themselves out of work. Bob Cratchit fortunately was not one of these.

*Why must it be so?* I wondered as I walked to the office one morning in late November. It seemed to me that modern civilization, for all the mechanical and scientific progress attained, was still helpless in taming the flow of money. The Scotsman Adam Smith wrote a great deal on the science of commodities, but he offered no advice on how to prevent these periods of want, which came and went, sometimes for no apparent reason.

In this meditative state of mind, I thought back to the last major one I endured, when I was a young solicitor and newly married. I was sorely challenged that year and sacrificed much during the period. Seven years ago, it was.

Then my heart skipped a beat. *Seven years?* I could not help but recall my mother's belief in the timing of our family fortunes: *Every seven years behold a shifting of the earth.* She did not mean by this motto, or whatever it may be called, that the shift was always adverse. Nevertheless, that was often the case. I remembered my father died seven years after she did.

Upon arriving at my office, I shook off this melancholy state of mind. I bade good morning to the old gentleman who watched over the place during the night, and he tipped his hat to me as he went out the door. I was grateful he had lit the stove, for the chill seemed to have gotten into my bones.

Mr. Wheelwright, the senior clerk who was also my good friend, ambled over as if to gather some of the heat himself. "Good morning, Mr. Truelock," he said quietly.

I replied in a cautious tone, for I guessed he meant to say more. He held his tongue, though. He and I rarely discussed anything but business, and it was not his usual way to approach me in this manner. *Odd.* I waited patiently as I continued warming my hands.

Finally he glanced around to see if any other person was near by. None was.

"I wanted to apprise you of something," said the clerk under his breath.

"Yes?"

"Word is, there has been a falling-out among the partners. Mr. Chauncey will be leaving us soon."

I said nothing, displeased to hear the news. Chauncey had been my benefactor and a guiding light when I first came to the firm. But such changes occurred, I knew. At that moment I was incurious as to the reason. As Uncle often said, "it's only business." Surely, I thought, this event would not affect me personally.

He leant closer. "And Mr. Edloe is to rejoin us. He is to become a full partner."

"God help us," I said softly, for this was quite another matter.

Edloe was the man who worked on the disastrous slander case of the previous year. I once lost my temper and argued with him over a legal point. I had no confidence in the man.

"I wanted to warn you, partly because I know you do not revere the gentleman. Yet I think Edloe is a fair man, though a rather arrogant one. But mind, he will likely be looking for reasons to trim the staff. So if I were you, I'd be extremely circumspect in all matters. Watch your step."

"Trim the staff? Tell me, is that rumor founded upon something solid?"

"It is not a rumor," Wheelwright said with authority and left me to go to his desk.

As it happened, Mr. Chauncey called the staff together that very afternoon to announce he was departing to take a position in a law school as a lecturer. He made a short speech and then shook each man's hand. We gave him three cheers, and he immediately departed, trying to put on a brave front, though his jaw was set and his face red.

It would have been better had he made a longer speech, I thought afterward, for the ceremony was so quickly run through and done with that it seemed perfunctory and devoid of feeling. I felt ashamed, for instead of saying anything personal to him in parting, I had merely gone through the same motions as the others—and then watched the man walk out the door.

We who remained meandered back to our stations in varying degrees of distress. Some were indifferent to the gentleman's departure. Some were shocked, having had no advance warning. I myself was concerned for my own situation, given that Mr. Edloe and I were not especially friendly.

Chauncey was not the only casualty that day. Two younger solicitors, lately hired, were summarily dismissed within the hour.

As dire as the future appeared, little changed in the next week or two. Everyone carried on as before. But a tense air of waiting and watching blanketed all that was thought, said, or done.

A new calendar page brought us the month of December, and the weather brought us cold winds and freezing rain throughout the city. When I came home one dark evening, Emily was already giddy with plans for Christmas. She barely let me take the time to embrace her, so full was she with notions she wished to share.

"But, darling, we have only lately entered Advent," I pointed out.

"Yes, I know, dear," she answered, "but we should begin to think ahead. We ought to send out invitations early, so as to reassure each person that our dinner will be resumed this year."

"Oh, very well," I said. "But don't bother sending one to my uncle. In a way I've already invited him, though I promised I'd drop by on Christmas Eve to remind him personally."

Our dialogue was interrupted by Alice, who, dashing into the room unexpectedly, grabbed my arm and led me to the nursery, as she had many important things to relate about her day.

After dinner, Emily and I settled down in the drawing room, and I inquired about her plans. This time she hesitated, possibly thinking she'd spoken too much already. Perhaps she feared I would again cancel the dinner. After my prodding, though, her manner loosened and she began to speak. Her enthusiasm quickly returned. I nodded and smiled at each turn to show my solidarity, though in fact many of her notions seemed tiresome to me.

Then I kissed her cheek. "Tell me, darling, what has sparked such fierce industry so early?"

"I am not sure," she said. "The weather, I imagine."

"The weather?"

"It is so cold and wintry," she elaborated, "and that always puts me in mind of Christmas."

Taking her hand in mine I decided then and there I would not let anything deter our Christmas plans that year. Nor would I continue to complain of the economic bleakness or the troubles at my law firm—both of which had become my favorite topics of conversation.

*By Heaven*, I vowed, *I'll not repeat last year's mistake!*

——◆◆——

The precipitation cleared up in a few days, but the temperature remained stubbornly cold. I walked to work at a fast gait every morning to generate heat for myself, fairly sprinting until I reached the refuge of the office and its blessed stove.

Though the air inside was warm, it was as cheerless and stale as an ill-tended hothouse. We all sensed the firm was failing. Edloe now sat in Chauncey's office hunched over books and letters, speaking little to the rest of us. Generally he was absent during the middle of the day. Wheelwright told me he went to the courts, gentlemen's clubs, and even taverns to search for clients.

Yet the "curse of the baron" hung over us—for it was acknowledged by everyone in the law firm that the client who lost the slander suit blamed us for bad lawyering and because of his influence, we were short of business.

Many wanted to leave the firm. But one had to have a secure harbor to sail to before he left this port and it was not easy to secure a new position in those dark days.

One morning Mr. Edloe summoned me to his office. He had me sit down and a wait a moment whilst he read a letter. He did not face me when he began to speak, which was a peculiar mannerism of his.

"I would like to say," he began in his aristocratic drawling manner, "I have not forgotten that in the slander case we lost—which haunts us to this day—that it was you, Truelock, who advised Chauncey to interview more ministers of Parliament prior to the trial. If we had done so, I rather think we might have won the damned thing."

I was thrown off guard to hear him praise my small role in

that disastrous case. "Do you know why Mr. Chauncey thought it unnecessary, sir?" I asked.

"Oh, he was convinced we had enough witnesses already to win it. Adding others to the chorus, all giving similar testimony, might have taken up too much of the court's time and annoyed the presiding justice at least in Chauncey's estimation. Besides, these politicians are a surly lot; they never want to testify in civil suits, and it's hard to get them off their bums to do so. However, it now appears—by means of hindsight—that a preponderance of testimony might have resulted in a just decision."

I nodded, not knowing exactly what to say, for he'd paid me a compliment in a rather labyrinthine way. But I was wary as to whither this compliment might lead.

"Alas," he continued with a sigh, "we can't do a blasted thing about it at this point in time, now can we? That case is done with. It was not one of the best showings of this firm."

"I agree," I said.

Then he turned in his seat to face me, still holding the letter he'd been perusing. "Truelock, a certain peer of the realm wants to bring a libel suit against someone who has accused him a dastardly thing."

"And what is that?"

"Cheating at cards in a gentleman's club."

"May I ask the identity of the peer?"

"The Earl of Archwood."

For a moment I could not breathe. I must have gone pale. "Another defamation suit," I said at last. "Sir, I wonder, if it is wise for us to embark on another case of this type. And one so conspicuous. Surely it will be followed closely in the press. If we should lose—"

"We will not lose!" he cried, as if insulted. "That can not happen. And a victory will restore our reputation, don't you see?"

I looked down to avoid his piercing eyes. My thumbs were pushing against each other. "May I ask what sort of card game the earl was engaged in?"

"Ha! Absurdly, it was a game of whist. Whist, mind you!" He laughed. "Can you imagine that?"

"I'm afraid I can, sir," I said. "It might be more prudent to advise his lordship not to pursue this action."

"What? Come, now, Truelock! The earl bears one of the most revered titles in the realm. No jury would ever believe such a distinguished man would stoop to something so vile as cheating at cards."

"Yes, Mr. Edloe, but a few years ago a similar libel suit was brought by Viscount Thornsbury against a man who also accused him of cheating at whist."

"Thornsbury?" He cocked his head and thought a moment. "I think I did hear something of that affair. What of it?"

"The viscount at that time was the Earl of Archwood's partner at whist," I said.

He considered this a moment. "Really? How do you know this?"

"It was written up in a newspaper at the time." I did not mention, of course, that I had not read the piece myself, but only heard it second-hand from my uncle. I explained how the viscount had accomplished the trick of voiding the cut.

"Very interesting. But you read it in a newspaper, you say? Let us not be swayed by anything printed by the fourth estate. They're rumor-mongers, the lot of 'em."

"Yes, sir, but the plaintiff *lost* the case. I do not think the *Times* misreported the verdict. The viscount was so humiliated he left the country—for Holland, I think—thoroughly disgraced."

Edloe glared at me in a most imperious way. It must have been hard for the man, I thought, to admit it was possible someone accused an English lord of cheating. And further that a member of the bar had been able to persuade a jury he had.

"Well, the defense must have had an excellent barrister, for it is damn difficult to prove in court that cheating has been done," he said, somewhat flustered. "In this matter I do not think they will be able to prove a thing as to the alleged cheating. Not a bloody thing."

"Mr. Edloe, in my opinion we should not take this case."

His face contorted. "My word, do you realize how desperate we are for clients?"

"I do, sir, but we cannot risk another catastrophe."

"That's quite enough," he said, staring at me as though I were to blame for the firm's situation. "Here is what you must do: you must interview his lordship at his earliest convenience. Get all the facts—*facts*, Truelock—and then return and make your recommendation."

"Yes, sir."

"We need this case. We must restore our reputation."

## CHAPTER 16

### PICCADILLY

I could not interview the earl right away, for he was currently at his estate in the country. However, his lordship intended to spend Christmastide in town, and I was able to arrange an appointment with him in two weeks' time.

Until then the only evidence I had to study was the letter from the earl's secretary, which was heavy with indignation and light on facts. It seemed that the source of the alleged libel was the same newspaper which had accused Thornsbury of cheating, *The Satirist*. This was puzzling to me. Was the earl referring to the very same piece that named his former whist partner a cheat? If so, his claim was past the statute of limitations for libel. Nor did I recall that the newspaper named the earl as a participant in the fraud. Surely after all this time they would not print anew something about that closed case.

What else might have caused the earl's displeasure? Uncle Ebenezer told me the earl gave up playing whist in gambling clubs like Gillingham's and Crockford's. Had he lately returned to those silver hells?

I could hardly wait for the interview to find out.

In the meantime, the firm limped along toward an uncertain future. Three other solicitors left us, one to take a position elsewhere and two who, sadly, had no choice in the matter. It was going to be a bleak holiday for the latter gentlemen.

For myself too, possibly. Only time would tell.

Yet I was determined not to worry about money. Not this year. I was never again going to dash Emily's plans for the annual party. When I arrived home of an evening, after darkness had fallen, I usually found her busy with some activity or at least considering a new notion related to the holiday. Her fervor was contagious. Alice too was in constant high spirits.

One evening Emily showed me a magazine that featured the royal family. In it was a recent picture of the Queen and Prince Albert, their two children, and a magnificent Christmas tree in the background.

"You see, darling?" she said. "The new custom has caught on quickly. The article maintains that Christmas trees are all the rage this year and not merely for the royal family."

"I am sorry for ever doubting you, my dear."

"Perhaps this year we should get a larger specimen than the 'little shrub' you so detested."

"By all means! Get one as big as you like," I said merrily. "Let it touch the ceiling!"

She gave me a sidelong glance and a smile, wondering, I assumed, if I was being a bit facetious. In that momentary pause I squeezed her hand and kissed her cheek.

Everything remained in a steady, unchanging state for days. Emily and I shopped for items we needed, planned the menu and parlor games, and decorated. Replies from the invitations were positive, and we expected a large group of visitors.

At work, too, things were static. But this would soon change. My appointment with the Earl of Archwood drew nigh.

Finally the day of our appointment arrived, exactly four days before Christmas.

I took a coach to his London residence. At my side rode a

capable clerk, Mr. Hastings, and in his valise was a list of topics, documents, and notes I had made. Though eager and intelligent, Hastings was something of a raw youth. He could not hide his unbridled enthusiasm for the ride into Piccadilly, a neighborhood he revered as much as Mount Olympus.

At Hyde Park Corner he grew excited. "There, Mr. Truelock! Isn't that the home of the Duke of Wellington?"

"No idea," I answered, barely glancing out.

As we rode along he continued to point out the lavish homes, dropping names like Rothschild, Cardigan, and Rosebery. I never learned whence he gained such knowledge of the neighborhood; he, on the other hand, quickly discovered I could confirm none of his suppositions and stopped asking me questions. His childish wonder did not help my mood. I was already daunted that I must confront the holder of "one of the most revered titles in the realm."

I must admit the earl's mansion was imposing. Four massive Doric columns, interspersed with facades of red brick, set atop granite foundation stones. It was all very grand. The columns gave an antiquarian and massive look to the residence, though it was not something an ancient Roman would have recognized. But it was enough to intimidate a solicitor and his clerk. After the coach pulled into the yard, Hastings fell as silent as a clam.

A footman opened the door of the coach, and the air that rushed in was damnably cold. As we stepped out, I noticed snow flurries drifting into the street. Some of the flakes moistened the back of my neck as we walked up six broad, slippery steps. A silver-haired butler opened the door.

I was glad to get inside. But we were kept waiting in the drafty marble-floored hall a long time. I had hoped to be shown at once into the drawing room. The butler finally reappeared and led us into the library, a large but informal room smelling of stale cigars. Newspapers and magazines were strewn about, but actually there were few books in the room, as most of the shelves were empty. Perhaps, I thought, the earl kept a more imposing library at his estate. I was grateful, though, to see a tremendous fire blazing in the hearth.

We stood before the fire for a while, not speaking to each other,. At last a tall, balding man wearing spectacles entered the room.

"Gentlemen," said the man. "You've come from the law firm, I hear?"

"Correct, sir," I answered.

"I'm afraid his lordship is rather indisposed this afternoon, having only arrived in town yesterday evening. He asks you to please return tomorrow at this same time."

"Excuse me, sir," I said, "but this appointment was made some time ago. For today."

The man gave me a haughty look. "I'm aware of that, sir. But your client is fatigued."

I sized him up. "And may I ask who you might be?"

"I am Mr. Upton." Then, after a pause: "His lordship's secretary."

"Ah, yes, 'Upton'—I remember the name now. We have your letter asking us to call *today*."

He did not reply, but only stood there stiffly, giving me a hostile stare.

"As you wish," I said.

Hastings quickly turned to go.

"But I should point out, Mr. Upton," I continued, "that his lordship is not yet a client of our firm. Therefore, it seems to me it may be better for the earl to come to the law office tomorrow. In that way the interview can be done at his complete leisure and on his terms. He may drop in at any hour. You have the address."

"Now see here," Upton said, "let us not be insolent, Mister . . ."

"Truelock is the name. I am the person who wrote to you. Let me give you my card." I was aware I was being cheeky, but the man irritated me, as servants of the rich often did.

"Visiting the law office is not an acceptable alternative," he said.

"Mr. Upton, I am not a tradesman come to deliver coal. I am a member of the legal profession. If he is serious about this proposed lawsuit—"

Upton interrupted me: "I have no idea whether he is serious or not!"

Interesting, I thought, since it was Upton who had written to our firm in the first place. "As I was saying," I continued, "if he truly wants to pursue the matter, then maybe we can have a short interview today. Then we'll leave. Is that acceptable?"

"Wait here a moment. I'll have a word with his lordship although I am loath to disturb him." He took a deep breath. "All I can do," he said in a clipped tone, "is put your question to the earl." Then he turned on his heel and walked out.

"Remain calm, Hastings," I said. "You may as well warm yourself thoroughly before we're tossed out into the freezing cold."

Hastings, looking red-faced and awkward, made no reply. Most likely I embarrassed him by speaking to Upton with disrespect. Now he fidgeted, as though he'd rather be outside in the aforementioned freezing cold than in that room.

In less than five minutes the earl himself breezed in, trailed by the secretary. He did not look tired to me. He was dressed to go out and looked impeccably groomed to do so. The man was in his late sixties, I estimated, and possessed a copious amount of gray hair and a Vandyke beard.

"Mr. Truelock," he said cheerfully and extended his hand. "Delighted to meet you."

I saw a twinkle in his eye and smiled. In my experience, titled persons are often more approachable than their servants.

"My lord," I said with a little bow.

"I'm told," he said, "you're anxious to get down to business."

"With the waning of the year, one feels a certain compulsion."

"Then let us sit down and have an informal chat." He turned to his secretary. "That will be all, Upton."

The secretary stalked out of the room in retreat.

"I'm going to have a whisky," said the earl. "Would you care for one?"

I declined, and then introduced Hastings to the earl. The former, mortified to hear his name spoken by a nobleman, only managed to voice a single incoherent syllable.

"I suppose you want to know something of my grievance," the earl said as he poured himself a small amount of whisky.

"That would be helpful," I said, trying not to smile.

He motioned for us to sit and then sat down opposite us. "I'm a man who enjoys life, Truelock. And nothing pleases me more than a game of whist. Do you know that wonderful game?"

"Only a little."

"It is a game of skill, you know," he said with a steady eye. "And it has been played throughout England, her colonies, and even on the Continent, ever since it was codified by Mr. Hoyle a hundred years ago. These days it is nearly a social requirement that a gentleman—or a lady, for that matter—be familiar with the game in order to succeed in society."

"I'm aware it requires skill," I said. "But is there not also a degree of chance?"

"Of course," he said with a shrug, "as in all of life." He sipped his whisky, seeming to consider how best to enlighten me.

"My lord, if I may, let us get to the crux of the matter. Has someone accused your lordship of actually cheating in a game of whist? One where money was at stake?"

He did not respond. I took his silence as a yes.

I turned to Hastings, and he handed me my papers, his hand shaking. I glanced through them, though I knew them by heart. "May I ask where this charge was published?"

The earl did not reply.

"Oh, here it is," I added. "*The Satirist.*"

"Yes," he said quietly. "In case you are not familiar with the rag, it is the worst scandal-sheet of our times and the cause of many a suit in the law courts."

"Yes, sir, I've heard of the publication."

"Well, there you have it. What else do you need to know?"

"When was this allegation published and what exactly was written?"

"It was printed three months ago."

"Do you have the issue in question?"

The earl looked a bit put out. "I suppose I could have my secretary dredge it up, but I can tell you what was printed. 'We have heard the sad news of the passing of Gerald Greyfair, Viscount Thornsbury, in Rotterdam of a boating accident'—et cetera, et cetera. That was the sole nugget of news. But then the editor saw fit to remind his readers that five years ago the viscount sued Mr. John Edmonds, who in an interview had told *The Satirist* that the viscount cheated him at whist. He went on to say the suit was won by Mr. Edmonds. And that having lost his suit and been proven a cheat, the viscount fled the country, his reputation in tatters. Lastly, he mentioned myself. . . ."

Here he took a deep breath.

"Yes?"

"The editor took pains to point out I was the viscount's partner at whist in those days and that, following the verdict, I retired from playing the game in public card rooms."

I nodded compassionately. "Terrible thing," I said. "Is that all they wrote, my lord?"

"Isn't that enough, man!" the earl thundered.

"I had the impression he accused you of cheating."

"Of course he did. By implication!"

"Tell me, is it true you no longer play in the various clubs?"

"Yes, that is true. I felt it would be vulgar to do so, especially after my friend left England as an exile. And I knew that some players would be afraid to play against me. As absurd as it may sound, many of them felt that I, too, was somehow complicit."

I shook my head earnestly. "Have they no respect?" I asked. I paused a long moment, then added, "I suppose they cannot overlook the fact that—though you were not in league with the viscount—you nevertheless profited from his deceptive maneuvers."

The earl gave me a steely look.

"In truth, my lord," I continued quickly, "if they only mentioned that you 'retired' from gambling in public, it is hardly actionable. Especially since, as you said, it is a true statement."

"But they made the statement immediately after saying the viscount left the country in disgrace! As if the two events had the same cause, thus implying that we *both* cheated."

"Still, they did not call you a cheat. Frankly, I would advise you not to sue."

"I cannot refrain from it," he said, as if in pain. "It's a festering sore with me. They link me with the late viscount—poor chap, to have died so young—and insinuate they take credit for removing me from the card rooms. The idea! As if to imply I was his willing accomplice."

"You would bring suit against the newspaper editor in this case, I suppose?"

"Yes. The vile man's name is Barnard Gregory."

"I know the name. He loses a great many libel suits, I'm told. But he wins some too."

"Someday they'll imprison the lout and forget where they stowed the key," the earl said with contempt.

"I agree with that sentiment, my lord, believe me. But I'm afraid this would not be the lawsuit that incarcerates him. On legal grounds, it's too flimsy."

I glanced over at Hastings. The boy was sweating like a pig.

"Are you saying," said the earl, crestfallen, "that I have no case? None at all?"

"I'm afraid I am, my lord," I said, passing the papers back to Hastings. "It would be a waste of your time and money. And in the end, what would you have to show for it? Not much, except to remind the public once again of the earlier affair."

Thinking about that, the earl stood and poured himself another whisky. He faced away from us, from the fireplace, and looked into the dark, cold recess of the far corner.

I rose cautiously and remained still, respectfully waiting to be dismissed. Hastings also stood but could not cease trembling.

"I've seen the way my friends look at me, Truelock. When I'm visiting the homes of the high and mighty, or even the low and hungry, even at my own estate . . . it's always the same. We finish dinner and have our cigars, and repair to the game room to join the ladies. Everybody wants to have a go at something— backgammon, whist, euchre, cribbage. But no one cares to wager a farthing should *I* join the game. Nor do many wish to play with me as a partner, though they disguise it with patter and clever turns of phrase." He turned to face me. "Everyone reads these scandal-sheets, you know. If not the *Satirist*, then *Town and Country* or one of the others. Lurid tales of upper-class misadventure is their staple—love affairs with servants, mainly. Petty crimes or some other social misbehavior. Shocking stories, served up for the enjoyment of the masses. Why such scandalous doings appeal to the lower class I'll never know."

He finished his drink and turned back to face us.

"Lately things had improved. I thought I was nearly out from under the black cloud that has hovered over my head these past five years. I tell you, Truelock, everyone assumed I was as crooked as that fool Greyfair, the viscount. The little ass could not master the game, so he turned to cheating to prove himself a prodigy. Then, years later, after people had forgotten the whole affair . . . there appears this obscene little footnote in the *Satirist*. And the whispers begin all over again."

"I am truly sorry for your situation, my lord," I said sincerely, for at that moment I pitied him. "Perhaps after a while the whispers will subside."

"I'll be dead first," he muttered.

Then he cleared his throat. "Would you like my butler to summon you a coach?"

"We would be most grateful," I answered.

"Wait here, and I'll have him come get you. Good day,

gentlemen."

The Earl of Archwood left us standing by the fire. He did not move as speedily going out of the room as he came into it.

Once in the coach, Hastings began to prattle. He raved about the architecture of the earl's house and the furnishings of the rooms, as if we had toured the building but had not met its owner and witnessed his misery. No doubt Hastings was only venting the pressure of his stored-up anxiety. Noticing that I paid no attention to his babbling, he finally changed the topic. "Mr. Truelock, are you certain his lordship cannot sue that dreadful newspaper?"

"Oh, he may sue, but it was our duty to advise him not to."

He shut up then, and we rode the rest of the way in silence.

---

The next day began well enough. I came to the office fully prepared as to what I would report to my superior about my visit to the earl's town house.

Looking back, I find it odd I had no qualms about reporting the results. My mood was sanguine and my heart light. The evening before, I'd told Alice the story of the Christ-child in the manger and then helped decorate our flat. In spite of the gloom that I knew awaited me at the office, I was determined to maintain my spirits throughout the holiday. I knew Edloe would be unhappy that the visit bore no fruit, but I felt certain my handling of the situation was the proper one. I did the ethical thing, and, as it happened, the smart thing. It would have been foolish for all concerned to encourage the earl in such a tenuous libel suit.

That morning I found Mr. Wheelwright by the stove— understandably, for outside it was a bitterly cold day.

"Good morning, Mr. Wheelwright," I said with relish, happy

to see him there. I always enjoyed our exchanges.

The clerk merely nodded.

"Come now, are things as dismal as all that?" I asked in a rather teasing manner. My mind was full of Christmas, which was now but three days hence.

"Look around you," the chubby little man replied. "There is much space in the office these days. And a surfeit of empty desks. We have but four solicitors left, not including Mr. Edloe, and only two barristers. And yet, they seem to have little to do."

I sobered quickly. "Is there some new disaster of which I'm unaware?"

"No, I merely woolgather in a somber vein this morning." Then he turned to me and smiled broadly. "Ah, but you seem lively today, Mr. Truelock, despite the freezing weather. I take it you have snared us a quail or grouse? Something to fend off starvation?"

I stared at him. "What do you mean?" I asked, for I was confused by his phraseology.

"You are nearly the last hope of the firm. Did you not know that? And from your demeanor, I assume you have saved the day. Bravo! We needed that new client."

Before this statement could register in my brain, I heard Edloe's voice loudly calling me to his office. In that moment an icy hand gripped my heart, for I realized it was not a quail but myself that had been snared. . . .

I was done for.

*How could I have been so blind?*

There have been only a few times in my life when I felt I might be approaching my doom, so to speak. This was one of them. Yet, like Mary, Queen of Scots, I went to the chopping block with dignity, fully accepting my fate. I have no idea how I managed it.

As I entered his office, Edloe quickly scanned my face for some sign or other. Then he told me to sit down.

"Perhaps it would be better if I remained on my feet," I said with resignation.

"Sit," he commanded, and so I did.

He fiddled with some papers, that nervous mannerism of his; but he finally shoved the lot of them aside and looked me straight in the eye, anxious to learn the result of my call on the Earl of Archwood.

"Report."

"I'm afraid the earl has no case against the newspaper," I said evenly. "They merely mentioned that he ceased playing whist in the gambling clubs following the self-imposed exile of his partner, Viscount Thornsbury, who has recently died."

"Eh?" he said, apparently confused by so much information at once.

"You remember I told you the viscount sued a man who accused him of cheating."

"Of course, of course, but what has that to do with the earl?"

"The earl took offense because the *Satirist* recently reminded its readers, in a perverse obituary of sorts, that the late viscount was proven in a court of law to have cheated at cards five years ago. Then the editor also mentioned that the Earl of Archwood, his partner in whist, gave up the game afterwards. In the earl's mind, that is tantamount to accusing him of cheating as well."

Edloe still looked befuddled. "I shall never understand this fuss about honor and games of chance," he sputtered. Yet he appeared to be turning the problem over in his mind.

"If I may point out," I said, "it is not merely a point of honor."

"What do you mean?"

"The two of them, as a team, won thousands of pounds in the period of time they were trouncing their opponents in the card rooms. They depleted the fortunes of many men. Some were ruined." In saying those words, I thought of poor old Jacob Marley, who had lost everything to the pair.

"Bah! They shouldn't have gambled, then," he said. "Gambling debts are unenforceable."

"I agree that no one should gamble. Yet, those of a lower station," I added, "might have expected better treatment from a viscount and an earl. They might have expected fairness and decency."

Edloe's brows crushed together and his eyes bore into mine. "Are you saying that the earl *was* a cheat? That—that the current bearer of his ancient title—"

"Without question he was a cheat," I interjected. "There is no way that the viscount alone could have perpetrated the fraud."

"Damnation! Didn't you tell me something about the younger man, the viscount, that he was adept at card manipulation? Dealing from the bottom of the deck or some such trick?"

"Yes. Many people witnessed it."

"Well now, the earl is advanced in years, is he not? His, uh, manual dexterity must be somewhat diminished and would have been so five years ago. I doubt he would've been capable of such legerdemain."

"He did not have to do any manipulation himself to collude with his partner. It was also attested to in court that the cards were marked using the fingernail as play progressed. I know not who *marked* them, but it seems likely that both players would be able to *read* them."

Edloe pounded his fist on the desk. "The Earl of Archwood a common cheat? I do not accept it! I don't believe a word of that rot! Impossible!"

"In any case," I pointed out, "he makes a rather frivolous accusation. It will never stand up in court."

He seemed not to hear me. "We will take the case," he said unequivocally, and then faced away from me and once again began shuffling the papers on his desk.

"I heartily advise against it, sir," I said, merely for the record, for I doubted my words would sway him.

"Noted," he said, not looking up.

I sat there stupidly. I had pointed out the drawbacks in the case. Edloe had made his decision. What more was there to say?

At last he said, in a matter-of-fact tone, "You may go."

I rose and turned to leave. My heart thumped wildly as I dared to hope I had escaped the chopping block after all.

"Truelock," he said.

I turned back. He was still hunched over his desk. "You need not worry about having to prosecute this case yourself," he said. "I shall have Hapgood take it. Kindly give him your notes. And see Mr. Richards to pick up your severance pay. We do not need the kind of man at this firm who has no respect for his betters."

He never looked up at me; he only kept pretending to read his letters and memoranda.

My anger swelled, but somehow I denied it release; there was no point in making a stir. It would only cause him perverse pleasure to hear me rant and would avail me nothing. So I made no response at all to the pompous ass. I merely turned smartly on my heel and left him to his aimless paper-shuffling.

I soon found myself once again outside in the cold.

## CHAPTER 17

### WORSENING WEATHER

I had left the office in haste, saying not a word to anyone, not even Wheelwright. In the street I discovered my greatcoat was not all the way done up, so I wound my scarf tightly and trudged off down the street. A few personal items of mine were tucked in my valise. No papers, though, for there was no need. I was no longer a practicing solicitor.

I was proud to have stayed calm during the final interview. Now I discovered—perhaps because of the chill air—that my feelings remained cool even now. I was in fact completely numb. I plodded like an automaton in the direction of my home.

This inertia in my inner being ruled me for many a street that I crossed.

Then I came upon a familiar place: the pub in which I tarried during those sad days of the previous year, when I delayed returning home night after night. I had not stopped there since. All at once, I fancied a pint of beer, despite the early hour. I decided to go in. A short time later I was conversing freely with the barman, who remembered me and listened patiently to my tale of woe. He had few customers at this hour.

After relating my dismal story I then surprised him by letting out a laugh, for I now spied a bit of humor in my situation and felt compelled to explain it to him.

"When you consider the problem, Charlie, it's really quite amusing," I told him. "You see, I could not succeed either way. If I had recommended taking the earl's case, the failure of it would have crashed down about my head eventually—mine alone, for the matter was certainly doomed to failure. On the other hand, since I did not recommend taking the case, I was immediately deemed a fool for declining such a wealthy and important client—not to mention castigated as a detractor of the nobility, which in Mr. Edloe's estimation is the worst sin an Englishman can commit."

"Sounds like a proper blackguard, your Mr. Edloe," Charlie said as he wiped the bar.

"Proper?" I cried. "By Jove, you've hit the bull's-eye! He's a blackguard, all right, but oh-so proper—as proper and prone to fawning before 'our betters' as any man in the kingdom."

I wondered if the barman had followed anything I told him. It was doubtful. Most likely he did not even believe I'd gone to Piccadilly the day before and chatted with a lord. Yet Charlie was an amiable man and a most-accomplished listener. We had two gins together as I drank my second pint, and then I left.

Yes, it *was* amusing in a dark way. And since Edloe was eager to take the case, the disaster would devolve on him in the end. Ha! I was sorry I should not be there to see his downfall. Ah, but since the whole firm was likely doomed, it was better for me that I'd left it. It was time to think of the future, not the past.

My feelings, even if a bit misplaced, were gradually returning. The air warmed as the sun grew higher, and I tramped on, trying to reflect on what course I should take. Serious reflection, though, was not easy. I did not want to nudge my mind in that direction quite yet; I was enjoying the satisfaction of being in the right and reveling in the recently-bestowed appellation of Edloe as a "proper blackguard." Ah, but sobriety began to creep in, and I accepted, finally, that I had to do some deep thinking.

First of all, I had to decide what to tell my wife. Should I tell her the whole truth straightaway? No, I decided, I would not spoil her Christmas again. I needed to think about the matter. As to what exactly I'd say when I got home . . . well, I'd leave that to the moment. I would improvise.

Luckily I had the last of my salary in my pocket. That would get us through. I wasn't sure how many days it would get us through—but it was something.

I had to think ahead, though; beyond the holiday, into the new year. A gentleman had to have *some* income. *Gentleman . . .* I was not sure I could be called a "gentleman," even though I had a profession and could append "esquire" to my name. I had used up my father's modest inheritance on my education. Now, like a blacksmith or plumber, I needed a steady job, plain and simple. How would I find one in such times as these?

What of the other solicitors who had already left the firm? Not long ago one of them, Nickson, was not dismissed but resigned voluntarily to take another position. Yes, of course! At the time everyone envied him. Whither had he gone? Perhaps I could follow him; I had to learn the name of his new firm. Wheelwright might know.

What other avenues were open to me?

*I could consult Uncle Ebenezer.*

No, not that! I was ashamed to have even hatched the idea. Having acted morally superior to him with regard to Cratchit a few months ago, I could not now approach him on my knees, a supplicant. What would I ask for, anyway—money? advice? No, Uncle Ebenezer would be my utmost resort. I did not even want to consider it. In fact, I did not want him to hear of my reversal of fortune.

I walked on briskly, yet the cold steadily crept back into my bones.

The faces of others came to mind: men I'd met from other

firms during trials; former teachers; businessmen I knew. Some of them might help me, or point me in the right direction. I would make a list, yes, and then talk to every one of them.

Then I halted, surprised to find I had in that moment arrived home.

I went inside the building and then upstairs to our flat, giving Emily a start as I opened the door. She was standing by the mantelpiece, and nearly dropped some green holly leaves.

"Fred!" she cried. "My, but you gave me a turn!"

"Sorry, my love. What are you doing over there? Need help?"

"I'm only decorating a bit, mainly with holly and ivy." She came over and kissed me. "Why are you home so early?"

"I—that is, I thought . . . I could help you with the preparations."

"Oh?" she intoned with doubt. She cocked her head.

"I've been given some time off today. Nothing is afoot at the office. It's quite dull there."

"Well, that's only fair," she said, "since you were out late yesterday, paying a call in Piccadilly. You look ashen, though. Is everything all right?" she asked, as her left eyebrow ascended.

"Perfectly, my dear," I said. "I've only been walking in the cold. Where's Alice?"

"Doris has taken her to the park," she said, referring to the girl who helped out. "Don't worry, she's wrapped up warm. It'll do her good to run around a bit."

*Doris.* Soon we must tell Doris we shouldn't need her. This brought to mind last year's misery, when I canceled the party out of financial worries.

"You needn't look so sad, dear," Emily said. "They should be back any minute. Let's have a bite to eat."

I forced myself to smile. "Good. I'm hungry."

She made sandwiches and tea. Soon Doris and Alice returned, and we all had a jolly time. The novelty of my being home so early delighted my daughter to no end and she could not sit still.

After Doris left us, Emily took my hand in hers.

"'Tis a shame," she said, "that we have no plans for this

unexpected leisure time."

"There *is* something we can do," I said. "Something important. Something we absolutely *must* do."

Alice was agog with curiosity. "What is it, Father? Oh, tell me! Please!"

"We must obtain a Christmas tree! A fine, tall, straight one. There's a man down the street who has cut down a few and put them up for sale. Let's go and seize one quickly, before they're all gone."

Alice squealed her delight.

"Oh, he wants too much for them," Emily said flatly.

"Then we shall haggle with him. Come, now!"

"Yes, but Alice has only just come out of it. Need we all go?"

"But I want to go!" exclaimed Alice. "I want to pick it out! May I?"

And so we all went to buy a Christmas tree—a foolish thing on which to spend money in my predicament. I could not even get the man to lower his price by much. Nevertheless, it was a delightful excursion, and we secured a handsome spruce.

We spent several wonderful hours decorating it. In so doing, I remarked to my wife that I had come to embrace this new custom. She smiled at me, radiant with a satisfied glow.

That evening, after Alice was put to bed, Emily and I sat by the fire on the divan and reviewed the details of the dinner, mostly to see if there was anything we had forgotten to buy, for the bulk of the shopping had already been done. There were long pauses in our conversation. During these we merely kept holding one another, feeling no compunction to speak.

Once, rousing herself and yawning, she said, "Why did you insist on buying that tree?"

"Did you not want it?"

"Of course I did. It's beautiful. But can we afford it?"

I made a smile she could not see, for this was an amusing reversal in our former attitudes. "My dear, you convinced me we must keep up with the times."

"Yes, but we might have purchased a smaller one."

"This tree will bedazzle our guests. They will talk of nothing else for days."

She gave me a kiss on the cheek. "I love you," she said, then rose. "I am ready for bed."

"So soon?" I said.

"The fire is nearly out."

I stood up reluctantly, poked the grate a little. I did not want the evening to end, afraid of what the next day would bring.

She took a step, then turned back toward me abruptly. "Oh! I forgot to ask you: Could you possibly visit Alice's godfather tomorrow and ask him to come to the dinner? I only realized today that I completely forgot to send him an invitation."

"Yes, I think I might have the time to do it," I answered.

"Marvelous," she said. "He's been so kind to Alice, you know." She yawned again. "And then there's your uncle."

"Eh? You did not send an invitation to him either?"

"You told me I need not bother! Remember?"

"So I did. But as you once pointed out, dear, he never deigns to come. Never in all these years. I'm surprised you want me to personally encourage him. As you have said to me, he's passing eccentric."

"Doesn't matter what I said," she said smartly. "He may be an odd duck, but he's the last of your kin." After a pause she added, "And my opinion of him has risen since he rehired Mr. Cratchit."

I recalled the last time I saw him, in the spring. I'd promised the old coot I would call and ask him to come to the dinner.

"Very well. I'll go to his place of business and get down on my knees one more time—perhaps for the last time. But not tomorrow. I have much to do tomorrow. I'll visit my uncle after I leave work the next day."

"On Christmas Eve."

"Yes, exactly. On Christmas Eve."

Despite the comforting warmth of our evening, I did not sleep well. It's hard to rest easy when one harbors secrets and indulges in lies. In the morning I went off to work as I always did but left earlier than usual. This was not exactly a ruse because I needed to return to the office and get there early.

When I arrived, there were but a few clerks present, most of them still sleepy and warming themselves by the stove. I greeted them pleasantly and quickly explained I had forgotten to collect a book of mine, one I'd lent to Mr. Wheelwright. Then I went directly to him and, keeping my voice low, asked what he knew about Nickson's present situation. He whispered in my ear the name of the firm the man had gone to. That was all he knew, however. He wished me good luck. I thanked him warmly and, having gotten the information I needed, left forthwith, not even pretending to have retrieved the mythical book.

From the office I went to a nearby coffeehouse to pass the time. A number of prominent men habitually gathered there, and I happened to see a barrister come in, one whom I knew slightly. He scarcely remembered me, but was kind of enough to tell me the street of Nickson's law firm. I would have asked more of him, but he was desperate for his coffee and left to sit with friends.

As for me, I sat down by myself in a corner. I knew nothing of that firm. Nor, indeed, did I know Nickson well, though we were on cordial terms. Young and bright, he was said to come from a family of lawyers. Although I jotted down names of other men I might seek out, Nickson seemed the main chance. Making the list helped pass the time, though.

At mid-morning I left the coffeehouse and set out.

My route was to take me a considerable way, over to Westminster. The day was overcast and gloomy, but the air not as cold as the day before. I could not help but notice that on every street, sometimes on every corner, there was some sort of peddler hawking something to do with Christmas: holly, fruit, poultry, fish, and, of course, evergreen trees, though none of these trees was as handsome as the one already erected in our drawing room. These street folk were trying to earn a bob or two from the holiday, and who could blame them? Especially in these hard times! I felt a cheerful energy as I passed by the peddlers and the well-dressed gentlemen who stopped to chat with them.

"Merry Christmas" echoed from diverse quarters, and usually there was a reply.

Shop windows and doors displayed greenery around their edges.

Where groups of people loitered, laughter sometimes broke out at random intervals, and snatches of singing occasionally rebounded from the eaves.

A rather grungy man of the street, who tended a small coal brazier on a corner, invited passers-by to have a roasted chestnut and adamantly declined any recompense.

*What in the world has happened?* I asked myself. The somber religious holiday I knew in my youth had been transformed into something new. My mother never considered this time of the year an occasion to make merry, nor even to relax the severity with which most men and women travel the road of life. It was my theory that some country vicar had imprinted on her mind the idea that Christmas was an extremely solemn time; for the birth of the Savior meant that He took on human form and thus would later sacrifice Himself in death.

Death is grim to consider, though. Nowadays it seemed people wanted to fix their minds on His birth, rather than His death. What had wrought this change? Was it inspired by the young Queen? Had her husband or the Lutherans changed the game? Or was this but an ancient pagan impulse, rooted in the winter solstice, rising anew in our blood?

I supposed no one knew. But I liked the change; I was now converted to it.

Snow flurries began to blow about me as I walked on. Eventually I located the law firm I sought and entered into reception. It was very quiet inside, very orderly. I could not guess how many rooms it might encompass, but I wagered the office was far larger than the one I'd recently left. As luck would have it, Mr. Nickson was said to be present and available to speak with me. He came out and greeted me warmly, pumping my hand vigorously. Then he detected in my demeanor that I was not in the best of spirits and suggested we repair to a tearoom down the street.

There I told him my story, and then we discussed the merits of the Earl of Archwood's case awhile. Nickson was of the same mind as I, and he thought Edloe was a fool for dismissing me. He told me plainly that my chances of getting hired at his firm were not good. He'd gotten his present position through the influence of his grandfather, he told me. However, the firm was overstaffed and not taking on new solicitors.

"Ah, well," I said, looking away. "I had to try something, you know. It seemed a good idea to contact you. My apologies. I did not mean to impose myself or disturb your day."

"Nonsense, man, I understand completely," he said. "I don't mind your coming here in the least. Renfield and Glaston have already been to see me."

"Oh?" *This young man has grown used to this sort of petition,* I thought.

"Well, thank you, anyway, Nickson. You're an able and fair-minded man."

"Truelock, even if there were a position, I have no influence at all in the firm. Perhaps in a year or two I might." His face hardened. "I must say, Edloe is a bloody beast for dismissing you so near to Christmas Day."

I nodded in agreement and smiled. Then I rose, shook his hand, and left.

In the street the snow was beginning to fall—quite heavily.

Because of the worsening weather I hailed a hackney cab to get to Mr. Evans's house. It was a fair distance from Nickson's firm.

As the horse clopped along I perused the list of names I'd made in the coffeehouse. My heart sank, for suddenly it seemed to me my situation was hopeless. Discouragement replaced optimism. Some of these men I knew but slightly and I also lacked the addresses of most of them. A few might be in a position to help me, but as I watched the snow falling, I knew they'd be able do nothing today or tomorrow. The stars were simply not aligned for it. I would have to wait until after the holiday. I'd been too optimistic about securing a position prior to Christmas.

The greater truth was that I might not get a new position until after the new year began. I closed my eyes, trying to calm my roiling emotions.

Before long we arrived at my destination. I paid the driver, and he disappeared into a white curtain of snow. I stood there awhile, taking in the facade. I had visited this house five years before, when I came to renew my acquaintance with its owner and to ask him to become Alice's godfather. The memory of that occasion cut deeply, for it was a much happier time.

I forced myself up the steps, then paused on the stoop and took several deep breaths, letting the wet snow gather upon me as it would. How could I face this gentleman? Evans was shrewd. I had to recover myself somehow, regain my composure, or he would detect in his visitor a broken man. If that was to be the case, it was better I turned around and left this house there and then.

An idea occurred to me. Why not pretend to be the man I was two days ago, before my visit to Piccadilly or my dressing-down by Edloe? It would be a mere trick of the mind, and if I could manage that trick, all would go well. I need not stay here long.

I turned the handle of the doorbell.

An aged manservant answered. After I entered, the old fellow brushed the snow off my coat before he took it from my shoulders. Then he remarked on the weather and said I must be glad to be out of it. "'Twill make a chilly custard pie of things if it lasts till Christmas," he said.

"Right you are," I replied with good cheer. "Let us hope it stops soon,"

"Wait here, sir, and I'll announce you. Master's in the library."

"But I have not given you my name," I pointed out.

"Oh, I know who you are. As I recall, you came by a few years ago, and I marked then, as I do now, that you are the very image of your late father."

He walked off in a rather shuffling gait.

Evans himself soon appeared in the hall, wearing a dressing gown and holding a pipe. "Frederick! What a happy surprise! Come in and warm yourself by the fire."

I followed him into his library, which he told me was his favorite room in which to pass the time.

"Ah!" I said, going directly to the hearth. "This is heavenly!"

He poured two whiskies without asking what I preferred. No doubt he considered this the best remedy for a frozen caller.

"And what are you doing abroad in such dreadful weather?" he asked as he handed me the glass.

"It wasn't so dreadful when I set out, you know. Winter has crept up on me."

"Excuse me a moment," he said and abruptly left the room. I heard him telling his man something. He soon returned, and our conversation continued in a trivial vein for a few minutes, each of us inquiring politely after the other's family.

His two sons were doing well. One now lived in France, in Bordeaux, whilst the other still lived in Croydon.

For my part, I assured him that Emily and Alice were healthy.

He especially wanted news of his godchild. I went on at length about her, explaining her excitement over Christmas.

After a few moments there was a lull in our back and forth. "Had you an appointment in the neighborhood?" he asked.

"Uh, no, sir,"

His question caught me off guard. He assumed I was in the neighborhood on business, it being the middle of the week. Otherwise, how was it I was not in my office, my place of work? I felt I should have answered in the affirmative, but I could not lie to Evans. I sat down heavily into an overstuffed chair.

"Well, it doesn't matter your reason for stopping here. I'm delighted you popped in. I have so few visitors these days."

"Oh, have you retired from the wine trade, then?"

"No, I still work, though not as much as formerly. And how is your uncle? Does he still run his business? Or has he perhaps sold it?"

"He runs it still. But see here, I must apologize! I haven't told you the purpose of my visit. Mr. Evans, My wife and I would like to invite you to my home for dinner on Christmas Day."

"That would be lovely," he answered, "but I shall be dining with my son in Croydon."

"Perhaps you could stop by on your way? If only to have a glass of eggnog or punch?"

"I'll certainly think on it. For then I might see young Alice! She must be quite tall now."

I spoke of Alice some more, detailing her excitement over the Christmas tree.

After that, I knew I should immediately rise and take my leave. My mind was unsettled, though; I felt like a fraud sitting in that room. I was weary of feigning good cheer and knew I could not maintain a sanguine facade much longer. Yet I lacked the energy to get to my feet. It seemed important to finish the whisky in my glass first.

"Fred? What's wrong? Is something the matter?" He sat down directly across from me and leant forward, searching my face.

"Oh, it's nothing but a chill from this horrid snow. I'd hoped for clear skies today, but that was not to be the case, as we see, eh?" I tried to smile as I said it.

"You shall go home in my carriage."

"Please don't bother. I can walk home."

"Don't be ridiculous! You'll catch your death if you go on foot in this blizzard. I've already told my butler to have them bring around the carriage."

I drank from my glass, lacking the willpower to argue.

"That's very kind of you, sir," I said. Yet his assistance made me feel even worse. The nicer he was to me, the worse I felt for concealing my misfortune.

Evans said nothing for a while, and I avoided looking in his direction. I lost more and more of my morale the longer I sat in that warm room. Yet my body wanted nothing more than to remain there, in that chair, close to the fire.

He refreshed our drinks. The silence between us stretched longer and longer. I sensed he was waiting on me to speak, to explain what was bothering me.

"Has something happened, Fred?" he said at last, his voice now soft but tempered with concern.

I knew not how to answer. I dredged my mind for an excuse to put forth, any excuse at all. It was as though I was again a boy and had been summoned into the schoolmaster's office, flustered, afraid, and unable to deny an accusation.

"You said a moment ago that your family is healthy. Is that truly the case?"

"Oh, yes, Emily and Alice are quite healthy. I, too, am healthy. The whole lot of us is healthy!"

"Then, why are you so distressed? For I can tell that you are."

I shot straight to my feet, now feeling overwarm from the embrace of the fire. I knew I could not dissemble any further, for my manner must have betrayed me. "It's nothing, sir. Please! It's a trivial matter I do not wish to discuss."

"My dear boy!"

He stood and approached, but I turned my back on him.

I rushed into the hall. The old manservant was waiting for me, smiling serenely, and informed me the carriage was awaiting me in the street. Before Evans came out of the library I was out of his house and flying down the steps.

When I arrived home the snow had ceased but still lay thick on the cobblestones and pavement. I took my time in tramping up to the flat, feeling worse than ever for having visited Evans. Had he thought I was looking for sympathy? It wounded my pride.

Once inside the flat, though, a surge of sentimental affection swept over me, and I hugged my darlings tightly. They assumed my tears were tears of happiness.

## CHAPTER 18

### CHRISTMAS EVE

Next morning, Christmas Eve, I ate a scone and once again prepared to leave my flat as usual. I hadn't yet told Emily I'd lost my position. Telling her now would spoil Christmas for everyone, especially Alice. And hadn't I ruined last year's holiday? The previous Christmas was no longer discussed, but surely Emily must have a sore spot about it. How secure was her trust in me? Perhaps if I told her now it would cause her to again flee to Greenwich.

As I sipped my morning tea, I reflected as to when I might make my confession. Perhaps on New Year's Eve? Ah, but to do that I would have to keep up the sham of going to work for a full week! No, no, that notion was intolerable; I would drive myself insane trying to maintain such a lie. I then realized the longer I delayed, the worse the situation would become. So I resolved to tell her the very next day, as soon as our party was done and we'd muttered our last Merry Christmas. Yes, that was the best time.

Not that the task would be easy! But I'd have some time to work up the courage to do it.

I finished my tea and kissed her good-bye, saying I might be late in getting home as I had to visit my uncle's place of business to entreat him to attend the dinner.

"Oh," she said with a frown. "Perhaps Mr. Edloe will let you leave early to accomplish your errand. It is Christmas Eve, after all."

I regarded her a moment. She was as beautiful as ever. "One never knows," I replied, holding her close to me for a little too long.

And so off I walked off in the direction of the office. Though the day was cold and breezy, the sun shone weakly through the clouds. Yesterday's snow had been mostly cleared by shovel or blown aside into drifts. I went first to a coffeehouse, for I judged there was little point in looking for a position on this day. In reading a newspaper there, I became interested by an article about archaeology and decided to visit the British Museum. I had never seen the inside of it and was curious about some of the antiquities, particularly the Rosetta Stone.

This turned out to be a good choice. The museum was a fascinating diversion, and I was able to while away the entire morning inside its walls.

The only other task that awaited me was to pay my annual call at the firm of Scrooge & Marley. I started for the warehouse about one o'clock, stopping along the way to buy a bit of bread and sausage from a street vendor. I was nearly there when I happened upon the tavern my uncle frequented for his meals. Normally I came from the other direction and would not have run across the place, but now it lay before me. I decided to stop in for a minute.

I'd been there once with my uncle—though I can't remember the reason—and the place had impressed me then as sinister, merely because it was where he and Marley had plotted the latter's disappearance. I wondered at which table they sat seven years ago.

Today there were more customers than before, but little cheer.

I likened the place to a small cave, a cave with dark woods and deep-blue pennants, wherein no one cared to speak in a strong voice. Even on Christmas Eve there was an air of listlessness.

I ordered a glass of stout. When the barman brought it, I thought to give him a holiday greeting; but before I could, he uttered a curse and called something over his shoulder to another customer. There was little of the new Christmas spirit in this shadowy tavern.

Two men came in shortly after that, talking more loudly than was customary in that place. Several tipplers at the bar scowled at them for their lack of propriety. The two sat down at a table to continue their nattering. I smiled, glad to see a breath of life in that moribund tavern. As I sipped the heavy brew, now and then I caught a word from the pair. I got the impression that both of them—younger men who looked to me like clerks of some stripe—had got off early on this day, the day before Christmas. They were in a lighthearted mood. Then I heard the unexpected name of "Cratchit" fall from one pair of lips. I turned toward the table and attuned my ears so I could hear more.

". . . and he must stay at his desk until the regular closing time, for he'll not be let go a single minute sooner," one man declared.

At this his companion laughed and shook his head.

"What else might he expect," the first man continued, "considerin' the sort of taskmaster who drives 'im?"

At that moment the barmaid brought over their two beers. I sauntered over to their table and said, "Gentlemen, pray, may I inquire about something I overheard?"

They cast suspicious eyes at me, afraid they'd said something impolitic.

"Here," I said, turning to the barmaid and paying for their beer. "Allow me."

At this gesture they greeted me like a long-lost friend and bade me sit with them awhile. Harry, the one doing most of the talking, told me they were off work for the holiday, and he named the shop where they were employed—a place I'd often passed by. It sat only a few doors down from my uncle's warehouse.

"I, too, finished work early," I replied, "and I feel quite full of the holiday spirit."

They both agreed 'twas a fine and lucky privilege to have time off. The quiet one said he hoped to have more spirit inside him very soon. They both laughed loudly at this *bon mot,* so much so that a loud oath shot forth from the direction of the bar.

"If you please," I said confidentially, "I was surprised at your mention of someone named Cratchit. I am acquainted with a man of that name."

"Oh?" said the loquacious one. "Well, our Cratchit is only a clerk at a warehouse. Certainly not your sort of mate, for I can see you're a gentleman."

"Still, it ain't a common name," suggested his companion, looking to the other.

Then I said, "My man's name is Robert Cratchit. Sometimes called Bob."

They looked at each other in surprise.

"Well, so's ours! How 'bout that!" exclaimed the loud one.

"I take it Bob couldn't leave early today," I said.

"And how could he? Why, he works for old man Scrooge, which is by way of sayin' he's the only clerk in that man's employ. He's worked to death, day in and day out. Why, he's lucky to get off for Christmas Day itself."

"The only clerk, you say?"

"There was another, but he was sacked a while back."

"Really," I said. "I wonder the reason."

Harry leaned over slightly. "'Tis because Scrooge is the most tightfisted man in this city. Ask anybody. He wouldn't give a penny to save a drownin' child."

"Or clerk," interjected the other.

"I doubt he can be all that hard-hearted," I said, smiling.

"Oh, sir, you don't know 'im," added the quiet one in an ominous tone.

I coughed. "I did meet him once, this Mr. Scrooge," I said. "And though he seemed a flinty man of business, I did not take him for the devil's own henchman."

"It may be your meetin' with him happened in a rosier time, perhaps in the merry month of May," said Harry, waxing poetic. "Neither of us thought so ill of him in past days—did we, Jasper?—but he's gone downhill in his deportment, so to speak, make no mistake. I don't know the reason; perhaps it's only because he grows older and richer. And, mind you, there's rumors afoot all down the street that his business, which you mentioned, ain't doin' so well."

I shrugged. "Well, not many are," I pointed out. "Not in these uncertain days."

"Mind you," he pressed, "we do not work for Mr. Scrooge ourselves. But we hear things, you know. And we see him on the street, and there is no more frightening figure to behold as he goes to and from his warehouse, a walking scarecrow."

"My word," I said. "Perhaps I'd better go see him for myself and take the measure of the man."

Both of them looked at me strangely.

"That is, go see my friend Bob, I mean."

"Oh, please, sir, do not go! I beg you! You may cause the man a heap of trouble without meanin' to do so—goodness, a friend stoppin' in to see 'im? Grounds for dismissal!"

The other man, Jasper, weighed in again: "If not that, old Scrooge may make him work the whole of Christmas Day."

At that moment the barmaid brought another round, including another stout for me. One of them must have signaled her, for the two were anxious to stand me a drink. I decided to remain with them awhile, thinking it might be a good notion to brace myself before proceeding down the street. As I sipped the stout, I tried to follow their meandering conversation, but I was so shocked by what they'd told me I could hardly manage. I was more alarmed about Scrooge than I was about Cratchit. Somehow I doubted the little man would slip up again. But what of my uncle? What had happened to him?

In listening to them speak, however, I concluded that the loquacious one, Harry, was inclined to magnify everything he said by several degrees. Perhaps he rendered a somewhat distorted picture of my uncle—in other words, his reportage was only tavern talk. I could hardly believe my uncle had become a complete beast and the scourge of his employees. He had always seemed fair-minded to me, though he acted by his own rules.

I spoke little, only a syllable here and there, to pretend I was listening to Harry's prattle. In truth I followed him not at all. The barmaid appeared again to ask if we would have another round. At that, I should have departed immediately, but it suddenly struck me that the report about my uncle had so upset me that for a few precious minutes I'd forgotten what a dire predicament I was in—for I was the one who no longer had an income and would soon be exposed and derided as a failure.

And so, feeling a bit better, I ordered yet another stout.

I tried to stay diverted and enjoy the moment. Harry was going on and on about items printed in the newspaper. He also tried to convince Jasper he should erect a Christmas tree in his home. I weighed in on the matter, extolling the beauty of our own Christmas tree. We all talked a great deal about the holiday from then on.

Finally, I set down my glass with a noticeable thunk, having drained the last of the stout. They looked at me inquiringly, their eyes bright. But I realized I could no longer delay my duty and refused another round. I had to face the truth that lay ahead.

Outside, a fog had rolled in and made the street as dark and full of gloom as the inside of the tavern. As I walked along, the cloud I was wrapped in grew thicker, and I noticed candles flaring in the shop windows. Somewhere a clock struck three, which was shortly confirmed by far-off chimes in the distance.

As I neared my destination I looked for the faded sign and finally caught its ghostly lettering through the fog. I halted at the door to take a breath of courage. Far down the street I heard carolers. Instead of rushing in at once, I joined them in a few notes of *God Rest You Merry, Gentlemen,* singing it as lustily as I could manage. I must admit that by then I was a little tipsy.

When I reached for the doorknob I heard a muffled cry of "Humbug!" from within. Nevertheless, I burst into the lion's den with singular brashness (perhaps due to the stout) and called out "Merry Christmas" loud enough to wake the dead. Bob, sitting on his perch, smiled at me but uttered not a sound. Uncle Ebenezer appeared at once from his inner office, looking harried and distraught.

"You!" he cried, as if affronted by the salutation. "What right have you to be merry?"

"What right have you to be dismal?" I countered and laughed.

"What else can I be," returned my uncle, "when I live in such a world of fools? 'Merry Christmas.' What's Christmas-time to you but a time for paying bills without money, a time for finding yourself a year older and not an hour richer, a time for balancing your books and having every item, through a round dozen of months, presented dead against you? If I could work my will," he said indignantly, "every idiot who goes about with 'Merry Christmas' on his lips should be boiled with his own pudding and buried with a stake of holly through his heart."

"Uncle!" I cried in protest. I was wounded by his verbal thrust more than he knew.

"Nephew!" he returned. "Keep Christmas in your own way and let me keep it in mine."

"Keep it? But you *don't* keep it."

"Let me leave it alone then." He stared at me coldly, then added, "Much good it has ever done you."

I had never seen him like this. His gray and white hair hung lank about his lined face. Only his eyebrows retained their black color. He was thin, too, and I found I concurred with Harry's description that he was a "walking scarecrow."

"It has done little for me, I suppose," I answered, profoundly saddened at both his appearance and his extreme attitude. "Yet it's the only time I know of, in the long calendar of the year, when men and women seem by one consent to open their shut-up hearts freely and to think of people below them as if they really were fellow-passengers to the grave and not another race of creatures bound on other journeys. And therefore, Uncle, though it has never put a scrap of gold or silver in my pocket, I believe that it *has* done me good and *will* do me good; and I say, God bless it!"

Bob applauded wildly, overcome with enthusiasm, then quickly reined himself in, realizing he'd overstepped his bounds.

"Let me hear another sound from *you*," Scrooge said to him, "and you'll keep your Christmas by losing your situation!"

I stepped forward. "I see you're again down to one clerk, are you not? At least, so I've heard."

"It's my business to run as I please."

"Don't be angry, Uncle. Come! Dine with us tomorrow!"

"I'll see you in hell first."

"But why?" I cried.

"Why did you get married? Why did you have a child? I know you squander your resources to the limit, Fred, and even overspend—given that the income of a young solicitor is not large. I wonder that you can still be solvent. Here, now: would you like a glass of claret? It's the least I can do for a man who has braved this nasty fog to come and sing me a carol, even as he toys with own destruction."

The last remark cut deeply. Did he already know I'd lost my position? Did he think I came to ask for his help? Perhaps he thought me a fool. It was all I could do to maintain my rosy outward attitude about my purpose on this day and not break down in tears. His miserable attitude had sobered me up.

But I held up my head and gathered myself together.

"I am sorry, with all my heart, to find you so resolute," I said. "We have never had any quarrel which we could not resolve. I'll keep my Christmas humor to the last. So, a Merry Christmas,

Uncle!"

Brave words! At least I had managed to say them, if only to spite him, whereupon I returned to the wet embrace of the fog, wondering what the old man really thought of me. As I walked along I tried to recall every word he'd spoken during our encounter, beginning with *"What right have you to be merry?"*

What right indeed? Perhaps he somehow knew I was a condemned man.

## CHAPTER 19

### ON THE MAKING OF PUNCH

As I lay abed in the early morning darkness waiting for Emily to stir, I cast my mind back by the span of a year, when I woke up alone in our flat, miserable after sleeping on the divan without a pillow and uneasy of stomach because I'd drunk too much sherry the night before. I put a loving arm over my wife's waist, touching her but slightly so as not to disturb her slumber.

All that was a bad memory, a regret, a lesson learned.

Now a year later, Christmas Day saw an even worse catastrophe upon my house, and, though I could not blame myself for the extent of this one, I nonetheless felt a failure. Why hadn't I accepted Edloe's point of view? The suit might work out better than I assumed. I tensed muscles in despair and in so doing must have pushed a bit, for Emily gave out a drowsy moan. Then she abruptly sat bolt upright, throwing off my arm.

"What time is it?" she asked.

"It is still very early," I said, my own voice sounding dull and sleepy. "Did I wake you?"

"No matter. Come, dear, we must get up. There's so much to

attend to."

I had other ideas of what we might attend to. I said, "Just now I was remembering how empty it was here last year, without you." I encircled her and drew her body close to mine, "The sun has not yet risen, you know." I nuzzled her neck and kissed the lobe of an ear.

It was in vain. She threw off the covers and got up.

I sighed, saying, "Emily, everything is arranged and planned. What is left to do?"

"A great deal, silly. Now get up."

We got up, dressed, and made a pot of tea. I could see she was anxious over the dinner and its various details, much as I might worry over an upcoming trial.

It was fortuitous we rose early, for we had hardly finished our meager breakfast when we heard a loud knocking. I hurried to the door. Though it was early for him, I thought it might be Topper, so loud were the blows; and as Alice was still asleep, I was afraid he'd wake her. However, when I opened the door I beheld my mother-in-law and Emily's two sisters standing before me, the girls giggling and rosy-cheeked. I supposed they'd all lent a fist in banging for our attention.

"Mama!" Emily cried, coming over. "My, but you're early."

"The better to help you prepare for the barbarian horde," she replied. Then she turned to me. "Take this, Frederick." She foisted on me a large wicker basket, which from past experience I knew contained plum pudding and other delights.

The four of them began to jabber at once, though none seemed to listen. The chattering swelled as Emily embraced her mother and sisters. I carried the articles they handed me into the kitchen. There I drained my teacup, for I knew I would soon be banished from that room.

When I returned to the drawing room, Emily smiled at me and said proudly, "Darling, this year they've traveled here by locomotive!"

"How bold of you, Mother," I said, trying to sound impressed.

"Well, dear me, it's not so bold any longer," she answered. "Folks dash back and forth along the rail line all the time these days."

Rose, the plump older sister, turned to me and said brightly, "Oh, but I did *so* enjoy the ride! It was my very first time to travel by rail."

Betty, the younger one, only sixteen, asked if she could go wake Alice.

At this they all laughed. Soon they were speaking as if in biblical tongues once again as they moved, en masse, toward the kitchen. I merely stood there and watched them squeeze into the other room, realizing there would be little for me to do now except answer the door.

I knew the pattern well. My mother-in-law would try to take command of things and she and Emily would quarrel most of the morning. They would declare a truce by the time food was served. Most of our guests would not eat with us at all, of course, but would arrive later, after fulfilling obligations in other dining rooms. I estimated we'd have about twenty assembled when the parlor games began.

Thus it occurred to me I should relish the quietness of the moment. Looking around the drawing room, I deemed we had done a creditable job in our decorating. The tall spruce was catching a bit of the early morning sun, and the tinsel sparkled a fiery gold within its branches. Holly and ivy found themselves strewn in clever places, and mistletoe hung from the crossbeam. In lieu of coal, I'd procured wood for the fireplace. I meant to tell each guest that these were my "yule logs," though in point of fact I did not know what yule logs actually were, nor for what pagan purpose they served for our ancestors at this dark time of the year. We had a spinet in the corner and Emily would certainly be called upon to play a few carols. Many of us would sing, most off-key.

It struck me I might slip into a bleak frame of mind before the revelry started, considering my general situation—that of having no employment nor any income. *I must avoid that,* I thought. It was better I threw myself into the spirit of the day and kept busy. My altercation with my uncle yesterday had turned me into an ardent advocate of the holiday—hadn't I lectured the lion in his own den about "opening our shut-up hearts freely"? So I resolved not to think about tomorrow, only of today.

Yet there I stood, idle, with nothing to do.

I woke up Alice myself, to create a distraction. She soon galloped through the rooms in her nightgown, boisterous and untamed and overcome with the novelty of finding her grandmother and aunts in the kitchen. I wondered if she remembered the Christmas of two years ago. Probably not. Then she was but four and probably had no memory of it. To keep her out of the kitchen, Betty and I led her to the tree and pointed out various little boxes there—articles which had somehow appeared overnight—and we watched her unwrap them. They were only trifles: candies, paper animals, rag dolls, oranges. But they stimulated her sense of wonder. More than the items themselves, it was the opening of the boxes she enjoyed.

Doris arrived in a little while to help out, and some time afterwards several dinner guests appeared, apologizing for arriving early. They all had their various excuses, but I was pleased to see them. By that time I'd already made the punch and had only to entertain our visitors with my charm, if I could muster it.

Luckily, then, I managed to stay busy throughout the morning. One thing after another needed my attention. Either I was helping the ladies in the kitchen, or setting out on an errand, or taking Alice outside for a brief walk.

The guests were never so eager to get started with the revels as they were that day. Was it due to the bad times? Or perhaps it was the change in the general tenor of the holiday itself. At any rate, I did not object to their eagerness, for I, too, was keen to distract myself in making merry.

Arthur Trumbolt bumbled along soon enough and was in fine

fettle. He had with him his customary bottle of sherry. I reckoned he'd already had a nip of something stronger.

"Merry Christmas, Fred!" he boomed in his usual manner.

"Topper, my lad," I said and embraced him.

I saw him glance around, apparently surprised he was not the first to to arrive. He must have been relieved to find others present, considering the awkward situation the previous year. Yet I frowned and laid a hand on his shoulder. "Well, Topper, old boy, I'm sorry to have to tell you bad news," I said.

"What is it?" he said, alarmed.

"We could not get a turkey, and the dinner itself has been canceled."

After a long pause, an onlooker broke into laughter, and I think Topper, whose face had fallen, nearly struck me. But his good nature won out, as it always did, and he caught me up in a bear hug that nearly winded me. The other guests applauded and came over to welcome him.

After things settled into a quieter mood—as much as they could with Topper in the room—he and I went to the punchbowl. He turned to me and said in a low voice, "I say, aren't Emily's relations coming today? Are they still angry with you?"

"No, no, they're merely slaving away in the kitchen, except for Betty, who's playing with Alice in the nursery."

"I see," he uttered. Then in a casual way he added, "What about the older sister? Is she also in the kitchen?"

"You mean Rose? Of course she is."

He smiled.

"Oh, I see. You have designs on the young lady."

"Well, I'm not sure, old man. I haven't seen her in two years. What's she like now?"

"Well, she's filled out nicely."

"I suppose that's good," he said, "within limits."

"Her limits are fetching enough. Shall I retrieve her?"

"No, no! Let me down a cup of punch first."

Other guests trickled in, bringing all kinds of Christmas

anecdotes with them. Some had already taken dinner elsewhere and were only here to drink punch and play the games. Listening to the general hum of conversation, I began to feel redundant, for our guests were now entertaining themselves. All of them remarked on the tree.

Then Emily and Rose emerged from the kitchen and greeted the newcomers. Emily whispered in my ear that dinner would be served in half an hour.

"As soon as that?" I asked, caught off-guard. The time had flown by quickly.

"We mustn't delay," she answered. "The barbarians seem ravenous this year."

"Is your mother in a dither? Is she fretting too much?"

"Only as regards the turkey. She's basted it to death, not that it wasn't dead already. Don't worry, darling, we haven't said anything we can't take back."

I noticed that Topper was now conversing with Rose near the punchbowl. They both appeared to be getting on together, if giddiness was any sign. Funny that he'd harbored amorous thoughts about this young lady. She was attractive in her way, but I never found her a witty conversationalist. But then, neither was Topper. Perhaps they were meant for each other.

After we ate dinner and returned to the drawing room, I found the larger group there to be in a genial mood. They were discussing some of the games we would soon play. In the interim Rose went to the piano and began to play. This surprised me, as I didn't know she had that skill. Everyone gathered round to listen, impressed. My knowledge of music is slight, but I enjoyed her performance of a tuneful piece by Mendelssohn called a "song without words."

Then more guests arrived. I observed that the punchbowl was now but half-full. I'd have to make another batch soon. In the meantime, I sat down by another solicitor that I knew slightly and chatted with him about a notorious murder case then covered in all the papers.

Soon afterwards Doris returned to the flat from an errand Emily sent her on. She came over to me, her face unreadable.

"What is it?" I asked, standing up, worried that someone in another flat—someone not as merry as we were—might have complained about the noise.

"Sir, there's an older gentleman downstairs. He asked after you but seems reluctant to come up."

My heart skipped a beat. "Mr. Evans," I said. "He's Alice's godfather." Doris regarded me strangely. No doubt my face had gone white as I remembered how I left him last.

"Are you well, sir?" she asked.

I cleared my throat. "Show him up, please. He's never visited before."

She went to fetch him, and the merriment of the moment vanished for me. I sat there a long moment, unable to move. What could I say to the man?

Then I roused myself and I slipped into the kitchen. Emily was the only person there at the moment, as her mother was lying down to rest. "Can you spare a moment, love? Mr. Evans is here. I thought you might like to meet him. I doubt he can stay long."

"By all means," she said, her eyes shining. She wiped her hands on a towel, brushed back a strand of hair, and came forward as I held open the door.

In the other room, several persons were gathered round the newcomer, obscuring my view. But as I drew closer I perceived that the white-haired man was *not* Mr. Evans. . . .

"Who *is* that?" whispered Emily. "I do not recognize the gentleman."

Then I manged to get an unobstructed look at the newcomer. "Dear God!" I whispered. "There's no reason you should, dear. For that is my uncle, Ebenezer Scrooge."

She gasped in shock, perhaps because the man's appearance did not fit with her mental image of my uncle. Last night I had described him to her as unkempt, ill-clothed, and stern of countenance. I went on and on about his recent change of appearance. Yet the man who now stood in my drawing room was well-groomed, dressed in his best Sunday clothes, and smiling. He appeared in good health, if a bit slender. And I saw a cheerful twinkle in his eye.

"Welcome, Uncle," I murmured softly, knowing not what to say after our heated colloquy the day before.

Ignoring me, he locked his gaze upon my wife, took her hand, and kissed it. *"Enchanté,"* he said. "You must be the niece I've long wanted to meet."

She curtsied by habit, confused but smiling, obviously won over by his courtly manner. "Pleased to meet you, Uncle Ebenezer," she said, flicking her eyes toward me as if requesting assistance.

"Uncle," I began again, "I must say, uh, I must say I'm surprised . . . nay, I'm overwhelmed to find you here. After all these years! Welcome!"

"And I am delighted to finally step foot in your home, Fred. Dear Fred! Above all, I am overjoyed to meet your lovely wife."

I marked that his hair, which yesterday had been shot with gray, was now a snowy white *in toto,* including the eyebrows, which kept no trace of the old dark color that menaced so many of his hirelings in the past. Yet his face shone radiantly, blue eyes sparkling. I could not account for the change. I was mystified! Where was the vile man who berated me yesterday? Who was this impostor?

Emily took his arm. "Would you care for a cup of punch, Uncle?"

"I would be delighted," he answered, folding her hand over his wrist.

As I watched them move away, I noticed that the room had gone silent, for every guest was puzzled by the newcomer, whom they had never met and only knew by a not-so-flattering reputation. I myself did not know what to think of him. Yesterday he had excoriated me, calling me a squanderer and a spendthrift. What was I witnessing? A sarcastic masquerade?

Could this really be the horrid man with whom I debated the day before?

I had no time to marvel further at the change in my uncle, for the whole flat was soon awash again with talk, laughter, and song. I was about to set about replenishing the punch, when there came a knock at the door. Puzzled, I opened it and found Mr. Evans, dapper and smart in his traveling clothes, the last person to arrive.

We looked at each other for a brief moment, each trying to take the measure of the other. I had worried all morning about what I would say to him should he pop in. Now I merely extended my hand to him.

"Come in, sir. Merry Christmas!"

"The same to you," he answered uncertainly. "I'm glad to find you cheerful, Fred. I was worried about you after your visit the other day."

"There was something on my mind," I said quickly. "Nothing important. But I must thank you for the use of your carriage. It was quite generous of you."

"That was nothing. I was happy to do it."

"Are you still bound for Croydon?"

"Oh, yes. My son prefers to have a late dinner on this day." He drew me aside. "Fred," he continued in a quieter voice, "I have found out what was troubling you."

"Oh?"

"Yesterday I called for you at your place of work, hoping to speak with you."

"I suppose they told you I'd been sacked?"

"Yes. The day before you came round."

"It was not unexpected. You see, the Earl of Archwood wanted to bring a suit of libel, and I—"

"Hold on, Fred. The reason doesn't matter to me a whit."

I felt my color rising. "Sir, it's only that I want you to

understand I did nothing wrong! I merely advised my superior to refuse the case as it had no merit."

He nodded as he considered what I'd said. "Libel, eh? I assume you know the Earl of Archwood is a card cheat," he said. "Of course you do. The whole world knows. If the suit had anything to do with cards and gambling, then you were correct to advise against pursuing it."

I could not believe my ears. "Yes! The earl wants to sue a newspaper. You say you're acquainted with his reputation?"

"Directly, for I am one of his victims. Once upon a time I played against him and that thieving partner of his at Crockford's. I saw what they were doing. But that's not important. You mean to say your superior at the firm wanted to take the case? To prove him innocent?"

"He is still keen to. And he was appalled by my lack of respect for the nobility."

"Listen carefully, lad. Don't think you will be taken back into the firm because of what I've said. I would be happy to repeat it, but the real reason you were fired is more likely that we—all of us—are enduring at this moment a very bad season in all walks of life. It has even affected the wine trade, which is not generally the case, since often in bad times more wine is drunk than usual. I'll tell you something else. There are always too many lawyers. And in times like these, many young ones are winnowed out of the legal profession. It has less to do with a fellow's ability and more with the scramble to survive."

I stared at him, amazed at his wisdom, then said, "The problem is, sir, I don't know what to do."

"What you will do is let me help you," he said. "I'll lend you enough money to get you safely through these times. For I'm sure you'll practice law again."

I did not know how to answer. It uplifted me that he was willing to help—nay, I was exhilarated. But the prospect of a loan did not appeal to me. Yet because of his generous spirit I must have appeared near the verge of tears, for the gentleman embraced me.

"Come, now, lad, pour me that cup of punch you promised," he said cheerily. "I don't have that much time to linger."

I glanced over at the punch table, where the entire group had congregated. They were now quiet.

"That might be a problem," I said, thinking to offer him whisky or mulled wine instead. "It appears our punchbowl has been drained."

"Really? My, but it looks to me as though the problem is in the process of being rectified." He was gazing across the room to where the punchbowl sat on a large table.

I turned around and was astonished to see my Uncle Ebenezer busy in the task of mixing a new batch of punch. A small group watched him work and listened as he explained his process in his paternal, didactic way.

"Mind you, never go too light on the brandy. It is the soul of the concoction," he said.

His audience tittered. Then he ladled some punch into a cup, sampled it, and nodded in approval of his own handiwork.

I escorted Mr. Evans to the table and proudly introduced him to all as my daughter's godfather. Scrooge broke into a smile and shook Evans's hand vigorously. "I'm delighted to meet you, sir. Elated! I've heard so many good things about you."

"Oh, but we've met before, many years ago," Evans replied. "At the home of Fred's parents. You visited him one Christmas, as I remember, along with your business partner—a Mr. Marley, wasn't it?"

"Right you are!" exclaimed my uncle. "I had forgotten you were a business associate of my late brother-in-law." Then Scrooge poured them both a cup of the punch, and the two of them went off to chat in a corner.

Emily came over, smiling. "Your uncle has charmed the entire party."

I was so full of conflicting emotions that I could not comment though I almost blurted out the terrible news of being sacked.

However, she turned and went back to the kitchen.

A few minutes later Doris brought clean glassware to the table. I asked her to fetch Alice from the nursery. She had refused to come out when earlier summoned. Several minutes later, when my daughter reluctantly appeared, she was fawned over by all the guests and then had no desire to resume playing at bricks with her Aunt Betty. She allowed her godfather to kiss her cheek and she hugged his leg as he patted her head.

She was less certain about my uncle.

"Well, now, who might this be?" said he. "Dear me, I think it must be a fairy who has flown down the chimney!"

"I'm a little girl, not a fairy," she answered solemnly. "And besides, if I'd flown down the chimney, I should now be nothing but a cinder!"

We all laughed, and Alice permitted Scrooge to embrace her.

A few minutes later Mr. Evans took his leave and wished us well with our festivities.

⟫◦◆◦⟪

When the parlor games were to begin, I asked my uncle if he would like me to summon a carriage to take him home.

"Certainly not!" he exclaimed in mock indignation. "You'll not get rid of me so easily."

I chuckled. "It's not that. But we are about to enter upon the silliest part of the day, when grown men and women behave like school children."

"Precisely! I can hardly wait."

I expected he would merely drink his punch and laugh at the antics of the young people. But he took part in several of those games, including a new one called Yes and No, a guessing game that allowed only yes-or-no questions. Scrooge excelled at it to everyone's delight, including his own, and his comic remarks during the progress of the game elicited much merriment. When it came to Blind Man's Buff, however, neither he nor I chose to participate, even if it was the most amusing of all the games played that day—that is, for those not blindfolded. It was especially enjoyable to watch Topper stumble about the room. Although he was fairly convincing in his temporary blindness, I noticed he seemed always to stumble into Rose and one time caught her beneath the mistletoe.

Uncle Ebenezer stayed all afternoon. Finally, with the games done and the daylight waning, our guests began to take their leave in ones or twos. Several of them told me my uncle had made the party more enjoyable and one called him a "merry old soul."

Then nearly everyone still present got up to leave at once—the herding instinct, I imagine—and I asked Topper to go summon a hackney for my uncle, who was putting on his greatcoat.

In the meantime Uncle pulled me aside to a quiet corner of the room.

"Fred, I do not know when I have enjoyed myself as much as I have this day."

Before I answered, I glanced around to make sure there was no one within earshot, for I intended to be candid with him, having held my curiosity in check for so long.

"I must say, Uncle, I'm truly mystified by your enjoyment. Twenty-four hours ago I saw you in a most unflattering light, to put it mildly. I would use stronger words, but I dare hope there's some accounting for that wretched display. When I left your office, I was crestfallen. Yet here you are today, an entirely different man."

He said nothing in his defense. Instead he actually bowed his head, as if in shame. It was a gesture totally foreign to my experience of him.

"Mind you," I continued in a gentler tone, "I welcome the change—completely. But in my heart I fear your transformation, if I may call it that, is too extreme to be permanent."

"As well you might," he said, raising his head to look me in the eye. "I scarcely considered how such a transformation might strike you or even alarm you. You must fear I've contracted a rare malady, and that henceforward you will never know which mad Scrooge you will encounter when we meet: the bitter complainer or the merry optimist."

"I never said you were mad."

"Such mental ailments exist, I've heard. But let me assure you that I do not believe I am so afflicted. I may be wrong in that, of course. I suppose I can only wait and see what tomorrow brings."

"Now you are jesting with me. Are you not?"

"A little, Fred, and as you are a man of reason, one who brooks no illusions, I am bound to tell you this: I sincerely hope my present condition is permanent. It will be, if there's anything I can do about it. Either that, or I am truly mad."

"I know not what to say."

"No matter. Now that we're discussing yesterday's encounter, it has occurred to me I wounded you unintentionally on one point. I now judge that some of the hateful things I said were taken by you as a personal affront."

"What do you mean?" I asked.

"When I said to you, 'What right have you to be merry?' I did not mean that lacking money to pay bills applied to yourself. I meant it in the most general way."

I cleared my throat. "I really don't understand your point," I said weakly, for I had an inkling of what he implied.

He leaned closer and lowered his voice nearly to a whisper. "Mr. Evans—a fine, genial chap he is—mentioned you have lost your position in the law firm. Now, now, do not fault him! He did not mean to tell me a secret. He assumed I already knew. The gentleman also informed me he wishes to advance you money in your hour of need."

I could feel the heat in my cheeks.

"I have a better solution, Fred, for I know you do not want to take out any loans. I want you to join me as a partner in my cloth business. Don't refuse me out of hand! The truth is, I need your help. I really do! I haven't time to explain it all now. Let's discuss it at the office tomorrow."

At that moment Topper bounded back in.

"Hullo! I have a hackney cab for you downstairs, Mr. Scrooge," he said, out of breath.

"Thank you, son. Mr. Trumbolt, is it?"

"Yes, sir."

Scrooge bent toward his ear. "Good luck with that charming girl. I wish you every success." Topper turned crimson and moved away.

Scrooge smiled benignly and turned back to me. "At least, Fred, be wise enough to drop by tomorrow, so that I may 'present my case,' as it were. Will you come?"

I nodded.

Then he clapped Topper on the shoulder. "Take me downstairs, son, and show me the cab."

They both went out. I heard Arthur's heavy footsteps clattering on the boards and the swell of their voices reverberating up the stairwell.

My friend soon returned but only to get his coat. We said our good-byes, and he left.

I surveyed the room. It was empty now; everyone had gone. I could hear my mother-in-law's voice droning in the kitchen. It sounded rather strong though I could not make out the words.

I knew what I must now do. Though I'd resisted it for days, I took a deep breath and went into the kitchen, where Emily was drying dishes and trying to ignore her mother as she dished out advice to Rose—something concerning Arthur Trumbolt, I was sure.

I asked my wife to follow me and then led her to our bedroom, where we could be alone. Taking her hands in mine, I explained in great detail how I lost my position in the law firm. This was a risk, for her mother and sisters intended to stay overnight. But I could not keep the truth from her a minute longer.

Emily was brave but cried a little from the shock of it. Then I held her close, assuring her that all was not lost and explaining that we had not one but two benefactors who wanted to help us. She soon recovered and then kissed me fervently. As for me, I was relieved to feel like an honest man again, and I held her all the more tightly in my relief.

Thankfully, she never told her mother of this calamity.

## CHAPTER 20

## A NEW YEAR DAWNS

I decided to go to work for my uncle.

It was the better choice, for I hated to go into debt, even to Mr. Evans. Uncle and I agreed that if for some reason I could not tolerate the textile business, I could wait until the proper time and then resume my law career. Thus my joining the business would be a trial, a trial that would last for six months or a year. After this period if I wanted to leave, he would not deter me. Nor was he obliged to keep me on should I prove inadequate. The prospect caught my fancy. I was curious to see if I might flourish as a businessman. Certainly I had misgivings with aspects of the legal profession.

Uncle insisted I start working for him immediately, and so it was that my life changed greatly during the first month of January. He said he would put me on salary, but later, if we were both agreeable, he would have papers drawn up to make me an equal partner.

The prospect pleased me, of course, and in short order Marley's old office became my own. Uncle proudly introduced me to every client who wandered in and to every worker at the warehouse.

The staff was now a most contented group, for he had recently given them all generous increases in wages. I already knew the two clerks, Cratchit and Smallet, a man he rehired, and soon got to know the "men in the back"—those who stacked, loaded, and unloaded crates of cloth and delivered the goods around town.

"You have more space in your warehouse than I imagined," I observed the first time I saw it. "It's like an enormous cavern."

"Ah, Fred," he said sadly, "we have entirely too much space and not enough cloth. I've refrained from ordering much from Manchester in these bad times. That's but one of the challenges we face. We've also lost customers to younger purveyors with bolder ideas. They've found new kinds of cloth, some made by new methods, others new in design. I have dealt mainly with cotton all these years. Some of these fellows import their wares from the Continent or even the Orient. After you learn the business, perhaps you'll help find new suppliers. We must keep up with the competition."

We had luncheon almost every day at his favorite tavern and there continued to talk about business as we ate. The place was still poorly lit, but it no longer seemed so gloomy to me. The food turned out to be quite good.

I tried to absorb everything he told me, for I was eager to prove myself.

Once, as we lingered over our meal, he said, "Someday we should go to Manchester."

"Oh? And why is that?"

"I think you should meet our suppliers, men I've dealt with for years. I haven't seen them much of late. And there you can see the great mills."

I did not respond but toyed with the last of my potatoes.

"What is it, Fred? Are you tired of all my yapping? Perhaps you're pining for the quiet of the law office or the drama of the courtroom."

"I must say I feel somewhat daunted," I answered, "for I'm unsure I possess the right skills for business. To be honest, I think the law suits my nature better."

"Ah, perhaps that's because you possess a superior intelligence. The law requires much concentration of the mind. Not so a little business such as ours. All we do is buy a commodity, mark it up, and sell it again. And keep scrupulous accounts of our transactions. But really it's quite simple, don't you think?"

"So it would appear."

"Perhaps you relish the challenge of the law."

"It's not that," I said. "Legal work is frequently dull. Rather, it's because a solicitor deals in concepts and words. I suppose I'm more comfortable with those than solid merchandise."

"Words can be slippery," he observed. "Unlike dry goods."

"I never told you, but I've always fancied I might like to write pieces of prose for others to read—essays, biographies, sketches of city life."

"My goodness! Well, my boy, you should have gone to Oxford."

"Oh, I'm no literary type," I said. "My scribbles would be better suited for newspapers or magazines. Someday I'll give it a go when I have the time. For the present I'll learn and apply myself as best I can."

"I'm sure you'll take to business as a duck to water."

"There is one other bothersome duty. From what you've told me, I must hobnob with other men of business, and frankly that worries me. Clapping a man on the shoulder, making clever remarks, pretending to be merry—I have little talent for that. You see, Uncle, I am not a gregarious person by nature."

At that he threw back his head and laughed loud enough to draw baleful glances from the other patrons.

I smiled at him. "What is so amusing, may I ask?"

"Fred, do you really think that I am a 'gregarious person'?"

"You were not a few weeks ago. And I recall you relied on Mr. Marley to deal with your clients. But now! Why, today you call no man a stranger."

His smile had vanished when I spoke Marley's name. "I

suppose I have become more outgoing," he said. "At least I am easier to get along with." He dabbed a napkin to his lips. "But don't worry, I still have a head for business."

I studied him afresh, marveling for the hundredth time at the recent change in his demeanor. I leaned across the table. "Uncle Ebenezer, will you at long last explain to me what happened to change you so profoundly?"

He tilted his tankard and finished his ale. "Oh, don't exaggerate, nephew. A man has many sides, after all, and he may show one or t'other to the world as befits his mood."

"Is that so? I would argue that to disguise one's true character is damned difficult! I only know that in the space of a day you underwent some sort of 'metamorphosis'—for I know not what else to call it—an astounding one, too, worthy of the poet Ovid. When I came to see you on Christmas Eve, you were the very model of the sharp pinchpenny and in the worst mood imaginable, complaining of every jolly person, every good wish, and the annual holiday itself. 'Bah, humbug!' was your watchword. Yet on the following day you appeared at my door as if you were Father Christmas come to call and you proved yourself to be a most entertaining guest. My friends could not believe you were the oft-mentioned uncle who so reviled Christmas, for you radiated such joy on that occasion."

He nodded, then said softly, "I admit something of a miracle occurred."

His eyes locked on mine.

I stared into their blue depths, trying to glean a clue. There was none to be found.

"Very well," I said, giving up. "I accept your explanation and say I am heartily grateful we are not yet out of the age of miracles."

"My dearest Fred, the whole explanation is quite lengthy. Nevertheless, I will tell it to you someday—someday very soon, I think." His tone was genuine. "That is a promise, for you are the only person in the world to whom I *can* relate it."

"It must be quite a tale," I said.

He smiled. "Let us get back to work, shall we?"

❦

Profits had been off for the last six months, but by February our sales began to pick up, much to our delight. According to the newspapers, conditions were improving for the country in general. The hard times now were mentioned as an occurrence of the previous year. Trade flourished, and even common laborers found they had money in their pockets at the end of the week.

As my apprenticeship continued, my confidence grew. There was not so much to learn after all. Uncle was correct, the basic model of the business was quite simple. We gathered and transferred goods, charging our customers for the trouble of it. Gradually I ceased to worry over the mysteries of the business.

Yet I felt that my presence in the firm was only due to my uncle's generosity, and it vexed me that I brought nothing of value to the enterprise. Then a small incident occurred that made me feel better. One day as we were eating at the tavern, my uncle told me, quite in passing, that he occasionally used a solicitor down the street to review agreements or contracts for him.

"He charges by the number of signatures I must make," he said disdainfully. "The man often overlooks items—ambiguities and those provisions which some call 'loopholes'—and that has cost me dearly at times."

"Is that so?" I asked.

"I would be right obliged, nephew, if you would review some of those documents before I sign them, at least the more important ones."

"I'll do more than that. The solicitor down the street is hereby discharged!"

"What do you mean?"

"From now on, you have a lawyer on staff," I added. "If there's one thing in which I am proficient, it's contracts."

"Marvelous! My, but it never occurred to me when you joined the firm I'd also gain a legal department."

"I'm happy to offer something of value, though the aforesaid department is rather short-staffed."

"I'm content with the staffing," he said.

After that I felt more at ease working for my uncle. He in turn gave every indication he was happy with my progress. He still talked about making a trip to Manchester but decided to delay it indefinitely. This was quite amenable to me.

That year, Easter fell in late March. Uncle Ebenezer consented to dine with us after church on that day. Strange as it may sound, he had begun to attend services regularly.

"Not because I have changed my mind about the church, mind you," he explained at the dinner table. "It's a problematic institution, in my opinion. But I have come to believe the church does indeed effect some good in the world, and so I've decided to see if perhaps it can wring an atom of good from this old sinner."

Whereupon he winked.

My wife and I exchanged puzzled glances and not for the first time. These days he was generous with his winks. If not winking, he was likely to be smiling or laughing that strange cackle of his. When it came time for him to depart, he asked for his coat and pulled me aside. Emily, noting this, bid him adieu and left the room to look in on Alice.

"Once again," he said, laying a hand on my shoulder, "I've had a delightful time at your home."

"I hope you return soon. It does not have to be on a feast day."

He gave me an inscrutable look. "Nephew, I'm not sure you have fully accepted the 'metamorphosis' you spoke of in the tavern a while back. You still cast your eyes on me in perplexity when I say or do something out of character for the 'old Scrooge.'"

I laughed. "I must admit I sometimes worry you'll suddenly and without warning revert to your former self."

"'Twould be a terrible calamity," he said and laughed heartily.

"I must say," I continued, "I have never heard of such a complete transformation of the spirit in so short a time. Possibly one could find examples in stories from mythology or the Bible."

"The conversion of St. Paul, perhaps?" he suggested. "But I remind you I am no saint, nor have I ever aspired to be one."

"All the more baffling."

"Hmm," he said, "Perhaps the time has come to explain what happened. Why don't you come see me next week? We shall sit down and have tea and biscuits as we've done before, and I shall at long last share with you the story of the so-called miracle."

"Wonderful! I am dying to hear it."

"I am keen to tell it. You may come anytime after the clock strikes the noon hour."

———⊳◆⊲———

So it was that the following Sunday afternoon I once again walked to my uncle's house. As I turned into the cul-de-sac, I felt anew the chill of the little street, even though I ought to have been inured to the shady corridor by then.

At the end of it I was pleased to see that April sunlight gilded the eaves of Scrooge's house. The old pile looked more inviting this afternoon. I marked that the eaves, window frames, lintels, and the doors had all been painted. Then I noticed that the shops of the stationer and tobacconist were out of business. The window of one the shops was empty of wares and the other was boarded up entirely.

I went up the steps and took hold of the knocker, observing it had been polished. My uncle answered the door in a short time, dressed in clothes he habitually wore to the office, an indication he was quite serious about his purpose on this occasion.

"Come along, Fred," he said and led me into the hall.

"I could not help noticing you have undertaken some spring cleaning," I said.

"Spring cleaning? No, no, that's not what you see, though the excellent Mrs. Dilber has worked hard to clean every corner of the house."

We entered the drawing room, which shone brighter than I'd ever seen it. Every pane of the large windows was scoured clean, and the drapes were parted wide to let in more sunshine.

"Here you are," I said, handing him a basket of sandwiches Emily made.

"Wonderful," he said. "Most likely we'll need a bit of nourishment later. Excuse me a moment." He left to make the tea.

After he returned I said, "Well, Uncle, I approve of your renovations, no matter the reason."

"It does make for a pleasant change, doesn't it? I should have done it years ago. But I'm such a stick-in-the-mud, Fred. I grow accustomed to the way objects are and leave them alone."

"Then why have you lately undertaken the task?"

"Why, because I am selling this house. Therefore, I must do all I can to show its best face to the world."

The news surprised me. To me, my uncle and the house seemed linked, each reflecting the aging nature of the other. "Is that why the two shops are closed?" I asked.

"Yes, I did not renew their leases this year. But don't worry, both merchants have found new venues."

"These days you astound me at every turn. Where will you live now?"

"I've decided to return to my old rooms at Mrs. Abernathy's. I was content there. The only reason I moved to this dreary place was that it lies closer to the warehouse, though as I told you it saved me no money whatsoever. And now—as you will shortly hear—I truly wish to be rid of it."

"Why is that?"

"Because in my considered opinion, the place is haunted."

I stared at him a long time, intrigued by the word "haunted." I recalled how he entered the house the day after Marley's disappearance and felt a strong sense of foreboding. I judged that was what he meant. And following his profound change of heart, I could understand why he would not want to remain in this mausoleum of a dwelling.

Uncle took forever to arrange things—the teacups, the biscuits, the sandwiches, the claret, his pipe, and an odd-looking bottle of whisky—but at last he seemed satisfied and sat down in his wing chair.

Having done so, however, he fell silent as he arranged his thoughts.

A minute or two passed.

"Aren't you ready to begin?" I teased. "There is only so much time in the day."

He did not smile, but exhaled a deep breath and nodded in agreement.

"I hope," I added, "we won't be disturbed by agents come to take stock of the house."

"I have not yet engaged a broker. Nor will the charwoman come today, nor anyone else."

"Good. No one will disturb us, then."

"Exactly," he answered softly, "and that's the way it must be. Yours are the only ears that shall ever hear this account, Fred. You are beholden to keep it secret."

I was somewhat abashed by his tone. But again he fell silent and stared into a dark corner. The clock struck two. After the sound died away, I coughed and gave him a look of impatience. Finally he rose and drew the drapes nearly all the way, saying too much sunlight would spoil the tale.

"I don't really know how to begin, Fred. Perhaps I should first apologize again for the rude way I received you on Christmas Eve. I must avow I can be a difficult character in the best of times, and those times were the worst. I had become a crude effigy of myself."

"Let us not discuss that awful day. It's over and done with."

He sat down. "No, I must talk about it, as well as the days and weeks leading up to it. You must allow me to tell my story as I see fit."

I nodded in agreement. He seemed to have found his voice, so I sat back and waited for him to continue.

## Chapter 21

### Scrooge's Narrative

You should know, nephew, that in the last quarter of last year, the enterprise of Scrooge & Marley lost so much money that I feared it might be dissolved by year's end. Most of the problems were due to the hard times, of course. But, as I mentioned to you earlier, younger competitors were faring better than my firm. I was merely doing what I'd always done and that was no longer sufficient.

Because I worried so, I could barely sleep at night. Nor could I concentrate enough to read a book, and reading was my only diversion. My digestion and general health suffered. Furthermore—and you may wonder at this—I also despaired for the men I employed. Though I was not generous in what I paid them, I hated to cause a complete stoppage of their wages through mismanagement. To me that would be like defaulting on a contract.

On the morning of the day before Christmas something else dogged me: a superstitious dread of the coming night. You see, I was acutely aware it was the seventh anniversary of Jacob Marley's departure. Previously I disparaged your mother's homely maxim about a "seven-year curse" when you brought it up. But deep in my countrified bones, I half-believed in it. Would something terrible happen to me, perhaps that very day? I wondered. Hadn't I taken part in a conspiracy to falsify public records? At the time I told myself I was merely helping out an old friend, yet I broke the law, and my actions brought me profit, for didn't I gain complete control of the business? I was in effect a criminal. Thus I feared retribution must be coming—when and in what form I did not know.

I'm nearly finished with my excuses. I merely wanted to explain how on that day I became a raving beast and was no longer the quirky, though tolerable, relation for whom you had to occasionally apologize.

My walk to the office on the morning of Christmas Eve did not improve my temperament. The snow, though in retreat, had left the pavement slippery, and I fell twice before I reached the office door. My hip throbbed the rest of the day.

When you appeared in the afternoon out of the gathering gloom, it was the last straw, so to speak. When one is miserable with his afflictions, nothing is more vexing than hearing a happy numskull singing a Christmas song—and off-key at that. I could not bear to hear another syllable about the day, whether it be spoken or sung.

I do apologize for my tirade. Ah me! I even told you that rather than attend your dinner, I'd see you in another place first. I'll not repeat the name of the place.

After you departed, my torture continued. On his own authority Cratchit admitted two portly gentlemen who were going about and requesting donations for the poor and destitute. Most assuredly they were honorable men—one showed me his credentials—but I turned a deaf ear to them and spewed vile words I now regret. Then I ushered them out. Surely they considered me the model of a miser. They were correct; on that day I was exactly that.

After I got rid of the two men, my spirit sank nearly to the point of collapse, perhaps because I knew I should be ashamed of my behavior. Yet I would not admit it to myself. I was stubborn.

In a little while, I managed to calm down. There was a warm silence in the office now. It was only Cratchit and I, for I'd sent the warehousemen home already. They had no work to do.

But the memory of the fateful night of seven years before weighed on my spirit even as I tried to add and subtract figures in a ledger. I constantly made errors and had to start over. After several attempts, I found I could not manage this simple task; I could not add two plus two! Soon I gave up on arithmetic and instead drank a glass of claret, longing for the day to end so I could squarely face the anniversary of the crime and be done with it. I felt I must confront it, even though I feared the coming darkness.

When it came time to close up shop, I instructed Cratchit to shutter the windows. He complied instantly and so rapidly that I had to suppress a smile. This was the first thing to amuse me during that long day. Wanting to draw out the moment, I'm afraid I gave him a difficult time about the holiday, as if the matter were not already settled. Then I gruffly assured him he would get the whole day off and gave him leave to go. The little fellow immediately dashed out the door, his silly white comforter dangling from his neck.

The fog grew heavier with the setting of the sun. It was a smelly, coal-laden mass of moisture, but I accepted its foul presence, for it seemed fitting that such weather should haunt me on this crucial day. It reminded me of the fog that had covered the city seven years before—you recall it, I'm sure. As before, it made an ideal setting for stealth and fear, no matter that every now and then one might detect in the distance a far-off note of "Silent Night."

If my walk to the office in the morning had been fraught with danger, the walk home was worse. Not because of ice, though; the ice had melted and the residual snow had drifted to the side.

It was the fog in league with the waning light that beset all who were making their way at that time. I could scarcely see a yard before me. I took small steps and depended on the glow of shop windows to find my footing. Lanterns across the street appeared spectral and far away. Many carriage drivers had halted altogether and sat with their horses nickering in the street. Enterprising lads offered assistance to the drivers, and a few were hired to walk ahead with a torch. Suddenly the bell of the neighborhood church struck the hour. I glanced up from habit, but I could not see the shrouded bell tower.

Though my progress was slow, I knew well the way to my favorite tavern, which was not far off. I expected the place would be full of customers seeking shelter from the cold and damp. The opposite was the case that evening; only two other solitary men sat in the semi-darkness, dining in silence. There was no sound except for the occasional clink of silverware. No one stood at the bar. I was disappointed, for I had hoped to see a crowded room on this dreary evening.

The food was not up to its usual quality, for the regular cook had gone home. I was able to order a half-loaf of bread and a bowl of beef stew, and that was enough for me. Afterwards I drank another pint and lingered over the newspapers awhile. Suddenly I noticed I was the last customer to be dawdling there and so bade a good-night to the proprietor and left.

The repast soothed me. But outside the cold had grown worse—much worse. I traversed the street as quickly as I could manage. Most people had abandoned it by this hour. Nor did I hear a single carriage clatter by. Occasionally a person would suddenly emerge from the fog, pass me, and wish me a merry Christmas, and I would nod at them in return. Once I paused at a corner where three men had set up a brazier and were warming themselves, chattering merrily. All were clad in rags. One of them tried to sing a carol with terrible effect. At least, I think it was a carol. They invited me to join them, but I walked on.

At last I turned into my own benighted street. It was deserted and even darker than usual. A smart breeze made me button the top of my coat. Its one street lamp shone ahead, a dim beacon in the enveloping fog. One or two intervening shops displayed candles, for which I was grateful. Keeping to the middle of the street, I hurried as fast as I dared. Soon I reached the solitary lamp and paused to have a look round. All was in order, yet I could see nothing ahead, not even my own house.

"Drat it, I should have purchased a torch," I said aloud. Only the wind replied.

Soon, though, I entered the yard before my house. There was, and still is, a little path amid the cobbles there, created from continual use, and I tried to find it. I judged I was about twenty feet from the iron railing of the stair. At last, probing with my feet, I located this path. Overjoyed, I walked the rest of the way too quickly and stubbed my toe on the bottom step. I took hold of the railing and went up. Then I inserted the key and entered, leaving the door ajar. On a table in the hall—you may have noticed it—I keep candles, sandpaper, and a supply of Congreve matches in a tin. I struck one and lit a candle successfully, thanking Providence I was home. As I blew out the match, I noted that my hand shook.

I had left the front door open to diffuse the fumes of phosphorous, which are particularly noxious in that narrow hallway. Then, carefully protecting my candle, I went to shut the door. It was then that a strange phenomenon arrested my attention. The light of my candle played over the surface of the dirty brass knocker, inviting the mind to conjure up all manner of fantastic bugaboos. I stood there rapt, ignoring the cold air, beguiled by flickering demons as they came and went. Then my eyes settled on a certain devilish countenance that appeared, a hideous face that expanded to cover the entire orb and stare back at me.

I fancied it was the face of someone I knew.

—◆—

"Humbug!" I cried angrily and slammed the door, almost extinguishing the flame of the candle. Regaining my composure, I slid the bolts and hurried to the kitchen, where I made a pot of tea.

I decided to go straight up to my bedroom rather than linger below. As it happened, I had no need to pause and search for something to read, for I already had a promising book up there, a ripping yarn by an American writer named Cooper. I set my candle on the tea tray and climbed the stairs, eager to reach the sanctuary of my bedroom.

A chill permeated the entire upper floor. But there was an ample supply of coal in the scuttle and plenty of kindling. I lit an oil lamp, started a fire, changed out of my clothes, and put on my dressing gown and slippers. Then I sat down in my reading chair. As I drank my tea, I felt satisfied and safe, and, above all, happy with relief that the day was over. I had survived it, hurrah! How silly I had been, I reflected, to pay so much attention to the anniversary, which, after, all was nothing but a mark on a calendar.

After the fire was ablaze, I felt over-warm, so I took off the dressing gown and picked up the book. Soon I was immersed in the adventures of Hawk-eye, a frontiersman, and his Indian companion, Chingachgook. At length my concentration became hindered by a dull throb in the area of my hip. When I looked under my nightshirt, I discovered a large bruise, the result of my fall that morning. I kept a bottle of laudanum on the mantel, and I took a dose for the ache, and another so I might sleep better. After reading another chapter my eyes began to shut of their own accord and I started to nod. Noting that the fire was down, I decided to retire, for I had all day tomorrow to read the book.

Then I was jolted out of my languor by the sound of a small bell ringing. *What is that?* I wondered. The sound was muffled, but unquestionably came from within the confines of the house. I conjectured it must be one of the old dusty bells in the kitchen, which were once used to summon servants. I was aware that former occupants of the house in its younger days kept as many as four domestics. Of course, I had no servants to summon, for I was alone—very much alone. *Perhaps a mouse or a rat brushed by the bell and made it ring,* I thought. I didn't care for that explanation, but before I could consider an alternative, a chorus of bells rang out wildly, as if all the bells in the kitchen were jangling at once. You would have thought a sledge was being pulled through the house.

These noisy bells filled my heart with terror. Could someone have broken in during the day, perhaps a thief looking for something to steal? Or perhaps the intruder was a vagrant who came in to get out of the cold. Neither was welcome in my house.

But why the Devil would he now make such a racket?

Then the bell-ringing abruptly ceased. I took a deep breath. Had it been merely an auditory display meant to frighten me and thus drive me from my own home? I cocked my head, straining to hear what might follow. But I detected nothing. All was quiet. Many seconds passed. Then a minute and another minute. The silence gradually became more unbearable than the jangling bells.

I turned up the lamp, added coal to the fire, and seized the poker. I stood and faced the door, listening for further disruptions. Though I knew I ought, I dreaded to leave my bedroom to investigate.

Then another sound came, a heady, dull clanking noise, as though a ship were hoisting a heavy anchor. It was assuredly the sound of chains, as if someone were rattling great links under the staircase. *Who? Why?* Then I recalled something I once heard, something Cratchit, a foolish soul, had told me: that ghosts in haunted houses carry chains about as punishment, each link betokening a sin committed during the specter's life. Humbug, of course, but I couldn't deny that the horrible scraping of metal was steadily increasing in volume . . . as if the bearer of those links was ascending the staircase.

The sound grew ever louder until it seemed to be on the landing, directly outside my bedroom door. Then I heard a piteous moaning, a caterwauling in the baritone register. Everyone knew ghosts were in the habit of moaning. Ghosts? What a ridiculous notion!

Nevertheless, my hands shook, and my heart beat wildly—despite all my practical-mindedness and belief in natural science and in the faculty of reason. The bruise on my thigh throbbed in sympathetic fear. I was frightened in every fiber of my body.

Then the door flew open!

I saw the vague outline of a man in the doorway. This specter did not yet advance, but continued to moan and manipulate his chain. I raised the lamp and took an unsteady step forward to get a better look.

The figure was dressed in the clothes of a former day, including waistcoat, tights, and boots. He and his attire were covered with patches of soot and white ash. As he stepped towards me I retreated. Once inside, he turned his head sharply from one side to the other, as if to take the measure of the room. By that motion I saw more of his head and hair. I tried to hold the lamp steady, but nearly dropped it—for the figure before me wore his thin hair in a pigtail.

At this I screamed. "Jacob! Is that you?"

The figure advanced still more. I continued to retreat. When he stood but three feet away, I raised the poker to strike.

"Beware, Scrooge!" the specter boomed. And it was Marley's own voice!

"How now!" I cried. "What do you want of me? Are you—or *were* you—my friend Jacob Marley?"

"Tell me what you see before you, Ebenezer," the figure

intoned.

"I cannot name it," I answered. "I *will* not name it."

"Then tell me if you can see through me. Do I seem to you transparent?"

I studied him carefully. The common belief was that ghosts were transparent in their makeup so that a living person could see all the way through them, from one side to the other. But that was not the case.

"No, spirit," I answered, my voice faltering. "I'm afraid I can *not* see through you."

"Thank heavens," he answered in a normal tone of voice. "That must mean I'm not a ghost."

My mouth fell open. I knew not what to think or say.

Then Jacob Marley threw back his head and laughed louder than I'd ever heard him laugh in all the years I had known him. He dropped the chains to the floor, unable to hold them as he vented his hysterical laughter. He wiped the chalk dust off his clothes and some sweat, too, and took a long breath to restore air to his lungs. I myself panted like a winded dog.

"Have you any brandy, Ebenezer?" he gasped.

"No, but I have whisky."

"That'll do," he said and dropped into a chair.

<hr>

My hands were still shaking as I retrieved the bottle of whisky from a lockbox in a chest of drawers, well-hidden from Mrs. Dilber's eyes. I was smiling now, or trying to, yet tears ran down my cheeks. I don't know if they denoted relief, fright, or amusement—probably all three at once.

After we drank deep of the whisky, both of us began to titter. Strangely, I found myself enjoying the humor of the Marley's prank. The more I laughed, the more my visitor laughed. We continued in this way for several minutes until we finally mastered ourselves.

"This is not at all proper," I said. "You are fully dressed, though somewhat shabbily, and I am in my bedclothes."

"Ah, but we're old comrades," he said. "It cannot matter if I see you thus. After all, you have seen me dead twice, seven years ago when I expired and now as a spirit."

That remark, though he clearly deemed it amusing, did not amuse me. It brought to mind our dark past.

"Don't jest, Jacob," I said. "We committed a serious crime together."

"Come now! 'Twas long ago," he said. "Some crimes cannot be prosecuted after seven years, you know, and presently we find ourselves at that juncture."

"I doubt our crime falls into that category," I replied. "But let us not quibble. The question is moot, for we must remain discreet about the matter, you and I."

He said nothing.

"By Jove, Jacob, I never expected to see you again in the flesh!"

"Not ever?"

"No. You fled headlong across the wide Atlantic, man. And I thought you most likely perished on the other side years ago."

"I'm a bit offended, for that shows little confidence in my capability."

"It seemed quite likely to me, from the rousing tales we hear. And did you not say you might push westward to Texas, a place where a revolution was then in progress? I feared you joined the rebels and that somehow . . . oh, but never mind. I'm happy to see that you survived it. Is Texas an agreeable place?"

"I have no idea. I never got down there."

"Indeed! How silly my notion was, then! Whither did you go, Jacob? North, south, perhaps west to the Rocky Mountains?"

"To tell the truth, Ebenezer, I never left New York City. I never needed to. 'Tis a great metropolis, old friend. Someday I think it will eclipse London in its size."

"Is that so?" I was skeptical of such an idea, for our capital was enormous.

He seemed not to notice my tone. "The Americans, at least those in the North, think of nothing but industry, trade, and money. They're the Phoenicians of our day. If we are not careful, they will someday buy England out from under us."

"In that case," I said, indignant at this absurd notion, "what made you return to this inferior island?"

Marley smiled. "A fair question. Don't you think I might simply have gotten homesick for these shores?"

"Not really," I replied. Then I caught a mischievous gleam in his eye.

"You haven't been there, my friend," he said. "It's a raw, barely civilized country. They're a crude lot—though Americans hardly see themselves in that light. They're complacent and self-satisfied."

"Perhaps they're born that way," I said.

"On the contrary," he said, "it's rare to encounter a person who was actually born there. Most of them hail from all corners of the globe. One must constantly rub shoulders with foreigners—Dutchmen, Germans, Frenchmen, and so on. The politicians call their country a 'melting pot,' as though a newcomer can easily be recast in the mold of a proper American in the twinkling of an eye. What rubbish!"

"I've read a great deal about America," I said. "And it seems to me that this drive of new immigrants to transform themselves is one of the country's strong points."

"Bah! I thought in going to America I would dwell in a country something like my own. Not so. Thankfully, they still speak English, though their dialect diverges from ours by the day. To my disappointment, I was accorded no special favor as an Englishman—to them I seemed no better than an Italian or a Pole. Indeed, some bore grudges against me because of bitter

memories of the war. And then there is this damnable preference
for coffee over tea!"

I laughed. "Jacob, Jacob! Perhaps you would have fit in better
had you *embraced* the melting pot—simply dove in and baptized
yourself voluntarily."

He glowered at me. "Sometimes, Ebenezer, you irk me with
such fancy talk. If there's one thing I like about Americans, it's
that they speak plainly."

I ignored his grumble, for it was an old complaint.

"So then, tell me, what did you do there?"

"I opened a haberdashery in lower Manhattan, near the
financial district. It was a lucky choice and I fared extremely well.
A lot of wealthy men came through my doors. It happened that
many of my customers were involved with the importing of rare
goods—ivory, lace, crystal, porcelain, and other commodities. In
that area of the city, so near to the harbor, cargo was regularly
unloaded and stored in huge warehouses—buildings ranging
row upon row by the hundreds."

"You don't say," I said.

"Now, these well-to-do gentlemen, my customers, could see
I was a seasoned businessman myself, both by my speech and
how I understood matters of trade. One day an enterprising
young man invited me to go in with him in a 'deal.' I was invited
to invest in a venture to distribute silk from Japan. Nowadays it's
the finest in the world."

"What? Better than Chinese silk? I must say I did not know
that. I've dealt mainly with cotton and linen all these years."

"You were never one to look far beyond the front door, old
friend."

"How could you invest with a complete stranger?"

"How could I sit idly by when there was so much money being
made all round me? The scale of it! It makes your enterprise of
moving fabric from Manchester to London seem like the work of
a girl selling flowers on a street corner."

"Is that so? I've said many times one prospers more by being careful than he does by being bold. You speak of scale. We may deal less in volume, that's true; but the business has provided me a steady income for more than thirty years."

He winked at me. "Truly? See here, old chum, I arrived several days ago, and word on the street is that your business—which for some odd reason still retains my name on it—is sinking fast."

His thrust cut deep, for he was correct. There was nothing I could say.

We both fell silent, each stung a bit by the other's words. After several minutes Marley sighed and stared down at his empty glass. "I don't suppose . . ."

"By all means," I said, and poured out more whisky.

"Oh, by the way," Marley said and handed me a tall bottle. "I have a small gift for you."

"What is it?"

"American whisky from the state of Kentucky."

"Ah, the land of Daniel Boone! Thank you very much." Though pleased with the gift, I was anxious to hear more of his story.

"All right, then, Jacob. What calamity befell your venture? Tell me."

"I wasn't swindled, as you so readily assume. My investment was only in the *distribution* of the silk. The cargo had already arrived from Japan and was stored in a warehouse on Pearl Street. Believe me, I would never advance money on the proposition of importing goods from the Orient. The Pacific is a vast ocean, and many typhoons sweep over it. In this case there was no need to worry, for the silk had already been brought to New York. I went to the warehouse. I saw the fabric, felt it, smelled it. Ebenezer, it was the finest material I ever laid hands on."

His enthusiasm impressed me. "Very well. But why did this man approach you, an outsider, if the cloth had only to be sold?"

"He'd had a falling-out with a former partner. They disagreed as to how much money to spend in the distribution. The other man wanted to confine marketing to the wealthier states, where high prices might be gotten—states like New York, Massachusetts, and Pennsylvania. But my new associate wanted to market it to all the maritime states, especially the southern ones, where wealthy plantation owners might be fascinated with this exotic fabric."

"Was your 'associate' an honorable man?" I asked.

"Without doubt. And he'd already bought out his partner. Although he now possessed a large quantity of silk, he found himself short of cash. He needed more capital."

"I see. And how much money did you invest?"

"Everything I had! I sold my store for a good profit and invested the proceeds to buy a third of the silk. Moreover, I agreed to help promote the fabric myself. As a first step I planned to travel to Virginia."

"Now, Jacob, allow me to hazard a guess. You had no luck down south in Virginia. Those wealthy plantation owners had no sympathy for this foreign cloth, a rival to their magnificent cotton."

"That wasn't it, Ebenezer," he said in a wistful tone of voice. "That wasn't it." He ran a hand through his hair. "I never went. The trip turned out to be . . . unnecessary."

"Eh? What happened?"

He drew in a sharp breath before continuing. "It was wintertime. A fire erupted in one of those buildings in the financial district. Firemen were called, of course, but it was so cold that the hydrants had frozen up. They had to draw water from the East River to fight it. I will not belabor you with details, but, suffice it to say, nearly all of those great warehouses—more than six hundred of them—were consumed, along with their contents. Fortunes were lost. Even the Merchants' Exchange on Wall Street burned to the ground."

"And your Japanese silk, I take it also went up in flames?"

"The entire stock. Once again, fate did not smile on Jacob Marley."

I laid a hand on his shoulder. "I'm truly sorry, old friend.

Rotten luck, I must say."

"Even my old haberdasher's shop was not spared," he added bitterly. "So you see, I would have been wiped out anyway."

Then he sighed heavily and looked away. "Life is a terrific gamble, don't you agree?"

At that remark it occurred to me I might tell him the truth about his gambling losses to the English lords, the men who cheated him at whist. But I refrained, not wanting to dishearten him any further.

"I read about that fire in the newspapers," I said. "That was some time ago. What did you do afterwards?"

"What could I do? I started over again, this time with no money at all. Mainly I worked for merchants in their shops selling dry goods. I also turned my hand to whatever additional employment I could find: running messages, bookkeeping, even teaching English to foreigners—including some Chinese sailors who'd come down from New Haven to see the big city of New York."

"My word, the place truly *is* a melting pot. Did those Chinese fellows settle in the city?"

"No, but I have a feeling they will. They told me they first had to return home and fetch their families. Who knows what odd customs they'll bring with them. 'Tis a strange country, America. Nobody is kept out and everybody who comes in changes the landscape to some degree."

I said nothing else for a while and let him catch his breath.

Downstairs, my big clock ominously tolled the eleventh hour. This caused me to reflect back on my guest's convincing impersonation of a ghost. "I must say, Jacob, you gave me quite a start, ascending the stairs and rattling your chains."

He chuckled and for a moment seemed to shake off his bitterness. "My jest was calculated to inform you that this house is possessed by evil spirits."

"I already suspected it was," I responded.

At this remark he gave me an odd look.

"Tell me," I said, "now that you've returned to England, what is it you intend to do?"

"Go to the north."

"Do you still have family there?"

"None, but I know some people living in the area. I hear Liverpool these days is akin to the city I recently left. Working men are flocking there. A horde of Welsh and Irish have descended on it, not to mention Europeans of every stripe. It's a busy port some call The New York of Europe."

I nodded, digesting this information.

He cocked his head and smiled. "Come now, Ebenezer. You did not think I would dare take up residence in town again, did you?"

"It has not escaped my notice that you still retain a key to the front door."

"Ha! Don't worry, I'll leave the key with you when I leave. I have some other business to take care of and I'll be out of the city shortly after New Year's Day."

"Other business? Mind that you take care, old friend. It makes me uneasy to have you around."

"Tut-tut!" he scoffed.

This nettled me. "You might at least take the trouble to lop off your ridiculous pigtail, so no one recognizes you. It's quite out of fashion, you know."

"Don't fret, Ebenezer. As I said, I've been in town awhile, staying elsewhere. I shall not return to this old house. I plan to acquire a new set of papers soon. They're in the name of a certain gentleman in Knightsbridge who recently passed away, God rest his soul. When I have my papers, I shall move on."

"My, but you've been busy—extremely busy."

"Come now, you are too suspicious. I'm well aware I cannot take up the name of Jacob Marley again. That fellow is dead and buried, as we both know."

"Yet somehow you seem to be forgetting it. Why did you not

sail directly to your destination? Why stop here? Was it merely to reacquaint yourself with the delights of the capital?"

"I only came to London to get those papers. It's more easily done here than up there."

I looked away, trying to remain calm.

"And what's more," he added more gently, "I wanted to see you. You're my oldest friend, after all. And you're the only person in England who knows I'm still alive."

"Yes, I am your friend," I answered, turning to face him. "But Jacob, you never answered my earlier question."

"What question was that?"

"The reason you abandoned America. Even after you lost your money in the fire, I'll wager you recovered. You always do, being so resourceful. In fact, you must have been doing fairly well, for you amassed enough money to book passage on a steamer and take care of 'other business' after you disembarked."

"I have enough money in my pocket, I suppose."

"Then what caused you to leave?"

"I thought it was clear. I left America because I'd grown quite weary of that paradise of fools." He stood and faced away from me, toward the fire.

"Really? I know you very well, and I can't believe you would quit a place where so much money was being made all about you, as you put it. My insight tells me you would have preferred to stay in the New World. Isn't that so? Answer honestly."

"Oh, damn you and your 'insight'!" he barked. I saw that I'd cut him to the quick. He sat down heavily and again ran a hand through his thinning hair.

"Ebenezer, I was happier there than I've ever been. It's true I have my complaints of the people and their customs. Their manners are atrocious, and I often thirsted for a decent bottle of claret. Yet, honestly, I loved the bustling island of Manhattan. The spirit of that place . . . oh, I'm not a man of fine words like you. You must go yourself there if you want take the measure of it."

"Jacob, my friend, if you were happy there, what on God's earth made you leave?"

"Necessity." He threw up his hands. "You see, I killed a man."

At this stark confession my mind went utterly blank. I took another sip of whisky.

He proceeded to tell me the story of a deadly altercation with a drunken butcher in a crowded tavern. As he told it, the stranger accosted him for no good reason. The man hated all Englishmen and was quite drunk at the time. Though Jacob did nothing to inflame the fellow's wrath, so he said, they soon quarreled and traded fisticuffs. Finally the other drew out a meat cleaver and swung it, missed, swung again, and in the same instant took a ball from Jacob's pistol at close range. I will not burden you with all the details he gave me, except to say Marley was a stranger in that tavern and soon realized the onlookers would bear testimony against him—a detested foreigner in their eyes. So he fled the tavern and began to make plans to flee the city.

I've no way of knowing whether this story is true. At its core, I believe it is. It's likely Jacob colored it to his own advantage—that would be typical. He mentioned that for a time he considered going to the frontier states but decided life was too rough there. New York was as rough as he could tolerate.

After much thought he decided to try his luck in the north of England.

We said nothing for a long time after that. Now I felt sorry for the man who sat in my bed chamber. He seemed only a shell of my former partner.

CHAPTER 22

THE EXPERIMENT

My uncle coughed and reached for a glass of water. "I must pause here, nephew," he said.

"By all means," I said. "You've been speaking quite a while."

He took a sip of water and relaxed in his wing chair, leaning back in a dreamy manner, as if to reflect.

I was enthralled by his story and wanted to ask questions, but I said nothing, afraid I might disturb his mood should I begin a conversation. I reckoned that his mind harbored thoughts half in the present day and half in the past. It seemed best to let him take his time. Yet I longed to hear more, for he had not even begun to explain how his inner spirit had been so altered that night.

A bit hungry, I selected one of the Emily's sandwiches. Rather than speak, I held out the basket to him, and he took one, nodding absent-mindedly. We ate the food in silence. After that he got up, moved around the room, and finally stood a long time in the weak light of the large window. Daylight was waning, and I wondered if we might soon need a fire.

"I suppose you want to hear the rest of it," he said at last without much spirit.

"Of course," I answered.

I sensed he was reluctant to continue, yet I dared not prod him. I merely sipped the wine and waited.

At length he smiled at me. "You're a patient man, Fred. But you must wonder, I imagine, why I hesitate to continue my tale. It's not because my memory is clouded, for I remember everything. No, it's because I am ashamed of something I chose to do; even though, in doing it, I received a great gift, one that has altered me forever."

I sat up in my chair, hungry to hear more.

Then my uncle resumed his narrative.

◆ ◆ ◆

Jacob assured me I would see him no more after that night. He only begged my indulgence in allowing him to sleep on the divan in the drawing room.

Strange to say, at that juncture of the evening I was not at all weary, despite the lateness of the hour. This unlooked-for intruder, my former partner, had brought with him a picture of the New World, and it was exciting to get it firsthand from a man who lived and worked there. My appetite was whetted for more. I wondered if he might have spoken with other men who'd traveled into the wilds of the interior and come back to the big city with fabulous stories to tell.

"Let us relax, Jacob," I said. "I am keen to hear more of America—that is, if you care to tell me. Would you like another whisky or some of your long-missed claret?"

He looked at me strangely. "I wouldn't mind a smoke," he said.

"Very well," I said. "Let me add another coal to the fire. Perhaps I'll have a pipe myself."

He watched in silence as I fed and poked the small fire in the grate. I took my chair again and, as there was a sip of whisky left in my glass, I downed it. "I rarely have visitors, you know," I said. "Sometimes my nephew, Frederick, comes over to hear me hold forth on the state of the world."

"Little Freddy? Goodness! I remember the lad from those days we used to visit your sister's house. He has grown up, I take it."

"Quite," I answered. "In the process of doing so he became a solicitor, married, and fathered a child. He remembers you with fondness and was saddened to hear of your 'unfortunate demise' seven years ago."

"What else have you told him about me?"

I hesitated for a brief moment. "Why, nothing the world does not already know."

He did not reply, and this created an awkward interval. I steeled myself to rebut any suspicions he might advance. Though I don't generally prevaricate, in this instance I cannot imagine what other course I might have taken, for I was not going to admit I told you the whole sordid truth.

"Come, now," I said in a jovial manner, "tell me more about the United States."

"To be honest," he replied, "I know little of what lies west of the Hudson River."

I groaned. "Pity! I confess my disappointment. I so looked forward to hearing a yarn or two." I glanced over at the novel I'd been reading earlier.

"I'll wager you know more about the frontier than I," he said glumly.

"All right then," I said. "You told me the reason you left America. May I ask why you dropped in this evening? Was it merely to play your ghostly prank? You must have enjoyed planning each detail whilst aboard the ship, then sneaking into the house to carry it out, eh? Very clever. You succeeded brilliantly, old friend. You nearly scared me out of my skin."

"Ebenezer? Are you sure you want to hear the real reason for tonight's visit?"

"I do, yes," I affirmed.

He stood up, shuffled aimlessly about the rug, then spoke. "I came to find out if you were the same smug fellow who wanted to be rich for no other reason than to have people look at him and say, 'There goes a true man of business, one who has accumulated a fortune.'"

"I care little about how others perceive me. We both wanted to be rich, Jacob. Don't you remember how we lingered in the taverns those nights, two rash young men plotting their futures?"

"You were never rash," he said. "But we made a good team: I, the daring one, and you, the cautious one."

"I grant we had contrasting temperaments."

"And still do."

"Yet I do not perceive what you mean to imply, dear Jacob. Smug, am I? In my career I have learned a lot and profited from the knowledge. Naturally, I have my own ways of doing things."

"And you're completely mired in them," he said accusingly. "I can understand the virtue of caution. But you are so enamored of your 'ways' that you reject new ideas. You cannot change. You can only wither and decay."

"Experience is the great teacher," I said. "Unfortunately, you yourself are not an apt pupil."

"Is that so? Then why, despite all your knowledge and experience, is the firm of Scrooge & Marley on its last legs?"

At this I blushed, because the accusation was undeniably true. "I've been hard pressed to do the work of two men these last seven years. I may also point out that you have landed on these shores in the midst of hard times. There is a general malaise in all trades and professions. Nevertheless my business will survive."

He shook his head, as if in disbelief. "I think you would do well to sell the company if you can get a fair price. It has no future."

"Oh, really?" I said, trying to put a touch of amusement in my voice. "And what would I do then to pass the time? I'm a man of ingrained habits. I cannot imagine what I would do in the mornings other than rise, dress, eat my porridge, and walk to the office."

He let fly a laugh. "Exactly so!" he exclaimed. "And you a wealthy man! Tell me, do you employ any servants in this old rat-trap of a mansion?"

"There is Mrs. Dilber."

"Ah, the laudable Mrs. Dilber! My former charwoman, now yours. Have you others?"

"No," I confessed.

"Have you ever taken time off from work to go on a holiday?"

"No."

"No servants. No luxuries. No holidays. Have you ever paused to consider your life? Or what the point of accumulating wealth might be? I don't think there is any point in it for Mr. Ebenezer Scrooge."

"Jacob, try to understand. When we first made acquaintance, I told you of my miserable upbringing—my exile at a fifth-rate boarding school; the drunken tyranny of my father; my utter poverty when leaving home to apprentice in another mill town. Is it any wonder that I am frugal? I should not be admonished for keeping a tight rein on my assets."

"On your purse, you mean."

"Very well, on my purse! But that is because I know there is always lurking around the next corner of my life an enemy—Complacency, the progenitor of Catastrophe. Therefore I keep a tight grip on my meager accumulation of capital."

"Meager?" he repeated and laughed again. "In hiding your wealth you invite others to deem you a miser of the worst stripe."

"Possibly I am, if the intelligent minding of one's money is to be vilified."

"Oh, I see you have not changed a bit," he said. "I was only curious to find out."

"*I* unchanged!" I said, then rose to my feet, though I felt silly doing so in my nightgown. "What of you, Jacob? You have not changed a jot or tittle. You still toss caution to the wind, invest in risky ventures, and squander your gains as soon as you have gotten them."

"Oh-ho," he retorted, "so you deem me a spendthrift?"

"Yes, that is exactly what you are."

"I've merely taken pleasure in the fruits of my energy and good fortune."

"Normally I'd not question the desire to do so," I said. "My own natural avoidance of ostentation doesn't mean I ever begrudged you that tendency. But Jacob, do you really think it was wise to gamble away your wealth in the gambling halls?"

At that he bridled. "It was my choice. I paid the price for the adventure of it. And yet, as a consequence, I have sailed off to see another world! Whereas you, you old coot, are still eating your blasted porridge and trudging to the office of a morning."

"Yet here you are, come back again in disarray . . . unsatisfied and a failure."

He looked away again. I saw I had wounded him this time, for his breath came short and hot.

"Ah, well," I said, "we'd better put our differences aside. We're getting on in years, and there's no use trying to refashion either of us at this late hour. Sit down, why don't you, and let's have another touch of whisky."

I proceeded to sit in my reading chair, but Jacob remained standing, struggling to rein in his temper. At length he gave me a strange look. "I want to show you something," he said and abruptly left the room.

He soon returned with an oblong case, the kind used for transporting a woodwind instrument, such as a clarinet or oboe, though larger. He laid the case on the floor and opened it, and I saw that it did contain an instrument, though I knew not what it was. Lying in a bed of felt, the item was about two feet in length, cylindrical, and made of a wood that I took to be bamboo or something akin to it. Also nestled in the case were several small metal accessories and boxes, strange to the eye. He lifted out the large wooden object.

"Are you going to serenade me, Jacob?" I asked. This brought a smile to his lips, and I was relieved to see he'd regained his sense of humor.

"Hardly, old friend," he said. "Did you mistake this for a flute of some description?"

"I thought that guess was as good as any other."

He handed me the cylinder. "Notice, there are no finger-holes on the body of it, nor any keys. It is not a flute; it's a pipe."

"A pipe? 'Tis a very odd-looking one and seems quite cumbersome. I myself prefer a simple clay pipe; I have several strewn about the house."

"Of course you do. You still use the old clay pipes despite the advent of new materials from the far corners of the earth."

I smiled and nodded. "You're correct there. I see many men on the street smoking those meerschaum pipes. They're very popular these days. What can I say? I'm old-fashioned and wedded to my country ways, as you know. The clay pipes are cheap and suit me well enough."

He grinned. "As they no doubt suited your father."

"Is there something amiss with that?"

"Not at all, not at all." He took back the cylinder and said, "I wonder, Ebenezer, if you would consent to a small experiment."

"What do you mean? What kind of experiment?"

"I would like you to sample this Chinese pipe—for China is its country of origin—and tell me if you do not agree it's better than any you've ever smoked. A Chinese sailor who was an English student of mine in New York gave it to me as a token of friendship."

"My, my, I suppose tobacco has conquered the entire world."

"That's true enough," he said. "But the Chinese have added native plants and herbs to suit their taste. That mixture is what I would like you to sample tonight. The vapor is entirely different than that of plain tobacco in its effect. You'll remember smoking this pipe long after I quit London for the north."

Though curious about this pipe, I waved a dismissive hand.

"I'd better not."

"Why?"

"It's late, and we should retire soon."

"You seem quite alert to me. Are you going to someone's house for Christmas dinner tomorrow?"

"I have been asked," I replied. "However, I doubt I will venture out into the cold. Since it is we men of business who must finance this yearly holiday, I might as well remain in my warm home and enjoy the day in my own fashion."

"I see."

"Furthermore," I continued, "as I've had so much excitement tonight, I doubt I will sleep well."

A glint appeared in Marley's eye. "Smoking the pipe will soothe you. The effect is quite relaxing, especially for one not used to the mixture's effect. I believe you'll find it easy to sleep afterwards and shall be better rested in the morning. In fact, I wager you'll enjoy the most sublime sleep of your life. Tomorrow you'll find yourself well-suited to engage in whatever activity you prefer."

I laughed. "Ever the able salesman, eh, Jacob?"

"Ha! But I speak the truth, old friend. You may never get another chance to use this exotic instrument. There's not a man on this island, I'll warrant, who has yet encountered the contraption—besides myself, that is. You, Ebenezer, would be the next!"

Something stirred in me. His proposal appealed to my latent sense of adventure. I wondered, would the fictional Hawk-eye have a go at this strange pipe? Likely he would. Old Mr, Fezziwig once told me a man should walk abroad among his fellow-men and travel far and wide as he could. All I had done in that regard was to remove to the capital. I'd never expected to behold such a tangible token of the Far East as the item brought directly into my bedroom that night. Here it was, and there was little chance I'd ever see its like again. Nor had I seen an Egyptian pyramid, the falls of the Niagara, the Taj Mahal, or a junk sailing in the sunset on the East China Sea; for I had never left Britain, not even to cross the Channel into France for a holiday. More than likely I never would. And now that Marley had summoned up the image of Far Cathay, I found I desperately wanted to do something—nay, anything—that would release my mind and heart from the prison I'd made for them, and that would enable me to fly into the outer world, if only for a brief moment in time.

Nevertheless, after a moment's reflection I again declined.

"I am not adept at learning new tricks, Jacob. It took me forever to get the Congreve matches to light without burning myself."

He came over and squatted down. His open expression told me he was pleased I even considered the proposition. "You do not need to master all the ins and outs of it. I will assist you at every step, for it's not as simple to use as one might suppose."

"Will you partake of it yourself?"

"Only after you're done."

My stomach turned within me. I wasn't sure if that was because I sensed danger approaching, or if, rather, a bit of undigested beef was playing havoc with my gut. I wanted to humor Marley and try the blasted pipe; but my strong impulse was to dismiss him, leap into bed, and draw the curtains.

"Won't you please give it a go?" he asked with childlike eagerness.

"Don't hurry me, Jacob. It's not every day I take such liberties with myself."

"Of that I'm well aware," he answered with a toothy grin.

*What are you doing, Ebenezer?* I asked myself in a panic. *This is madness!* Then, seized by the imp of petulance, I gave him a stern look. "I must say, Jacob, you seem to relish prodding me into doing a thing that is not in my nature to do."

He stood up and regarded me with a superior air. "My dear friend, I came here hoping to see you grown wiser with age. I don't think you have, but I do sense in your manner a vague yearning to explore something new and a stifled longing for new horizons. Because I esteem you a lifelong friend and owe you so much, I wanted to share this small experience—smoking the Chinese pipe—so that your door to the world may widen a crack, and you may gain something to remember of me, hopefully in gratitude."

I clenched my teeth but said nothing. At length he shrugged, muttered a curse, and returned the pipe to its case. Yes, this man certainly did owe me much. My pride urged me to blurt out the whole sordid story of the cheating lords and their nefarious ways, and to explain how they plucked him cleaner than a Christmas turkey. Oh yes, his monumental self-assurance would suffer a blow then, now wouldn't it? The crafty Jacob Marley duped by amateur card sharps—what a tale!

But that would be mean-spirited. Petty. I deemed myself a better man than that.

*And,* I reflected further, *he's absolutely right. I am smug and satisfied with myself, and have no higher aspiration than to accumulate money for its own sake.*

"Damn you!" I spat out. "Get on with it, then. The hour grows late."

His eyes widened and he drew back, puzzled by my sudden vehemence. Then I leapt to my feet, snatched the pipe up from its velvet home, turned it over, and stared down the bore, anxious to initiate the experiment before I could change my mind.

"Hold on there," he said, "gently taking it back. There are preparations to be made. In the meantime you may seat yourself on your bed. How convenient for us that we're in your bedroom, for it's best to be recumbent before one takes his first draft."

"Whatever for?" I asked, since this idea seemed stranger than the oversize pipe itself.

"Trust me, please. I've mastered the protocol. You see I learned the art of smoking the pipe from my Chinese friend."

I reluctantly moved to the bed and sat there with my legs dangling as I watched him. I felt extremely restless now. I could hardly control my hands, which wanted to flit about aimlessly.

Marley opened one of the strangely-made boxes in the case and examined its contents. He pronounced the mixture completely dry and fit for smoking. Then he moved my little night table slightly and asked me to lie back. He arranged the pillows so I would be slightly elevated.

As I made myself comfortable, Marley set a small metal oil lamp on the table. He proceeded to light it with a straw he'd stuck in the hearth.

"What is the purpose of the little lamp?" I asked, fascinated by this elaborate ritual.

"This will heat up the *chandu*," he said, by which I supposed he meant the mixture.

There was a metal appendage on the pipe, about two-thirds the way down its length, in the shape of a tiny bowl. Into this small receptacle Marley added the *chandu,* which I observed had more the shape of pills than the stringy consistency of tobacco. He told me it attained that shape from the way it was processed. He performed the task by using a little spike, for I could see now that the bowl was covered except for a small hole. He impaled each pill, pushed it through the opening, then withdrew the spike, taking care to prevent drawing out the pill. Jacob seemed quite proficient in this task.

I asked nothing more, for the whole scene was so suffused with the allure of the Orient that I knew that any answers given to my idle questions would only confuse me further. So I relaxed and waited as calmly as I could. I felt as if I were about to participate in some kind of sacred rite, much as a Christian child awaits his or her first communion.

Finally he came over to me, smiling, and asked if I were ready to proceed.

His eye held a mischievous spark I knew well. Suddenly I felt extremely uneasy. What had he said? I would enjoy the most sublime sleep of my life? My stomach flipped again. I nearly panicked to think he might poison me.

I placed a hand on his wrist.

"Jacob, I'm afraid," I said, hearing my own voice quaver.

"Do not worry, old friend," he whispered, "I'm here at your side. You'll suffer no harm. That's a solemn vow."

I recalled his harsh words to me earlier—and mine to him. Nevertheless, he was the same Jacob Marley I had known for forty years. I let go of his wrist.

I had decided to trust him.

As he directed, I received the pipe and put the ceramic mouthpiece to my lips. Then Jacob took the metal spike and again inserted it through the hole—to spread the mixture around, he said. Finally he carefully inverted the bowl over the flame of his little lamp.

The *chandu* began to heat.

In a short time, he said urgently: "Quickly, Ebenezer! Inhale the vapor, as deeply as you can, and hold it in. Begin now!"

I drew the vapor into my lungs. It was rich and satisfying, and soon I began to feel light-headed, but pleasantly so. I held the vapor in as long as I could. Then I heard him say to repeat the process. I tried, but I'm not sure I succeeded. My concentration was faltering. I might have managed to take another breath or even another. I'm not certain, for at that moment I seemed to leave my bedroom and the city itself behind me.

———◆◇◆———

The euphoria induced by the vapor truly soothed my restless spirit. But peaceful sleep did not follow as promised; for at this juncture the experiment took a mysterious turn. I received a series of visions—you might call them hallucinations—during which I remained awake and yet was transported to other places and other times.

Were they dreams? They were much more than that.

At first, I found myself standing upon an open country road

with fields on either hand. It was a clear, cold winter day with snow upon the ground. I knew exactly where I was, for I'd been a boy there. I looked about and found I was alone. Yet near me I felt the invisible presence of some unseen person—dare I say a spirit?—who spoke muffled words occasionally. Most of the time I could not make them out. This presence urged me to walk forward, more by tone of voice than English speech.

The way was entirely familiar, as only details learned early in one's life can be. Indeed, I remembered every gate and post and tree. As I walked on, a little town appeared before me in the distance, one I knew well. Soon I could make out its church, its bridge, and its winding river.

As I got closer to the town, I passed some walkers in the lane. None of them noticed me though I knew them; I could have called each of them by name. But they paid me no mind whatsoever. It was Christmas-time there, and these folk were merry and light of heart and they called out their Merry Christmases as they parted at cross-roads and by-ways.

Then I was taken to another place and time. I found myself on a road I knew all too well. At the end of it stood a mansion of dull red brick with a little weather-cock stuck on its cupola. It was my old school, and I soon espied a child sitting alone in its great hall. The students had gone home for the holiday, all but this one boy. It took me a moment to realize who he was.

It was not a happy picture. The sullen boy sat by the fire, reading the tale of "Ali Baba and the Forty Thieves." He knew that the harder he concentrated, the better he could escape the rude surroundings and the terrible loneliness.

That child was myself, of course. I was that sullen boy.

Then the muffled voice spoke again and the scene altered. I was set forward in time a year or two. I observed I'd grown taller—I mean my young self had done so, for I was only an observer of the scene and invisible to my younger self. Once, though, I fancied he caught sight of me from the corner of his eye. I wondered who was the real ghost—the bygone image I encountered or myself to him?

We were again at a time near Christmas, and now I was reading *Robinson Crusoe*, the only boy there. I did not remain alone, however. On this chilly day my sister, Fan, suddenly arrived at the school in a coach. She was still a child, but already wise and sure of herself.

I was overjoyed to have a visitor and greeted her warmly.

"But I have not come to visit," she said, laughing and putting her little arms around my neck. "I have come to bring you home, dear brother."

She told me our father had changed of late and had become more genial to everyone we knew. He had dispatched Fan to fetch me home. Father owned that I was now entirely grown up, a man and need no longer to remain there. At this news I cried tears of happiness.

I remember that day well. At the time the good news struck me as rather odd, for I could have been no more than fifteen years old at this time, not really a grown man. I was not sure how much of this change was due to Father's softening heart. It occurred to me he might be tired of paying my room and board at the school. No matter, I was overjoyed to be liberated from that prison.

Now the scenes flew past me so fast I could barely assimilate them.

When my head stopped spinning, I discovered I was now indeed a young man, full of the dreams and aspirations all young men possess. In a certain provincial city I had become apprenticed to a businessman named Fezziwig, who owned a warehouse full of goods. I was a bookkeeper there. Mr. Fezziwig was a kindly man, and on Christmas Eve he liked to shutter his warehouse, clear a large space in the middle of it, and give a little ball for his employees and guests, complete with a country fiddler providing the music. What a grand time we had! I saw myself dancing there, if you can believe it, dancing with a young woman to whom I was engaged.

Soon the unseen spirit spoke a word in my ear, and I was dismayed to learn we must leave the ball. The scene now changed to a still later time, in the springtime. I was a few years older now, in my prime, and still engaged to that lovely young woman. Her name was Belle. By then I was completely preoccupied with pursuing my career and saving for the future. I was inspired by Mr. Fezziwig's business success, although wary of his copious generosity. To me it seemed excessive and not at all prudent.

Belle and I sat together in the shade of an old elm tree. It was wonderful to be in her company. Whenever we met like this, I was in the habit of first apprising her of the latest value of our nest egg, which would someday enable us to marry. Then the both of us would sit close together, hold hands, and give voice to our dreams of the happy life we would someday share.

But on this day, Belle seemed nervous and told me she had something important to tell me.

"What is it?" I asked.

"I have decided to break off our engagement, Ebenezer."

The words struck me like arrows. I begged the reason for this, not fully believing she meant it.

"You have time and again refused to set a date for our marriage. I have come to believe you love the getting of money more than the getting of a wife."

I assured her the latter statement was untrue and told her I loved her without limit. But I also averred it was not wise to marry as yet. "We dare not risk it," I said, "until I accumulate a proper sum with which to begin our married life."

"I don't care if we are poor and remain so, Ebenezer," she answered hotly. "Our lives are slipping away, and we shall have nothing left but your 'proper sum' if we wait any longer."

In my stupidity, I thought the problem still had to do with money. "You are ashamed that you have no dowry," I said.

"Not true!" she cried in obvious distress. "It is you who are ashamed I lack it!"

And that was the end of our dialogue. She ran off and never

came with me to that garden again.

After that vision, I wished I had never taken hold of Marley's Chinese pipe. For as much as I enjoyed seeing the earlier scenes of my life, I was now utterly downcast with regret, burdened with a deep despair. For the first time, I perceived how ambition diverted the course of my life.

More muffled words urged me to move, and suddenly I found myself in my present place of business, sitting at my desk. Then you, Fred, came to the office warbling a noel. Again I observed my other self from a discrete distance, marking how I truly appeared to the rest of the world. I was forced to relive the unpleasantness of that long day.

I was in the full height of my anger, lashing out at all who approached me. I denied Cratchit enough coal to warm himself. I beat on the windows to drive away wandering carolers. In the main, I holed up in my private office, stewing over a glass of wine about the fools who made a fetish of Christmas and its silly customs.

My Lord, what vileness spewed from the core of my soul that day!

Once I might have explained myself by blaming the hard times, my failing business, Marley's absconding to America, my age, and various other causes. But I now saw there was no valid excuse that could be given. Seeing oneself as others see you is a terrible cure for arrogance. There I was, suggesting you should not have married as young as you did, when I myself had done the opposite thing and paid a heavy price for the choice. Now I saw that you were the wise one and I the fool.

Then let us consider the two portly gentlemen who asked me for a modest donation for the poor and destitute. Cratchit, you see, had let these two slip in even as you departed to go home. As I had no intention of giving them a farthing from the start, I could have merely shooed them out and got back to my stewing. I did not do that. Instead, I flung clever remarks at them in a haughty manner, saying perverse things about the poor. Now I had to hear again each and every cutting word that came from my lips. Inwardly I writhed in agony.

I've said I did not think Marley was with me; but someone must have been, for I clearly heard "shush" and "there, there" said over me as if I were being gentled by someone. Or by some spirit. If it was not Marley, then perhaps it was the spirit of your mother. She once attended me when I suffered a bout of the grippe. Oh, but I was in a whirlpool of distress as I observed this scene! I was full of misery for my condition . . . the condition of knowing I was a deficient human being.

At length the scene faded and the storm in my breast spent itself. I hoped I would now slip into a sound sleep. That did not happen, for I was immediately pulled along by a flowing tide into the next vision and soon found myself in a graveyard at dusk. No one lingered there but myself. No shadow of the past was there to disturb or shame me. This setting I found to be extremely soothing to my tortured soul.

I walked among the headstones in a haphazard fashion.

At first I deemed it a country churchyard, for it sat next to a rather homely house of God, the kind found in a rustic village. But then I noticed street lights shining through the bare trees and knew I was in no such place. Curious, I walked about in search of a clue as to where I might be, for I assumed this location must be a relic from my store of memories. How else, I thought, can one conjure up anything in a vision or a dream unless he retrieves it from the past, though it may be long forgotten?

It did occur to me I might be having a vision not of the past but of the future. Such revelations have been granted to mystics and holy men. And to fools. At any rate, I continued to feel at peace though I knew not the reason for it.

The more I looked around—and it was not large, this churchyard—the more familiar it seemed. I was certain I had been there before. I wondered if it might be where my father was buried. I did not attend his funeral, but once visited his grave to pay my respects. That was the only cemetery I knew where one might find the name of SCROOGE chiseled in stone. I did not find such a name here. After examining a few of the more legible inscriptions and not recognizing a single name, I walked to the perimeter of the yard to survey the city that enclosed it. Still thinking the city to be where my father, Fan, and I once lived, I was confounded by the dark, forbidding buildings I spied. Clearly I was not in that provincial city. Then I heard bells toll the hour from many quarters, and they informed me of my location, to wit, this immense, drifting sprawl in which we now live.

I do not go to many funerals, nor do I attend regular church services. Yet strange to say, I was certain I had once stopped in this particular churchyard. Some hazy memory told me this was an out-of-the-way parish, one with a dwindling congregation. I examined the less weather-beaten headstones as far as the fading light would permit. Not many were legible. I kept at it, though, determined to find some clue. At last I came upon one whose marble was relatively fresh. It bore no Bible verse, nor any inscription whatsoever, only the name of the entombed: JACOB MARLEY.

This discovery jolted me out of my peaceful state. I had forgotten the existence of this benighted place. It was the little graveyard chosen by Jacob himself, set in a parish whose vicar could be bought for a few pounds, sad little man that he was. Here I signed the guest book at his funeral as his sole mourner on the very day he ceased to be Jacob Marley.

Of course Marley himself was not interred there. No one was. It was all a hoax.

I felt quite alone as I contemplated the headstone. No comforting presence hovered near me as before. If the guiding spirit had been Marley himself attending me, then he must have departed my bedchamber by this time, perhaps to seek his own visions on the divan in the drawing room.

Why, you may ask, did it so disturb me that I found that empty grave? Was it because it brought home the travesty I helped perpetrate? Partially, I suppose. It certainly demonstrated the lengths to which I went to enrich my estate—for didn't I gain the whole of the company, a house, and a carriage to boot? I once told you I did the mischief to help a friend, and so I believed. But history teaches us that evil men have a way of deluding themselves.

As darkness fell, I remained rooted to the spot, caught in a dream, unable to extricate myself, even after shadow swallowed up the words on the stone. I could only weep. Then after my weeping, something deep inside my being began to wail, and it took me time to glean the real reason for my distress.

It was this: I was devastated that I had located Marley's gravestone *instead of my own*. You see, I had assumed this vision was a premonition of my final resting place, the cemetery where I myself will be laid to rest.

That is why I felt so much at peace there.

But it now seemed I was not to be released from my sins by an easy death, not at all. Instead, I would have to deal with my actions long after the visions ceased.

I had several others, but they were trivial compared to these. At long last, I fell into a profound, dreamless sleep—completely restful, without consciousness—and woke at first light, refreshed and in a neutral frame of mind. I sat up in bed and looked around. I was relieved to see the morning light stealing in.

Then I discovered my bedding was in chaos: pillows flung aside, some to the floor; covers kicked hither and thither; one of the bed-curtains ripped down.

I stepped onto the cold floor and tried to get my bearings. Because of the disarray, my own bedroom looked foreign to my eye. Then a familiar church bell pealed, and the sound told me I had indeed returned to the present time, to my own dwelling, alive, and perhaps with many years to live.

That being the case, I knew I could not live them in my former way. I had to transform myself; I had to become a different man. My soul depended on it.

Soon I would discover that Jacob was gone and all his

paraphernalia with him. And as he promised, he left the house key behind.

◆ ◆ ◆

My uncle and I sat silent in his drawing room awhile. Clearly, he was drained of energy from the ordeal of unburdening his soul to me.

We took some claret together, and I dared to ask how he felt.

He smiled weakly, told me not to worry, and added he would shortly regain his equilibrium.

In a few minutes, we began to discuss the details of his story. He told me he was of two minds about smoking the Chinese pipe. He was ashamed he succumbed to the adventure of drug-taking—for that is what he suspected from the very first—and yet he was grateful he had, considering the powerful visions that resulted. They changed his life.

In response I said, "I myself do not think use of the pipe was so great a vice. It strikes me that the drug, whatever it was, only prodded you into a state of extreme introspection. You already knew your life needed repair. Yes, and you may have reformed yourself anyway at some later date. That's my opinion."

"You are such a rational man, Fred. But I doubt I would have mended my character in the normal course of events, for I was an obstinate old bird, and held fast to the ingrained opinions of a lifetime. It was only when I saw myself as others saw me— and heard me—that the truth struck home.

"And there is something else that impressed me strongly. I truly did feel the presence of a guide—perhaps mortal, perhaps spiritual—who stood beside me as I viewed those scenes. And I felt this entity was urging me to change my life. That is the gift that was offered to me. And by then, I knew I had to accept it."

"A guardian angel, perhaps?" I asked him playfully. "Or perhaps it was only the genie of the pipe."

He chuckled. "Perhaps so."

We ended the long session by sampling the Kentucky whisky Marley brought from America. In it, I could taste the backwoods of the raw frontier, for it tasted nothing like the civilized spirits made in Scotland. If I had any doubt that Marley actually returned to England, that notion was dispelled by this exotic whisky. For there could be no other explanation for its being in the house.

Before I left, we drank a toast to Daniel Boone.

## Chapter 23

### The End of Scrooge & Marley

U ncle Ebenezer had charged me to keep secret all that he told me on that April afternoon. "Yours are the only ears that shall ever hear this account," he said at the outset of his narrative.

That, however, was not to be the case. Other ears would indeed hear about it.

It was not because I myself told anyone the story, certainly not. I did not even tell my wife what I knew, though she pestered me many times for a cogent explanation of the profound change in his character. I simply told her that Uncle remained secretive about it and that we should not look a gift horse in the mouth. Indeed, that would hardly be appropriate since we were the main recipients of his generosity following that remarkable Christmas. For example, later in the next year I became an equal partner in his firm—he even saw fit to replace that awful sign of his, changing the name of it to Scrooge & Nephew. He lavished gifts on Alice and Emily throughout the year. He virtually adopted Bob Cratchit and his family, though he still disapproved of its magnitude, and grew extremely fond of Tiny Tim, whom he sent to special doctors to cure his affliction.

Later that year, in the month of October, Emily and I were blessed with the birth of a son. Uncle Ebenezer immediately pressed us to become the boy's godfather. Indeed, he pestered me about it continually, even though I assured him we wanted him for the job. He repeated his request so often that it became something of a byword whenever we met. This familial bonding was in my opinion the greatest sign of the metamorphosis, and I thanked God for it. I never saw him so happy as on the day he recited those few words at the christening.

When Christmas-time again came round, he gave generously to the poor. Not only that, he helped raise money by soliciting contributions from fellow businessmen down the thoroughfare. In this effort, he happily worked in league with "the two portly gentlemen" he'd so rudely derided the previous year. By virtue of having undergone a notable change of heart himself, he in turn managed to open the hearts of others. In so doing, he became the talk of the street, for every shop owner and worker was astounded to see the startling change manifested, a change more commonly observed in the fervor of a religious convert.

In a short time, my uncle became a celebrity in certain pockets of the city, for he labored for many worthy causes. There is always curiosity about startling reformations of character. Skepticism as well. People demand an explanation for it. Gradually, though, they left him alone. But then midway through the following year, my uncle was "waylaid," as he put it, at a gathering of charity workers who had asked him to speak at their meeting.

In his remarks he acknowledged his own former failings, which were well-known to his listeners. Then he exhorted them to continue their good work and to never underestimate the latent human capacity to turn toward the good. Later he told me (for I was not there) that he was disappointed to discover he lacked the flair to put his own rare feelings into words of inspiration and that he soon found himself mouthing platitudes.

"I was relieved to conclude the speech," he told me one day in

the tavern. "But then a man in the back of the room stood up and
called out a question. 'Mr. Scrooge,' he said, 'surely if you could
explain how you yourself underwent such a "turn toward the
good" as you have called it, your words would not only inspire
us but might supply a matrix by which others might be reshaped
into kinder, nobler human beings. What say you?'

"I tell you, Fred, I felt the weight of the moon and stars
pressing down on me. He had chosen his words carefully, that
clever fellow, and they elicited immediate applause. 'Hear, hear!'
someone cried, and others took up the cry. I was at a terrific
disadvantage. I could hardly tell him and the others that I'd
found myself in a terrible situation due to my own folly, then
partook of a drug that altered my mind and caused me to see the
greater truth. That was no recipe that could be used by others!"

"My word," I said, smiling. "How did you respond?"

"I said this: 'Sometimes a man is granted a divine vision.
That happened to me. I have no explanation for it. As a result, I
saw my attitude toward my fellow man to be in grave error. Since
that day I have tried to rectify my former sins as best I can. I was
fortunate. That's all I can tell you.' Then I sat down."

"Well done, Uncle. You answered truthfully but revealed
nothing of substance."

"Yes, at the time I thought I was brilliant. But afterwards, the
man who asked the question sought me out in the milling crowd
and grabbed hold of my lapel. He was quite forward, this young
man, but there was something appealing about him—perhaps it
was his lively eyes and a clever tongue. He would be about your
age, I estimate. He proposed standing me a pint at a nearby pub
so he could ask me 'one or two minor questions.' I could see he
was not satisfied with the bland explanation I'd supplied."

"Ah-ha," I said. "Sounds like a very brash fellow. I'm glad
you saw through him."

"Yes, I knew he only wanted information. But the fact is,
Fred, I accepted his offer."

"You accepted? Good heavens, why?"

"I don't know why. He told me he wrote stories for the popular magazines—serials, actually—and wanted to write something regarding my change of character. He'd heard a great deal about my 'turnaround,' as he called it, and thought perhaps he could fashion a good tale from it. I wondered whether he could. Then for some reason, he mentioned he'd lately returned from a trip to America. Upon learning that, I grew curious to hear more about his trip—whence he went and what he saw. And the notion of a pint then seemed a rather jolly idea. I had no other business at that hour, so I went."

This was how my uncle came to tell his story to the man who first wrote it down. Of course the latter did not record it verbatim. Hardly! Instead, he changed nearly everything about the story to suit his taste and purpose. When the tale was published that year in December, I was shocked by the profuse liberties he'd taken and bristled at the effrontery of the author.

When I strode into the office the day after reading the little book, I found my uncle perusing the volume himself and laughing, apparently enjoying what he read.

I slammed my copy on the desk. "Are you not appalled? He's mangled everything! It's nothing but a ghost story."

"He's merely taken poetic license," Uncle said. "And I believe he has the right to do so. Why should I care, anyway? He's got the spirit of it down, close to perfection. And he extols the joys of Christmas quite wonderfully, don't you think? It doesn't matter if the details are—how shall I put it?—more *symmetrical* in the way he's made them. It's a work of art, not a newspaper article."

"But don't you feel he's taken advantage of you?"

"Not in the least. It's rather an honor, Fred. I have been

fictionalized!"

I struggled to see his point of view and for some reason resented his lack of outrage. But I soon calmed down. After all, it was his story, not mine.

"I admit," I said, "he did keep his word in the two matters you mentioned to me."

"Yes, he did. I knew he would. He had the look of an honest man."

I flopped into a chair. "Help me understand, Uncle. What possessed you to unburden yourself in that way? To a man of the press, of all people!"

"I really don't know. But he's more than a simple man of the press, Fred. Those serials of his have been republished as novels. I know, because he kindly sent me a few of them. I had heard tell of one, the story of the fictional 'Pickwick Club,' and I was delighted to finally read it."

"I see. Well, is the fellow a decent writer?"

"He's very talented."

"Still and all, Uncle—*really!* Did you not worry about the incident of the Chinese pipe?"

"Ha! Glad you asked. Fred, he did not believe me when I told him about the device! Even if it were true, he said, it sounded too fantastic, and his readers would not understand it. Besides, he was already set on his ghost story idea, and so his spirits merely appropriated the stuff of my visions. Like any artist, he wanted to remake the story in his own fashion."

Now I was somewhat amused and gave him a look of mild scorn. "You told me you didn't want anyone to know of these things. By Jove, you swore me to secrecy!"

"Aye, so I did. But what was it you said a moment ago? 'I unburdened myself '? That was exactly what I did, and I was glad to get rid of the burden. Besides, I wanted to talk to this man. He'd been to America, remember. And he traveled so far west that he beheld for himself a prairie in the state of Illinois. A real *prairie!*"

What could I say to that?

—◆—

In the following year, my uncle at last sold his house and moved back to his old rooms, which lay empty at Mrs. Abernathy's. I had never seen him healthier and more vigorous. His jovial character drew people to him, and many of them pressed him on the question of whether he had been the model for the miser in the now-famous ghost story. He deflected all such questions with good humor. Indeed, he became quite deft in his ability to change the topic of conversation, for he always had some cause about which he could talk endlessly.

The question of his relation to the fictional character became less and less a problem as time passed. He was only known in certain city boroughs, after all, and no one could be sure of the connection.

Then a miracle occurred. After several months of living in his new, or rather old, rooms, Uncle married the widow Abernathy. Incredible! My jaw dropped when he told me the news. They went to France for their wedding trip.

During this time, we managed to keep our company afloat though it did not thrive as it did of old. As previously mentioned, Uncle insisted the name be changed to Scrooge & Nephew after that first year. I had no objection to the change. That is, I had none until we made our long-delayed trip to Manchester.

My uncle believed I should see for myself the giant mills from which our supply of cotton came. We were, of course, mere distributors of their cloth and had no direct stake in these massive concerns, now grown highly prosperous in the Age of Steam. But they were in a way partners of ours.

"I think you will find it instructive," he said. "We can also examine any new products they have. Though we are not a large company, they are cordial to all their distributors."

I had long been curious about the mills. Their great engines were praised all over the world as a shining example of scientific progress. However, when I finally saw the conditions within the mills, I was horrified. So was Scrooge. The workers tended the enormous machines for long hours, and woe be to the person who let them go idle. There was no joy in the work; the laborers, many of them women and children, worked like automatons. And we learned there were frequent accidents. In fact we witnessed one, when a young girl had her hand bruised in a machine. Her distraught mother told us the girl's younger sister lost part of a finger in the same apparatus.

"I may be naive," I said to him as we left the premises, "but I have never seen such demeaning treatment of our fellow human beings."

"I must agree with you," Uncle answered dully. "During all these years, I've only cared about the machines; I never considered the plight of these workers. I was deluded by my attitude that they did not have to work in the mill, that it was their choice to do so, and that the mills provided work otherwise unavailable in this region."

"We must allow that all that is true," I said. "But consider that men, women, and children as young as six must work twelve-hour shifts, or even longer. It seems to me your factory men don't care a fig for their workers. They mean nothing to them. They might as well be livestock. Those fellows only want their magnificent machines to keep on running."

He did not reply.

We cut short our visit and returned to London.

After that excursion, my uncle fell into a profound depression and left the running of the company entirely to me. He came to the office only occasionally. Once again he was consumed with guilt for his former actions, or lack thereof, and blamed himself for failing to deal with what he now perceived as a grave human problem.

A few weeks later, as we were having luncheon at the tavern, he said, "Fred, I cannot continue dealing with the taskmasters of those factories."

I set down my mug of ale and stared at him a moment. "What shall we do?"

"I will transfer everything to you, Fred. Thereafter the company will be yours to do with as you see fit."

I said nothing for a moment although I knew it was my place to dissuade him from this momentous proposal. But I knew it was not a whim. He seemed completely sincere about this course of action.

"All right, if that is your decision," I said. "In that event, I will dissolve the company."

"As you wish," he answered without blinking an eye.

"That would not upset you?"

"No," he said. "Please take care of the men, though."

"Don't worry, I will give the clerks and warehousemen plenty of time to find other employment. I will also give them severance pay."

"But what of you, Fred? What will *you* do?"

"Return to the law. I have been invited to do so already, now that times are good. I believe it is the best course for me. You shall retire, I hope, and travel with your wife to exotic ports of call. Perhaps even to America, eh?"

He did not smile at this suggestion as I thought he would. "Perhaps so," he said, still in a regretful mood.

I kept my word. It did not take long. And after the company was liquidated, his mood changed for the better.

Uncle never did travel much though he had amassed a considerable fortune and could have done so. He was content to do charity work, accompany his wife to the opera, and dine with friends about town—and, of course, read of America through the works of James Fenimore Cooper.

Several years later, my uncle died suddenly of cardiac failure at the age of seventy-five.

I was afflicted with a powerful grief, for I would miss his singular nature, his wit, and his love for his fellow-man. How strange I should feel this way, I told my wife, considering our relationship had suffered so many ups and downs. Those are the bonds which are most precious, perhaps—the ones which are most complex.

His death signified the end of a bloodline, for he was the last older relative of mine to pass away. I recalled that when I needed a godfather for Alice, I could not locate any living relative, close or distant. It so troubled me at the time that I wrote many letters and looked everywhere for possible survivors by the name of either Truelock or Scrooge. None were to be found. Therefore, I was constantly mindful that he was my last family connection.

I must assert that I believe my dear uncle lived the last portion of his life in a way that entirely compensated for the shortcomings of the previous years.

The funeral was well-attended, and at the wake many spoke to praise him.

Afterwards I went to visit Bob Cratchit, who was getting on in years himself and was afflicted with rheumatism. He had felt poorly on the day of the funeral and could not attend. Thanks to my uncle, he was quite comfortable financially due to an annuity set up for him and his family. Bob told me that, when he was able, he liked to walk over to the old warehouse, which was by then a dress shop and millinery, and then stroll down the street, stopping to greet old friends.

During our conversation a stray thought struck him, and he turned to me sharply. "Oh, but Mr. Fred!" he exclaimed. "Did you not hear that Mr. Marley's old house, which were also Mr. Scrooge's for a time as you may remember, has been leveled to the ground? Aye, they have razed it completely, so they say."

"No, Bob, I did not know that," I replied. "I can't say I shall miss that old pile of stones."

"Nor I," said he. "I do believe, if you'll pardon my sayin' so, that there was a terrible curse on that house. By heaven, I do believe it!"

"Very likely, Bob. Very likely indeed."

When I departed, I thought I might go over and survey what rubble remained.

On second thought, I decided against that whim. I had no wish to enter that dark and sinister street again.

---

I myself have now retired from the law, as I mentioned in the beginning of this work. I must say I've had a comfortable and prosperous life on the whole and have enjoyed the opportunity to pen this modest memoir. Not much of my own life was truly worth setting down, and so I apologize for the inclusion of those portions, though my descendants may find them interesting. Surely the best scenes are to be found on the pages that center upon my remarkable uncle—and upon that other strange man, Jacob Marley.

Especially the latter.

If one wanted to write a popular sort of tale, he should look no further than the character of that rogue. Marley was decisive, and in retrospect that is something I admire. Nearly all of the events, turning points, and reversals I have recorded here were precipitated by him. In contrast, Scrooge was a creature of the *status quo* and not prone to change—with the sole exception of his extraordinary metamorphosis, that is. Even that event was precipitated by Marley's encouragement for my uncle to undergo the so-called "experiment." Readers of today will have recognized the Chinese pipe for what it was: a device for smoking the vapors of refined opium. I do not believe my uncle ever realized there was absolutely no trace of tobacco in the "mixture."

The opium Marley used in his younger years was in solid form. Although it was potent, no one in England at that time knew that the power of the drug could be greatly magnified when it was inhaled, nor did any other race but the Chinese work out the correct method for effecting that trick. Presently, of course, the smoking of opium is a scourge in its own right and plagues many who have fallen under its spell in our modern world, especially in London. I became curious about the habit when I realized this new vice was related to my uncle's experiment.

Some fifteen years ago or so, when I was still practicing law, I traveled by rail to Lancaster on a legal matter. After attending to my task and with some time on my hands, I decided to visit the nearby port which sits on an arm of the Irish Sea—Liverpool. I had been curious about the place ever since my uncle informed me it was a hub of commerce that rivaled New York City.

Sure enough, I found the place bustling; it was brimming with activity throughout. In my short tour, I found there were many lovely areas one might visit in the city proper. Other areas were not so proper, for example the waterfront, which was diverse and fascinating, but also crude and crowded with every type of riffraff one can imagine. As I wandered about the docks, a seemingly endless parade of seamen from many nations passed by me, some clad in colorful, outlandish costumes. Often they laughed and bellowed in loud voices, but seldom did I hear them use a word of English.

The harbor seemed like another world. There sailors drank and whored, spending their sea wages until the money was gone and they had to sign on for another voyage. In that quarter, I saw many opium dens, as they are now called. I'd read of these establishments but never seen one. They could be found in London, but in that city one had to ferret them out. Here they were manifestly visible, shockingly open for business to all comers.

My curiosity about these dark caves flared up as I wandered the streets close by the docks. Finally I got up the courage to enter one. I wanted to see the actual pipes and see if they were used as my uncle had described. The establishment I chose was small and appeared halfway reputable. At least its front door was newly painted.

Mind you, I only planned to observe the ritual of smoking the pipe. I did wonder, though, what harm there could be in smoking a small amount of the drug—one time only, say, as my uncle did.

No one questioned me upon entering. I advanced with caution through the narrow room. Smoke hung like a heavy blanket, and I coughed several times. Dim lamps revealed that the chamber was lined with sleeping bunks. In them men languished in all sorts of exotic attitudes—limbs stretched out or bent, necks craned up or down, eyes open or closed. In that place there seemed to be a specimen of every race on the earth; and each specimen appeared listless and devoid of energy. Here and there I spied a flame ignite and then pulse as someone drew on a pipe. Once I spotted someone manipulating the pills into the chamber, exactly as my uncle described it. Some of the men muttered low to themselves or others, but most were silent, enveloped in whatever sensation or dream occupied their minds.

*God,* I thought, *these poor wretches might as well be confined to hell.*

When I reached the back of the room, I found a man of the East, perhaps a Chinese, sitting on a high stool keeping watch. At his signal a shirtless boy of about twelve brought over a pipe to me.

"You want boy too?" the man asked.

"No, thank you," I said quickly, feeling flushed. "No boy, and, uh, no pipe." The child disappeared. "I was only—I mean, I was only looking for a friend of mine."

"Whozat?" asked the man, suddenly suspicious and glowering at me.

Now I was caught in a self-made web and had to think of something to say. "Uh, his name is Mr. Jones," I said, lying poorly. "He comes from Manchester. Do you by chance know if he's here?"

"Nobody here you want," he answered in a gruff voice. He stared at me belligerently, puzzled at the well-dressed Englishman standing before him. Obviously he was worried as to what sort of trouble I might make. He glanced over to a long club that leant against the wall.

Mortified, I turned and rushed out of the place. As soon as I was on the street, I threw back my head and heaved a deep, gasping breath, thankful to inhale the sea air once again.

At that precise moment, a well-dressed, respectable-looking woman walked by. What she was doing in this infamous section of town I could not imagine. She must have wondered the same thing about me, for she cast a thoroughly scathing look in my direction, narrowing her eyes as though to abase me for my patronage of the opium den. Now even more embarrassed, I dashed off, only to collide with a gray-haired man coming the other way. He was short, frail, and gaunt, and he cursed at me even as he swayed on his feet, his hands shaking. Though I politely asked his pardon, the man flung another gibe at me, spat on the sidewalk, and turned to enter the building from which I had a moment ago departed. It was only then I noticed the pigtail down his back.

I stared after him in profound shock and dismay as he disappeared into the blackness of that infernal place. Aside from my childhood days, it was but the second, and I'm thankful to say the last, time I saw Jacob Marley.

*Frederick Truelock, 1875*

## Afterword

As the editor of this memoir, I believe it necessary to add a few words to enlighten the casual reader who may come across it.

First of all, I would like to speak to the origin of the work.

The author, my father, was keen to write prose, as he once remarked to his uncle. Of course, he found little time for this pursuit in his day-to-day life. After his stint as a cloth purveyor, his friend Mr. Evans found him a position in a good law firm, so he returned to the legal profession. Thereafter he spent nearly thirty years at it and enjoyed much success. He retired when his health began to fail.

I can attest that he worked hard as a solicitor, something that did not please me in my early years, for I saw very little of him. But then I was packed off to school anyway, as are many boys, and spent much of my youth away from home. Father always made a big to-do of Christmas, however. That time of year was special in our family, and I have many glorious memories of it.

When he finally retired, he sought the solace of a pastime, for he was by then alone. My mother had died of influenza five years before. He decided at last to have a go at writing prose.

First he tried his hand at the type of city sketches he mentioned to my great-uncle, but he discovered that that sort of writing was out of fashion. Next he tried serious essays, whose grand topics ran to politics and religion. Again, no one was interested in publishing them. He even tried writing fiction, only to discover he lacked a basic talent for invention.

My father had to face the fact that his literary ambition had come to nothing. For a time he fell into a heavyhearted period of dejection and showed an uncharacteristic impatience with all those around him, even his grandchildren.

One December day, he was sitting in a coffeehouse when some idle chatter drifted his way. The talk concerned the famous Christmas ghost story, still a favorite with many readers at that time of year. One man asserted with force that in his opinion Jacob Marley was the scariest of the four ghosts that haunted Scrooge on Christmas Eve. At this declaration my father, as he told it to me, heard himself speaking in contradiction to this person, whom he knew not at all, even raising his voice to inform the stranger that, "Marley was not yet dead on that occasion!"

The man and his friends broke into laughter. One of them remarked loudly that only a lunatic would say such a thing about a made-up person, and they all laughed even louder.

As my father tramped out of the coffeehouse in a huff, he muttered to himself that someone ought to write down the true version of the story. Once this peculiar notion took root, it quickly blossomed into a full-blown idea. *He* could write it. *Only* he could write it. At last he'd found a worthy subject: a history of the real Jacob Marley!

He embarked upon his project with relish and finished the work in the space of a year. Although it primarily concerns two men who were better as friends than partners, in the course of it, he related some of our own family history, including details of his own life and marriage. It was necessary to sketch the background, he told me. His chief aim, he said, was merely to record the truth so that he could let go of the secret he'd kept for so many years.

However, since he mentioned persons in the text who were still living, he declined to publish the work. He bequeathed that task to me, his son, as well as the task of editing the manuscript. He said I should do with his literary opus as I saw fit. I should also add that by this time his health was precarious. He died the following year.

Though I hope the reader will find the above background interesting, my main purpose here is to clarify a certain part of my father's memoir by explaining what he meant in the last chapter concerning "the two matters" that were agreed upon by my great-uncle and the man to whom he gave the use of his experiences.

The so-called "magazine writer" was obviously smitten with the haunting visions which were described to him and wanted to create ghosts to present them. My great-uncle thought this a capital idea. But he had two stipulations.

The first was that the writer must unequivocally state that Marley died seven years before the story opened, precisely as the whole world thought he had. This would conform with the public record. Otherwise, the authorities might investigate and bring criminal charges against my great-uncle. The writer had no quarrel with that proviso. Indeed, he said he would turn Marley into a ghost as well and that Marley's ghost would introduce the other spirits. He promised he'd make certain the reader believed the man was "as dead as a door-nail" on the very first page. True to his word, he did exactly that.

The second stipulation was that the author must not use my great-uncle's real surname. This, too, was agreeable to the writer, for he knew the pitfalls of dragging the names of real people into print. As we have seen, this man had a genius for coining queer surnames for his characters—Twist, Heep, Chuzzlewit, to name but a few—and so he devised the unique and dismal-sounding name of "Scrooge." That name has by now become a veritable synonym for "miser." This was not my great-uncle's family name, of course; his real name was Mackinnick, and as far as

I know, there is no one alive in Lancashire, nor in all England, who bears the name of Mackinnick today. It is extinct, or I would not have mentioned it here. Therefore it was that name my great-uncle so eagerly sought on the gravestone in his eerie vision of the churchyard—not the name of Scrooge, which had yet to be coined.

The author, however, chose to retain the name of Jacob Marley, who by then was mostly forgotten. When the book was published, Marley's name no longer appeared on the sign above the door, but many people remembered when it had. Some of those saw in Mr. Mackinnick a person similar to Mr. Scrooge—for both were considered disagreeable men who reformed themselves late in life. And a few of them dared to mention this to my great-uncle. The old fellow laughed off the notion there was a connection to himself but remarked it was a marvelous coincidence that the rare Christian name of Ebenezer had been employed.

With time the suspicions melted away, and readers no longer pestered him with questions. Mackinnick & Nephew, as the company was then called, did not remain in existence much longer anyway. After my father closed its doors, it quickly faded from public memory. So did the name of Mackinnick itself.

The reader may wonder, then, why my father retained the name of Scrooge in his own memoir. He told me he did so because otherwise it would have made little sense to the average reader. The ghost story was by then celebrated in England and abroad, so this connection was the main point of interest. Furthermore, he had no wish to reveal his uncle's real name.

At this late date I judge that no one can possibly be harmed by the publication of this work as its writer originally feared might happen. Jacob Marley, the Fifth Earl of Archwood, Cratchit, Wheelwright, Evans, Edloe—they are all gone now. The world has moved on.

At first I thought to print a small run and keep the book only for family members and descendants. But as I pored over it, making small changes, I came to believe the story merited a wider audience. There is, of course, its link to the famous Christmas tale. But it also has a certain charm because of incidental innovations the narrator witnessed—for example, the advent of the locomotive and the Christmas tree.

My father strayed far afield in his portrait of Jacob Marley and manifestly did so almost from the beginning. But he ends appropriately, I think, with the title character. The disturbing final scene is a cautionary lesson, to be sure, regarding the use of opium.

Alas, disasters may come sooner than seven years and they always come unannounced. I am saddened to say I recently lost my dear sister, Alice, whose sprightly presence as a child enlivens some of these pages. It is a bleaker world in which I now live, for I miss her dearly. My wife and children give me much-needed strength, yet I feel more alone in the world than I did before her passing. It is now clear that I am the last man who will bear the name of Truelock. After I die, this name will also be consigned to the dustbin of history, for my children are all daughters.

I now sympathize even more with my father. He lost his parents in his youth, and it is evident that his story is less about Mr. Marley's doings and more about his own quest to forge a bond with his only living relative, the complex and aloof Mr. Mackinnick, my great-uncle and godfather. This was no easy task. Year after year, my father asked him to Christmas dinner, and year after year the man stubbornly refused to come. On one occasion, when my mother suggested they cease inviting him, my father's reaction betrayed his brittleness of spirit. He could not give up asking him, he told her, because his uncle was all he had.

I am happy my father succeeded in his quest. The bond forged between those two men lives on in this memoir; and, I may say, continues to endure in the person of myself.

*Ebenezer Truelock, 1890*